Shades of Desire

This is a work of fiction. Names, characters, businesses, places, events and incidents are either the products of the author's imagination or used in a fictitious manner. Any resemblance to actual persons, living or dead, or actual events is purely coincidental.

ISBN-13: 978-0-9961091-1-6

Cover design and book layout: Book Cover Corner, bookcovercorner.com

Fox, Mara.

Shades of Desire / Mara Fox — 1st ed.

Dedication

One day, I bought a print of a cowboy sharing his lunch with his horse and his dog. I had never bought a Western picture in my life but there was something extraordinary about that cowboy…

Little did I know that I was meant to meet a cowboy very much like the one in the picture, a man, both tender and tough, who had a horse, a dog, and a ranch to share.

So I dedicate this book to my cowboy, Rick Moretti who looks at me like I'm a gift in his life, even though I'm just a regular girl, and makes me laugh when our lives gets a little tough.

And I just want to say how proud I am of my son, Travis Mark Horstman.

Shades of Desire

by

Mara Fox

She'd wept, wailed, and watched
over the young souls
but evil prevailed…
So she rode the scorching desert winds into Last Chance
To discover why McKee hadn't come to release them
he couldn't dream, feel, or sense her there
a shade, a spirit, a ghost, lost
No partner to her pain and obligations
These nights she haunts him
The man with the gift to hear
as she stands for girls buried in red sands

"Please McKee…"

Chapter One

Jake McKee caught his reflection in the mirror behind the scarred, wooden bar in the Last Chance Saloon and raised his glass to acknowledge his own disreputable reflection.

Then he drained the chaser he'd ordered with tequila.

West Texas bars had the same things to offer-alcohol, TV, bar fights, and if he were lucky, women, any of which would offer forgetfulness. Not that he was in any pain.

He snorted at the thought.

Unfortunately, all of his liquid salvation was gone. He tipped the glass over to stack it on top of the other three, just to make sure.

Yep. Another empty.

As he reached for his wallet, a postcard slipped out to the scuffed wooden floor. He didn't reach for it; he'd memorized the damn, cryptic message in the old man's handwriting:

> winds of fortune blow,
> beware, shadowed man,
> the woman of desires.

What the hell. He'd definitely enjoy a woman of desire. She'd be brazen. Smokin' hot in a little skirt and cowboy boots. He'd take her out to his truck.

Where he'd lean her up against the door and put his hands on her dangerous curves. They might not even make it inside the cab before she'd wrap her long legs firmly around him, hiking up her skirt, and begging him to take her. Then he'd sink so deeply inside of her hot and yielding body he couldn't think. Long strands of silky dark hair would distract and entangle as they slipped sensuously over his skin.

If he started thinking again, she'd push him inside of the cab, down on the leather seat, raking her nails over his bare chest, demanding more, more of him, riding him again and again into oblivion…now that was his idea of dangerous desires.

"McKee."

"Shut up." He fought to hold the image in his mind.

It had been too long since he'd lost himself in the heat of a woman. As his Shaman uncle, interpreter of mysterious messages from the spirit world, and possibly high on peyote, had so enigmatically pointed out-women of desire were dangerous.

And sex was complicated.

"I wonder if he's objecting to the woman's tribal heritage. We're not damn dogs that we should keep the bloodlines fucking pure. The tribe's unrecognized…"

"What are you muttering?" Robbie, the bartender asked.

McKee thought about destroying the postcard. But he wouldn't let it matter that much; he stuffed it back into his wallet.

Right now he wanted to be anywhere else but here in Last Chance, Texas. Give him good kick-ass pursuit, or the adrenaline of a ferocious fight.

The only part of McKee's Indian-Scot-Tex-Mex mutt ancestry that appealed was how they'd raided in the Texas desert on horseback. McKee and his partner, Rider Blue Storm, had been attracted to a similar legacy of chasing down the bad guys…but he couldn't think about it, not tonight.

McKee signaled to Robbie, with the shot glass. "I'll have another and make it a double."

"Beer," Robbie insisted, warily.

Not daring to risk his old, skinny, chicken neck by coming closer, McKee noted.

"Now McKee, you've had enough tequila. You're talking crazy. Muttering in your native language and stuff. Just take it easy tonight."

McKee always thought Robbie looked as stubborn as the butt end of a mule. Or was it as ugly? "Tequila."

"Beer." Robbie slid a foaming mug across the bar. "Don't you have something to do besides get shitfaced? Like chasing some bad guys?"

McKee grabbed the mug, knowing it wouldn't be enough, nothing would be enough.

A beefy man with hairy arms sticking out of a black motorcycle shirt and a beer belly overflowing his filthy jeans yelled at Robbie, "Hey old man. Can't you move your ugly ass any faster? I ordered a beer."

"Robbie, who's the ape-man?" McKee asked loudly. Though he knew the man intimately, Dale Arranger, an unofficial suspect in McKee's ongoing case and a generally reprehensible human being. Nobody deserved a good ass kicking more than Arranger.

"Don't talk to him, McKee." Robbie hissed.

"Why not? That prick shouldn't be talking trash at you." McKee took a deep drink of his beer.

"Gimme a break. It's a bad night. Bad karma, full moon. I almost always get the place broke up on nights like this one." Robbie clucked like a hen. "Don't know why I didn't open a feed store. Cows are more civilized than the cowboys in this town."

"Robbie, don't be such a bitch. If you had a feed store you wouldn't be able to give crappy advice with your crappy booze." McKee toasted Robbie in the air with his mug.

The bar was full of familiar neon, the smell of whiskey, the clinking of pool balls, and the soothing ballad of profanity as a shot went wild and a pool ball hit the wooden floor with a loud clatter.

McKee almost felt at home.

"If I didn't owe you my life," Robbie lifted up his shirt to show off a scar on his abdomen. "I'd have called the sheriff the moment you came into my place. Why don't you get back on your Harley and ride outta here?"

"I'm not driving the hog tonight."

"Whatever, just go home and sleep it off."

McKee shook his head. "I didn't save your life, man, just your damn virginity, you don't owe me shit. Especially not any shitty advice."

"Hell with you, McKee." Robbie said. "But seriously, you gotta stop getting busted up in my bar. I can't afford it. You gotta understand. We used to be friends."

"Then give this old friend a shot."

Robbie snorted. "A shot at breaking up my bar again?"

"Haven't you heard the wind's changing?" McKee slammed the mug down on the bar.

"You gonna go and find those missing girls from the college? Poor things. But I guess you got better things to do." Robbie shook his head.

"Asshole, I've got my time off like everyone else." McKee defended.

"Why don't you sleep it off in the storage room before you get too drunk? I understand. Sure I do. I know it's been a year since we lost Anne. It's the anniversary of hard times." Robbie ducked; bobbing his head as if he feared McKee might burst into violence at the reminder.

McKee felt the familiar cold wind blow through his soul. *She haunts me. But I can't feel her. I can't hear her and I can't find her in the dream world. What good is a goddamned gift if I can't use it to find my best friend and avenge her murder? It's been a whole goddamned year of walking in the wilderness.*

Robbie slid the beer across the bar towards the jackass. "Hey, man, I'm sorry it took me a minute."

"Old fucker." The man said. "Like I fucking care what your excuse is."

"I'm gonna teach him some manners." McKee pushed the coldness away and eagerly grasped the distraction. There was nothing quite as useless as a warrior slinking home with no scalp, not that Arranger had much hair.

Damn the consequences.

"McKee, just take it easy." Robbie said.

All his life McKee had tried to make amends. He'd tried to balance the scales. But he couldn't even catch the guy who'd killed Anne. So what was the point?

"I'm gonna break his ugly, Neanderthal face," McKee predicted mildly. Not letting on he knew Arranger from his varied and violent police record.

"If you can't keep it together, I'm going to call Sheriff Foley."

"Hey, old man, this beer tastes like shit. Give me another mug. And I ain't gonna pay for no fuckin' flat beer." Arranger pushed the half empty mug of beer across the bar. "And gimme a shot of JD. Or I might beat the fuck outta you. "

McKee rose slowly from his bar stool.

"No, McKee. Here. Just one more." Robbie sent him a shot of tequila only half full.

McKee nodded as he accepted the shot glass. But he didn't sit down. Anne's death had ended things for him; it was just taking him longer to die.

He sipped tequila. Savoring the burn.

Robbie leaned in closer to ask, "Why don't you go to a shrink or a shaman, or whatever you people do for help?"

McKee thought of the postcard in his wallet and shook his head. "A shaman's just as worthless as a law enforcement shrink or a meddling bartender."

Arranger elbowed his way into their conversation. "Hey old man, you can't remember shit. Gimme the JD."

"Arranger you gotta pay first." Robbie said apologetically.

"You shitting me?" Arranger scratched his balls through the front of his jeans.

McKee wondered how he found them; they were obviously pretty fucking small.

"Now, don't make me come across this bar." Arranger lunged at Robbie and grabbed him by the collar of his red, cowboy shirt.

Robbie's face turned as red as the shirt. "I hit the panic button. The sheriff's on his way," he wheezed.

Arranger shook Robbie. "Fucking old man."

McKee asked calmly. "Robbie, you got a problem with me taking care of this?"

"No, McKee, you leave this for the sheriff. He'll be here any minute." More wheezing and a couple of coughs came from Robbie's florid face.

"Sure you can wait that long? It doesn't sound like you're getting much air."

The stubborn old man might have nodded. It was hard to tell.

But McKee had had enough of waiting. He reached over and poured what was left of Arranger's beer over Arranger's head.

Arranger immediately let go of Robbie, "Hey fucker!" He leaned forward and punched McKee in the face with a fist as hard as an iron-shod hoof.

McKee gave Arranger a smile that felt feral. The redeeming ache was better than wallowing in guilt and apathy.

"Stop!" Robbie demanded. "McKee wants you to fight...he's with the..."

"Fuckers!"

A shadowed man. His uncle wasn't particularly original.

McKee slammed a fist into Arranger's nose, burying his spiritual impotence in blood and flesh.

Arranger hit back; it felt like the cold anvil of fate. "You freakin' fucker," he yelled as he struck.

The pain sings in McKee's blood like a religious chant.

Hell with it all. No one's coming to rescue me

Arranger threw a punch, jerking McKee's head back on his neck. McKee kicked out with his left foot and grunted when he connected.

And he didn't want to be rescued.

The spirits might not care, but the tequila, the adrenaline, and pain, filled up the emptiness. McKee pounded on Arranger with a vengeance, but the man fought dirty, kicking him in the nuts so the world went gray.

"Fuckin Neanderthal." He spat out, huddled in a fetal ball. Robbie shouted.

McKee looked up through the red haze and stared directly into the barrel of a pistol.

Thank the gods.

It's finally over.

He heard Robbie shout.

Then, everything went dark.

Chapter Two

Kendall Waite sat at her desk in the Last Chance Law Enforcement office with her cell phone up to her ear, "Yes, Mom."

She crossed her legs, creasing her heavily starched khaki work pants. "Yes mom, I'm definitely staying in Texas for the summer." She tugged on the mass of hair she'd pulled up into such a tight knot it was giving her a headache.

"No, I really can't come this summer." The old guilt soured her mouth and acid trickled down her throat making her stomach hurt.

"I'm working as an intern to Janice Foley here at the jail. I'm observing as she does…ah…intakes on…ah persons of interest, for the county prison system."

I go along with Janice as she does psychological evaluations of people, not unlike you, Mom, when you were in trouble. Sometimes Janice incarcerates them, like when they took you to jail and then they took me away from you. And I don't know why I'm going down memory lane…But this little town, so far away from my life, is exactly where I need to be for the screwed-up undertaking I have in mind.

Since screwing's the goal. Ha Ha

Kendall smiled at her own pun, but then her mother's voice rose in her ear.

"Yeah, I know your opinion of psychologists."

"And I realize not everyone who goes to jail's a criminal." Kendall jiggled her leg.

"Yeah, this will be field experience for my work resume. Yes mom, I brought the cat. Yes of course there's a bar. And no, I don't go out much."

At least not yet.

She tapped her pencil.

"You're working, Mom. That's good."

After years of studying psychology Kendall understood her mother's many problems: plenty of fascinating possibilities, if you hadn't lived it firsthand.

"Yes, I'm sure it would solve all of my problems if I could just find the right man."

"Yeah, goodbye, Mom. I'll text you."

For a minute Kendall stood there looking at her orderly stack of papers on the otherwise scarred wooden desk.

"Mom's been singing the 'find a man' song so long, that's probably where I got this insane idea."

Abruptly, Kendall swept her hand over the tidy pile sending everything to the stained cement floor. For a minute, she just stood looking at the mess she'd made.

"Damn! Frik! Fricken! Damn it to hell!" Apparently, old wounds still ached.

"Why can't I reason my way past this?" she asked herself miserably. Bubba Houser glared back at her from a mug shot lying on the hardwood floor.

Kendall grimaced at his scowling face as she picked the photo off of the ground. "I wasn't talking to you. Bubba; even my mother wouldn't go for your ugly mug. I want to be cured not killed."

Ironically, she was about to do something crazy-something her mother might understand; because the fantasies still came to her, and vivid dreams, where she imagined having sex with a bad bad boy.

Sometimes the fantasy started with her bad guy in a prison cell...that's how she knew he was a bad guy...

In the fantasy, Kendall stood just outside the cell gazing at his handsome, misunderstood face, and those dark brooding eyes behind thick, iron bars. She inched as close to him as she could. Drawn by his obvious pain. Wanting to heal him and so much more...

He wanted her too; she could see his erection pushing up against the material of his pants.

He put his hands directly on top of her breasts thru the bars. It didn't take him but a second to find her nipples since she was wearing a daring demi bra.

Kendall wanted to pull away-he shouldn't be touching her--but his touch was a torch. Her flesh flamed and ached. She clung to the bars as her knees weakened, as did her resolve.

He reached for something. It was a knife.

That proved he was a bad man. Kendall flinched, but he only slashed open her prissy work shirt, avidly exposing the swell of her breasts. And then his hands slid roughly over her soft heaving flesh, possessing her hungrily, devouring her.

Then he discovered the key around her neck, dangling temptingly between her breasts, and he let go of her to open the door to the cell.

She expected him to flee, but he didn't try to escape.

Instead, he pulled her inside the cell where he pushed her up against the wall, and pushed up her skirt, wild to be inside of her, where she was naked and utterly open to him.

He thrust his huge, hard penis inside of her, filling her up, again and again and again. Until he was so deep inside of her that she had the orgasm. The big orgasm she could only seem to have in her fantasies involving her bad boy.

Inside that dream, she experienced a sexual release so intense her wild screams would make the other prisoners restless.

And she didn't care if they heard. She wasn't a professional. She was just a woman engaging in wild, forbidden sex with the black-haired bad man who haunted her dreams. She tingled at the thought.

I can't really be considering going through with this crazy idea can I?

The next mug shot lying on the ground was a man named Arranger who had lots of hair, but none of it on his head.

Kendall shook her head and spoke to Arranger's mug shot as she set the picture on the desk. "Now your type is evidence Neanderthal genes are alive and well and mixed in with the general population."

Stop this. Stop looking at these mug shots and considering this course of action. Meeting a criminal...and...just stop thinking about it, she ordered herself.

Even though she understood how dangerous this obsession could be, she might actually let it play out. Or eventually the uncontrollable fantasies might destroy everything she'd worked towards.

"You know how you have something inside your head that's stupid? Something dark and dangerous and yet you can't let it go?" Kendall didn't know if she was talking to Arranger's picture or to herself.

"It's a little chink in your sanity armor. If you ever had any sanity." This time she *was* talking to a mug shot.

Talk about a lack of sanity.

"It's a fatal impulse." She continued her one-way conversation with the sullen man glaring at her from the mug shot.

"For me it's a bad boy."

She sighed. "I need a cure because I know having sex with a bad man would be bad on so many levels . . ."

Physician heal thyself…

She'd always wanted to be a hero. Save people. It didn't take a doctoral degree to understand she really wanted to save her mother.

Certainly not emulate her.

Which made this course of action completely crazy.

She laid Arranger's picture down. "You're not at all like the man I dream about."

In fact she knew exactly what her bad boy looked like and that was even more terrifying.

Because her mother believed in any number of ridiculous things, a woman who'd spent most of her life being a victim and mostly homeless, actually believed in a benevolent creator, angels watching over her on the way to the homeless shelter, demons, ghosts, and psychics.

But I'm a scientist, a rational person. So it shouldn't bother me that I've seen my bad boy's face in dreams and fantasies. It's just an image I saw somewhere, probably on TV.

"But Arranger, you're way too ugly to be on TV. Unless you are the bad guy." She felt herself grinning like a crazy person as she spoke to the mug shot.

"Did I tell you how my mother dragged me to a palm reader? The woman told me I could communicate with other planes of existence. Only there are no other planes of existence. We went hungry after mom paid that fraud."

Kendall felt a strand of her hair escape to fall down on her neck and that was probably why her neck tingled at the thought of a supposed physic.

"So, I have weird dreams. I know where dreams come from."

She set the mug shots aside.

"Not even a crazy person would have sex with either Bubba or Bart Arranger," She sighed. "So, I guess I'm going to have to find another town. Because I need a bad guy I can stomach. I'll just have a real bad time, and get it outta my system, and then I'll be all right."

Her words rang out in the empty office.

They just didn't get enough crime in Last Chance.

The internship had been a great idea but the social worker, Janice was married to Sheriff Foley, and she did more socializing than assessing criminals.

Shaking her head, Kendall tried to loosen the messy knot of her hair. Had she really imagined she'd find the bad boy who haunted her dreams in a place like Last Chance, Texas?

The name had been like a talisman, promising her redemption from her demons. Now she realized the demons in Last Chance actually looked like they'd been through hell.

Gathered the files and papers up off of the floor, Kendall thought of how she'd spent nearly a decade in school and she couldn't give up now.

She'd graduated early, earned scholarships, and worked her tail off, all of which had allowed her to fulfill her dreams and walk across the stage last month to receive her PhD in Clinical Psychology.

Technically, she was Doctor Kendall Waite, but it still sounded presumptuous.

A young girl who'd once been homeless had a PhD, and might just land herself a prestigious job on the east coast.

Kendall organized the papers she'd retrieved from the floor.

She still had only to take the Virginia state certification tests, but she'd taken this break, and accepted this job to handle one final problem. . . only she liked to think of it as an assignment.

Placing the files in order inside the desk drawer, she carefully locked the mostly confidential information.

Then she realized she'd accidentally left the pictures on top of the desk. Arranger's ugly grimace appeared to mock her from his mug shot

I'm not so perfect as I appear on my resume. And a prestigious firm would have rigorous interviews and what if they uncovered my obsession?

She grabbed the water bottle from on top of her desk. She took a long sip to cool off. But it did little to put out the forbidden fire.

Take the fantasy she'd had on the verge of sleep last night, the one with a handsome, dark-haired convict who was very troubled. In an active counseling session, she did him right there on her couch, in her office with her hair falling all around them as she rode him to a cure. She'd come to a screaming, sweaty orgasm.

There was no board certification for that little pleasure trip. If anyone in her field ever knew, she'd find herself on someone else's couch as the patient. She had to get this stuff out of her head.

She took another sip of the water. It didn't matter which scenario because Kendall's intelligent mind had created them all. While her visions tantalized, they also terrified.

How could she become a responsible counselor when she couldn't even control her own angst? The fantasies came at the most inappropriate times. She knew she had to get it out of her system: when the man treated her like a hardened criminal would treat a woman, she'd finally be cured…at least that had been her game plan.

Kendall sighed, thinking she should have stayed in Virginia and taken a few summer courses.

Lacy, the law enforcement, administrative assistant came bobbing into the police station, her pretty curves barely contained by her casual, Friday jeans.

"Lacy, Please tell me there's something to do in this town tonight," Kendall inquired. She needed something to distract her from her spiraling thoughts.

"Hey, we got him," Lacy babbled. "He's right here in our jail. Arranger got away." She shrugged. "But they'll get him eventually. Anyway, McKee's sleeping it off as we speak."

"Who?"

"Jake McKee. He's, he's…" The woman wheezed out the last of the sentence.

Kendall handed Lacy one of the inhalers, which were located in every corner of the office. "Slow down. Breathe. Remember how you hate having to go to the clinic for oxygen when you can't breathe."

With practiced ease the young woman took a puff on the inhaler; a few seconds later the color flooded back into her cheeks. "Thanks. It's dusty out there"

After another deep breath, Lacy continued, "Unfortunately, McKee's not dating material."

"Who says I need a date. I just wanted to go out for a drink."

"McKee takes his walk-alone-Indian-heritage very seriously. He's made a vow to marry into the blood."

Kendall couldn't help but smile at her friend's enthusiasm. "I think I said I wanted a drink, not a mate."

Lacy gave her a scorching look as she took another hit off of her inhaler.

"Lacy, are you having second thoughts about your engagement? Is that why you're excited about this Indian guy?" Kendall teased.

"No, but he'ss prime." Lacy said with difficulty.

"Prime. Okay. He's prime and his name's Jake McKee. But isn't McKee a Scottish name?"

"Part Indian, all gorgeous. And tall. Did I mention he got the tall genes?"

"No." But I'm sure you'll mention it again.

"See if you can scoff after you take a look at this!" Lacy crowed, slapping a mug shot on the desk in front of Kendall. "Best thing to come through here in a hundred years. Not that the mug shot's really necessary. He's a lawman. Foley's trying to teach McKee a lesson-get his attention. Get him back on track. He's been pretty messed up since his partner died last year."

Kendall's attention was so totally focused on the mug shot she didn't hear a word Lacy was saying, "that's him." The words came from some place so deep inside of her that she was hardly aware she'd spoken them. "He can't be real."

"He's real all right. Isn't he stunning?"

Kendall nodded absently, focusing on the man in the photograph. Hadn't the Indians believed photos could steal your soul? This one stole her breath and her resolve. Even bloodied and bruised the mere image of the man made her heart pound in her chest. A man she'd seen in her dreams for most of her life.

Finally, the thought drifted across her mind.

Stupid thought. Weird shit again. Came from talking with her mother. He just looks like a famous actor or model…only rough, intense, seriously damaged and haunted…

"The boys are back in town because of the disappearances at the college." Lacy said.

Kendall still wasn't paying attention, or not much attention. The sight of the man, her man, made her tingle in all the right places.

This is the one.

Ebony eyes filled with such angry intensity she caught her breath at the sight. Glossy black hair lay haphazardly, almost touching his shoulders. Golden skin, high cheekbones, and a chiseled profile, with a noble nose, apparently previously broken, made him look incredibly masculine, dangerous, and so desirable.

She felt heat rise up inside her body.

This man's obviously bad to the bone, and just the cure for what ails me. In a few days I'll be back in Virginia with my head firmly screwed back on.

"Wow."

"Is that all you have to say? That little, understated, wow?!" "Okay, he's hot. Who is he? And what did you say he's in for?"

"Drunk and disorderly. He wasn't the only one. He rearranged Robbie's bar last night. Robbie said something about it being the anniversary of hard times. I think it's because of A…"

"Arranger?" Kendall interrupted. Foley had been complaining about the guy all week long.

Lacy nodded. "Bart Arranger's on the run for pulling a gun. Unfortunately, his twin brother, James, the highway patrolman, will arrive tomorrow to get him off of the hook. And Robbie didn't put cameras in the bar, so Arranger will probably slime his way outta trouble. Again."

"Hummm." Kendall looked at the mug shot.

"Now both brothers are gonna be gunning for McKee." Lacy wheezed. She took another hit off of her inhaler.

Kendall shook her head at the small town drama.

When she could breath again, Lacy continued, "I hope Foley doesn't keep McKee in jail for long. It'll keep him safe from Arranger. Sure. But he'll be real pissed off. I think Foley ordered the mug shot to wake McKee up. I swear Foley was so red-faced talking about the situation, I thought he might blow a gasket."

Foley was the very substantial sheriff of Last Chance. It took a lot to rile him. Kendall had gained a real working respect for the man.

"The Sheriff thinks McKee's bad?" Kendall mused.

"Oh, Foley was hot enough to cook a steak on. Threatened to keep McKee a whole year in the tank if he didn't get himself together."

Kendall had to keep herself from physically reaching out to touch the face in the photograph. The man was utterly perfect.

In fact it was probably good he looked so much like the face in her dreams. Gorgeous. Angry. Surly. There was no way he was just a misunderstood cowboy who'd been abused as a child. This one appeared to be bad. He was just the man to cure her of her forbidden fantasy.

Kendall took a measured sip of her water hoping she appeared calm and collected. She didn't want Lacy to know her plan. A droplet of water splattered on the mug shot, blurring it. Could she really follow through? Did she have the guts?

"I guess this is the best one."

"The best one? Has the summer heat gone to your head or what?" Lacy had no inkling of Kendall's problem nor her plan. No one in the world knew the successful student had a wicked dilemma. Lacy didn't know Kendall's plan to have sexual relations with a criminal and Kendall had no intention of telling her now. "I'm sorry. I was just thinking. What else do you know about him?"

"Why?"

"I just thought I'd get a closer look," Kendall said casually.

"Look, but don't touch, you're definitely not acclimated to Texas tough guys."

The thought gave Kendall a hopeful shiver. "Is he violent."

"No more than necessary. Arranger meant business."

"I could acclimate to Texas tough guys."

"McKee would burn you worse than your first sunburn."

Kendall's first sunburn had turned her skin such a spectacular shade of fiery red it had kept the law enforcement staff in a state of good-natured hilarity for a week.

"You can't even tell a rattler from a rat snake."

Kendall shuddered at the thought. "You're right. McKee is hot, but he's miles away from the kind of man I want."

Did Lacy look disappointed? "Well, I wasn't suggesting we do any more than cozy up to the bar for a drink and drool at the sight of him when he manages to crawl out of that cell. I'm actually only allowed to gaze and drool."

Kendall took a deep breath. "We could definitely gaze and drool."

"You'll have to let your hair down. Literally," Lacy suggested.

Kendall self-consciously lifted her hand to her hair. She always wore it wound up tight. If only she could control her libido so easily. "Do you think so?"

It couldn't hurt to look.

"Honey, take the hair down. Do you have a skirt? And some big hoop earrings?"

"Why do I need all of that stuff?" All of a sudden Lacy sounded just like her mother.

"Are you listening to me?" Lacy complained.

"Of course. What did you say?"

"Wear high heels. No stockings." Lacy counted it out on her fingers. "Make sure your top is tight and don't wear a bra. Do you even own a denim skirt?"

She has no idea I learned all of this stuff at my mother's knee and some additional tricks. "Okay. But I still don't see the point if I don't want to get his attention."

Lacy smiled. "You want to get his attention. That's fun. But you definitely don't want to take him home."

Kendall decided Lacy was the queen of understatement, since they were talking about a dangerous criminal who got rough and rowdy in a bar and had to sleep it off in a cell.

He sounded perfect.

"He's pretty dangerous? But not like the missing girls dangerous?"

Lacy shook her head. "He's mostly dangerous to a girl's senses. He's actually in town to investigate…"

"He looks like he's in pain." Kendall mused. Not paying attention to Lacy.

"You'd be in pain too, if Arranger had tried to rearrange your face." Physical pain or emotional pain, it couldn't matter, Kendall was determined McKee would do more than look at her tomorrow night, or whenever he got sobered up.

Kendall hoped by the time Lacy understood what Kendall really wanted from McKee, she'd be too full of alcohol to protest much. The only thing left to do was to come up with the feminine equipment she apparently needed.

Kendall carefully wiped the droplet of water off of the mug shot so she could see the hard expression on the face of her man. "So, when do you think he gets out of the tank?"

Chapter Three

Kendall sat on barstool in a black leather skirt, hair loose, bright lipstick, and for a moment she saw her mother's hopeful smile, on the face of the woman in the mirror behind the bar.

I'm not really like her. All my dreams are practical. And if this plan is crazy, well, it's for a good reason.

Lacy danced her way across the wooden floor, jamming to the music coming from the jukebox in the corner.

"I can't get over it." Lacy gushed when she got close enough to be heard over the classic country tune. "I wouldn't have recognized you. And look at those tan legs. I thought you'd given up on tanning after that sunburn."

"It doesn't take much Texas sun to toast a girl."

Kendall nibbled on a peanut. While the bar hardly looked sanitary the alcohol should kill whatever bacteria she might pick up. And it kept her hands busy.

"I like your hair the best. It's so long."

"That's why I wear it back. It's always in the way." Kendall hadn't ever confessed how wanton she felt when she let her hair hang down to brush her waist. And she'd always dreamed of a lover who was turned on by her hair.

So, she kept her hair ruthlessly knotted up. Just like she'd tried to keep her fantasies under wraps. Unfortunately, both her hair and her fantasies tended to slip beyond her control.

But I'll be cured of that problem after tonight.

"Your hair's gorgeous. And I'm going to give you one of my necklaces to go with that outfit and your eyes. Amber, druzy, and mystic topaz would all look great on you."

"I'd love one of your necklaces. You really ought to sell them online. You're wasting your talent as an administrative assistant."

"I'm thinking about branching out."

Kendall nodded. Absently she stroked the hair sliding over her shoulder. She felt restless, and anxious, and full of anticipation, she self-diagnosed. Was she really going to go through with this?

"Tell me more about McKee," she prompted Lacy. "McKee." Lacy sighed. "He's tortured by Anne's murder." "Murder." Kendall repeated. "Murder?"

"He didn't shoot her," Lacy shook her head. "And it wasn't like the missing college girls either; they found Anne's broken body in the desert shot through the heart. McKee's been looking for her murderer ever since."

"Right." Tonight Kendall had intended to eradicate her inappropriate urges. It was logical a criminal wouldn't be interested in anything but self-gratification and therefore a lousy, if not outright disgusting at sex.

On the other hand, what if he hit her, beat her up, or murdered her in the process? She felt like an idiot for even considering flirting with a crazed man who'd torn up a bar on a drinking binge and had something to do with a murdered woman.

"Huh Lacy?" Slipping off of the stool, Kendall decided to go home before she got in any deeper. Satisfying a neurosis wasn't worth getting herself killed. At the moment her super-charged dildo was definitely a safer alternative.

"I'm going to get something out of the car..." She made it as far as the edge of the bar when the door opened and McKee sauntered into the room.

Suddenly, she couldn't seem to inhale-air wasn't important--she just wanted to breath him in. The man was more breathtaking than his picture, and he absolutely exuded sex. He spat pheromones into the air.

It was the only explanation for her dramatic and drenched female reaction.

I don't recognize him. I just want him, there's a difference.

How could she have gone from wanting to sulk away to safety, to wanting to push him down on the pool table, slip her skirt up around her waist, climb on top of him and take a ride on his cock on top of the green felt?

McKee glanced her way and there was darkness in his eyes. His bruised and battered face mesmerized her.

Lacy rushed up to Kendall's side, her blue eyes alight with excitement. Her gaze said I-told-you-so. "You ready for a drink?"

Kendall nodded, shakily. "Sure. I'm really thirsty." Actually, she was ravenous watching McKee prowl up to the edge of the bar.

"Sounds great," Lacy said with a wink.

Kendall wanted to laugh at her friend's sweet naiveté. Apparently, Lacy thought Kendall was totally inexperienced in picking up a man in a bar; when in fact as a small girl Kendall had observed all the tricks first hand, at least until she'd fallen asleep in the booth waiting for her mother.

"Lobo Lito okay?"

Kendall nodded absently. All of her energy focused on the man at the bar. As she approached him she felt her hips sway in blatant female invitation. Would he notice?

I can't really be thinking of going through with this stunt? Can I?

While standing at the bar Lacy gushed. "McKee's even better than I remember. Maybe I should throw Jason over and go after McKee-the-hotty." She sighed, and then she gave a big grin to the bartender. "Robbie, we'll have a couple of Lobo's Litos."

Robbie nodded while grabbing two mugs. "Don't forget to tell your friend about the disappearances. Warn her."

"I know about the disappearances." Kendall said while surreptitiously looking at McKee in the mirror over the bar. She didn't want to remind Robbie that she worked in the law enforcement office, not in front of McKee. He'd probably leave immediately.

"Two girls from Texas Tech have gone missing and everyone's looking for them. Including the violent crime experts." Robbie said loudly, looking over at McKee.

Kendall swallowed a gulp of beer as she peeked over the edge of the frosty mug at McKee. What did the bartender expect from a criminal? More violence? Or was he mentioning law enforcement as a warning to McKee to behave himself?

"Make sure you don't become one of those sad statistics, pretty lady." Robbie's look turned sour.

"Some officers should try catching bad guys instead of acting like them."

Kendall shook her head. She shifted close enough to whisper in Lacy's ear, "Robbie doesn't seem to recognize me from the last time we were in here. Is he okay?"

"Robbie's only seen you in your work clothes, when you have that I'm-a-professional, don't-touch, look, and he probably thinks he'd remember all that hair."

"We sure need help around here." Robbie prophesized.

Kendall wondered if the constant grind of the jukebox had given him profound hearing loss. Either that or he was getting senile.

"Shut up Robbie." McKee's gravely voice flowed like hundred proof whiskey from the end of the bar.

Kendall immediately lost all interest in Robbie.

"You'll scare the tourist."

"I'm not a tourist." Kendall protested.

"What are you?" His gaze stalked her.

"McKee. Leave her alone. Haven't you done enough damage?" Robbie gestured toward the back of the bar where the remains of several chairs lay stacked against the wall.

McKee took a step towards Kendall.

Kendall backed into Lacy, who barely managed to keep the mugs upright on the bar.

"I've been here most of the summer." Kendall protested.

"Where're you from? You sure don't sound like anyone from around here," he drawled.

"I'm from Virginia. I'm ah…graduate student here on ah…internship." *And I sound like an idiot.*

"Well, good for you. A tight ass, back east, bitch." "Hey," Lacy protested. "Be nice, McKee. She's a friend."

But Kendall's spirit's soared. This was exactly the way she'd expect to be treated; she was surely on her way to a cure. "I can be a bitch." Her mouth curved upward, challenging him. "If that's what you're after tonight."

"Kendall." Lacy sounded shocked as she introduced them. "This is McKee."

McKee's gaze traveled over the front of Kendall's thin tank top where her nipples were thrusting against the material and then looked down the length of her legs. "Maybe I should say I'm sorry. I'm in a surly mood right now. Kendall."

All of Kendall's nerve endings sprang to attention when her name rolled off his tongue like he was savoring it. McKee was definitely interested.

"You should get the hell outta my bar for talking like that in front of the ladies," Robbie declared.

"Robbie, McKee." Lacy sounded flustered.

"Hey, Old Man, I paid for those damages."

"Robbie,' Lacy tried to pacify the bartender who'd gotten red in the face and began gesturing wildly.

"Come with me." McKee pulled Kendall by the arm to a table near the door. "It's too crowded." McKee gestured toward two stools in the corner.

Kendall followed him, enthralled by the way his tight ass filled out his worn jeans.

She climbed up on the stool, her equilibrium a little shaky, so she took a cleansing breath. Barely resisting the urge to rub her arm where it still burned from his touch.

"We don't need them clucking over us, unless you'd rather travel in a flock like the rest of the chicks in this bar."

"I definitely don't flock." "Why?"

Kendall floundered, knowing he didn't really care, yet yearning to bare her soul, lay all of her problems on his broad shoulders. Or reach out to smooth the deep groove between his dark eyes. This man sucked her in and made her ache with vulnerability. She shivered and pulled her hair around her like a shield.

She didn't answer him.

"Hi Jake." An older woman with ancient eyes stumbled against a bar-stool and then righted herself. McKee reached out to touch the woman's shoulder solicitously.

Kendall averted her eyes. Glad to see he exhibited tenderness for the woman, but feeling embarrassed for the stranger because she appeared to be dressed little better than a homeless person.

McKee said something kind to the woman and then she drifted away. "You don't like Maggie?"

"I didn't say anything."

"Honey, your body language said it all."

Kendall met those dark hypnotic eyes. "I definitely know her type." He looked wary. "Her type?"

"Can we talk about something else? Please?" They were getting way off track. They were supposed to be getting to know each other on an entirely different level--a physical one.

"I don't know. You're cute when you've got your nose in the air."

"Very funny."

He looked at her intently. "I really want to know." He coaxed. Kendall sighed.

"Oh, you know. Maggie seems to be the type who can't commit to any job or anyone, but she claims she loves you. Can't provide anything, but aren't we having fun camping in the park?"

McKee looked at Kendall. Waiting. Like he was actually listening.

"She won't ever grow up. She believes in fairy tales." The words felt bitter in Kendall's mouth so she took a cleansing sip of the beer, mostly to keep her mouth shut.

And here I'm following in my mother's crazy footsteps. If I'm lucky he'll tell me to shut up, and go away.

"That's interesting. And pretty deep for a beautiful woman sitting in a bar."

"Right. Sorry. You prefer your women vapid."

Those ebony eyes crinkled in the corners as he grinned at her. "Nope. I actually have a taste for an intellectual with a bit of a bite. I still don't think your talking about Maggie."

Kendall tugged on her hair. "I was simply speculating about a personality profile."

Jeeze. It seems this trip's about my mother after all.

"So you don't believe in anything like visions or fate?" Did he sound relieved?

"No. I believe in science not fairy tales." *Because if I believed in fairy tales I'd be wondering why I've been dreaming of your face for years.*

He nodded. "Good. Me too. Because when you start to rely on things you can't see they slip away, mocking you and fu…mucking up your life."

He reached out and stroked the hair lying on her shoulder over her breast. "So let's skip the deep thoughts? Shall we?"

"Okay," she nodded. Wondering. But she couldn't suck in enough air to ask any comprehensible questions with his fingers millimeters from her nipple. Apparently, despite the questionable origins of her desire, she wanted to take him to bed. She really really wanted him.

"Maggie's not comfortable with the restrictions of your world." McKee told. "I'm not very fond of restrictions either, especially right this minute."

He glanced over at where Robbie and Lacy were looking over at them. Maggie? Were they still talking about Maggie?

"What restrictions?"

"We're consenting adults." She blurted out.

Thinking about the size and warmth of his hands, she wondered if they'd be similar to the size and warmth of his cock?

"Maggie lives in the moment."

Kendall almost wept when he took his hand away from her hair. Live in the moment indeed. The man could convince her to get naked right here and now. The fantasy of them having sex on the pool table re-played like a movie in her mind.

"Maggie's honest and open to her impulses."

"Shall we be open to our impulses?" She encouraged him.

His eyes heated. "Do you want to stay here and have another beer, or do you want to take a ride?"

"A ride?" They were finally moving in the right direction. But where exactly were they going?

"Do you like motorcycles?"

"Yes." She knew she sounded way more enthusiastic than she'd planned. She loved bikes. They aroused her; so they'd been a no-no for years.

"Then let's get outta here."

She nodded. Her brain clicking away. Would there be sex without any preliminaries? He'd have to wear a condom at least. Was it possible he'd be bad at sex? Brutish. Selfish.

She hoped so.

It would be better if he disappointed her, or yelled drunkenly at her for disappointing him. Or immediately fell asleep and snored. All sorts of scenarios drifted through her head as she slid off of the stool and followed him toward the door.

Every one of the scenarios involved sex.

Though both Lacy and Robbie protested when she announced she was leaving, Kendall waved at them before the doors shut behind her. She didn't need their counsel. She already knew she'd started something she couldn't stop.

McKee stopped in front of a black and silver Harley. She bumped into the side of him; all thought fled, as he reached out and steadied her. The man was a live wire conducting raw sexual current.

He looked at her strangely. "Have you had a lot to drink? Maybe you should go back in with Lacy."

Wouldn't he rather take advantage of her? She wanted him. Needed him. "I haven't had enough alcohol."

"You sure you're sober enough to understand what I want from you?" Kendall lifted her face to his in the moonlight. "What do you have in mind?"

Lowering his head, he blocked out the light. His kiss landed hard and fierce on her mouth. There were no preliminaries: he demanded, opened, and ravaged her mouth and she met him every inch of the way.

He tasted bitter and sweet at the same time. She dove deeper into the kiss. He tasted amazing.

His large hands ran down the stem of her waist and then the slope of her ass. Where one of his hands hovered teasing the edge of the tiny skirt, almost sliding around the curve of her buttock, almost touching her flesh, he made her need more. Demand more.

He wrenched away from her. "Damn, girl. You can kiss."

"For a tight-assed bitch." She stammered, because she could hardly breathe.

"You're just right for what ails me tonight. You still game?"

She guessed those were the preliminaries. Funny, how she didn't care about anything other than getting her hands on him again. "You got a condom?" The blunt question that came out of her mouth should have made her blush.

"I got everything you're gonna need tonight."

It shocked her when he handed her the helmet. Bad boys didn't care about such mundane things. She started to protest, and then realized if she didn't wear the darn thing her hair would be a tangled mess when they got where they were going. With practiced ease she twisted the long sweep of her hair up and tucked it into the helmet.

"Damn shame." He muttered.

"What?"

"Nothin. Are you gonna take all day?" He climbed on the bike and started it with a roar without offering to help her get on.

Kendall looked at the bike and then at the skirt. This wasn't going to work.

"Just pull it up." He sounded disgruntled.

Thinking he'd just drive away without her, she pulled the skirt up so high it left nothing to the imagination, especially not the pretty peach thong she'd worn for the occasion.

He made a funny sound in the back of his throat. She looked up to see him fixated on the thong.

It was empowering.

They stood looking at each other for a long moment, the breeze fluttering coolly on her bare thighs; though not cool enough to sooth the heat from his gaze. This was similar to one of her fantasies. He had only to grab her and carry her away. They would…

The sound of voices jarred them from their mutual trance. Customers coming out from inside the bar.

McKee's arm snaked out and grabbed her at the same time as she stumbled forward to land awkwardly behind him on the seat. With a couple of tugs she got the skirt tucked under her thighs. He looked back as if to make sure she was secure. Then the bike took off from the curb.

Once they were in gear, the powerful roar of the bike subsided to a throaty purr she felt all the way through to her core.

Bikes made Kendall feel so hot.

The vibration of the engine rubbing her clit felt like the sensation of a certain electronic toy she often employed.

Riding motorcycles eroded her self-control. So she'd only been on a bike a few times. Never had she dared to admit to anyone how bikes stimulated her sexually.

"Hang on Sweetheart." His gravelly voice blended with the road. He'd probably been chain-smoking his entire life. Pretty soon he'd have a cigarette with the same careless arrogance he'd take her body.

Where would he take her? A field? The park?

The thought of those missing college girls crossed her mind, but impatiently, she pushed away her fears. What was better? To go missing?

Or to miss out on life?

I'm crazy. I'm as certifiable as any criminal might be and I'm not sorry.

Wanting to experience it all, she reached up and unhooked the clip holding her helmet. Then she slipped the cumbersome thing off of her head and held it by the strap. Tipping as far back as she could without loosing her grip on McKee, she enjoyed the sensation of the breeze catching and teasing the long strands of her hair.

McKee grabbed at her arm as if he feared she might loose her grip.

Too late, I've already gone over the edge, she giggled. She snuggled as close to her bad boy as possible.

The sweet purr between her legs, the wind whipping through her hair, and the heat of the man against the front of her all intensified her desire until it burned in her blood.

This time she knew she wouldn't be able to keep her perspective and take notes in her head. Perspective was already lost in a haze.

Kendall had no idea how long they rode but it didn't last long enough, and lasted way too long. She hoped it was a preliminary to what else Jake McKee could make her feel.

They pulled up in front of a motel. For a moment she sat, trying to catch her breath, which had wheezed out of her chest until she felt like Lacy trying to inhale.

He sat for a moment as well, she wondered if he felt anything close to what she felt.

The naive thought made her smile. He was an experienced criminal with a long sexual history and who wouldn't be affected by a bike ride with an anonymous woman.

McKee turned off the Harley. "Why'd you take off your helmet?"

"You know why. It feels better. Sexy." She raised a hand to her hair to feel for tangles.

He nodded. Without indicating if he understood what she'd been trying to articulate.

Then he surprised her by saying, "Sometimes safe just doesn't cut it."

Kendall smiled. Apparently he understood the rebellious streak she so rarely unveiled. What else would she expose tonight? What would she strip off with her inhibitions? "What room are you in?" she asked boldly.

McKee's smile flashed in a nearby streetlight. He swung off of the bike with a fluid movement, holding it in place while he did so.

"I'm in seven."

She nodded. Slipping off of the back of the bike then handing him the helmet.

The bike was secured with a minimum of fuss.

She shifted from foot to foot. What was she doing here? But she knew. Physician cure thyself. Soon, she'd be on her way, a full PhD with a prestigious placement in a firm. Jamming her hands in her pockets, she tried to keep her feet on the ground.

"It's this way."

She looked up at the building. The little motel wasn't exactly a Hilton, and it looked even more ramshackle at night than during the day. Still, it was the means to redemption, so she followed him up the small incline to the room. Keeping her eyes on the delectable view of his very fine ass. The man filled out his jeans in a real impressive way.

With one hand he dug into his jeans for what she supposed was a key. She couldn't help noticing he was already erect. Wow. That was great... good. Wasn't it? She didn't want a con who couldn't get it up. Did she? Oh no, she was going to giggle...

He caught her noticing. With a grin he wrapped his long arm around her chest then pulled her close.

Her breasts were tingling as she struggled to breath.

Bending close to her ear, he whispered, "Are you still up for this?" "Well, since you are..."

His chuckle was deep and sensual, as he pushed her hair over her shoulder, giving him access to the sensitive side of her neck. He nibbled on her ear. And she melted. "Mmmmm."

His large hands curled around the flesh of her shoulders, kneading for a blissful minute, before smoothing her hair down her back. For a second he paused sensually, at the indentation of her waist, before running his hands over the curve of her ass.

Kendall sucked in a breath. Would he touch her out here? How far would he go in the glow of the porch light? Her legs grew weak. Even if the only witnesses were the bugs throwing themselves against the bulb, it seemed wicked.

Dangerous.

He went for it. His fingers boldly explored the curve of her ass under the skirt and the outline of the thong, dipping boldly into the heated moisture of her body. She clung to his shoulders, trying desperately to stay on her feet.

She wanted to see if anyone was watching and at the same time she didn't care. The man's touch was tantalizing.

So wicked.

She shivered as he pulled her closer.

This time his exploration including the silk thong. Skimming the damp material. Finding the nub of her sex, and stroking her until she shuddered. The purr from the bike had sensitized all of her nerve endings, and his expert teasing brought her desperately to the brink.

Then he stopped.

McKee held her away from him as he opened the door. "After you," he said with a strange little smile on his face.

Kendall thought she would have followed him into hell.

The décor hardly registered. Only that there was a bed. Her legs were unsteady as she took a step in that direction, but he caught her around the waist. Closing the door with a thud, he pushed her up against the cheap door, which shuddered.

"Baby, you've got me so revved," he purred in her ear.

"A condom." She didn't care if he had her right there against the door. She wanted him. But, she needed to be as safe as possible. "I have one in my purse."

"In a minute, princess. First I want a taste of you."

He kissed her. Ravaged her lips, nipping, love bites. While his mouth explored hers, he held her in place with his knee planted firmly between her legs. She would have gone over the edge if she could have moved at all. Instead he kept her just shy of an orgasm.

When he finally let her slide down from being pinned to the door, he put both hands on her breasts. Pinching gently, from the top and bottom he teased her nipples into knots. Roughed them, kissed them, and then suckled until she quivered.

The soft leather skirt brushed her legs as it fell into a puddle at her feet. Kendall opened her heavy lids to find his gaze avid on the thong. "Pretty," he declared thickly.

She reached down to feel if his arousal was as intense as her own and found his cock thrusting forcefully against the denim of his jeans. "Hmmm." She said, stroking though the course material. "Pretty hard."

As if she'd asked, he pulled the tab, and let the jeans slide down. He had nothing else on, and he hadn't been circumcised. Some sort of tattooing decorated the beautiful golden skin above his hipbone. He was so obviously wild. She took hold of his cock with a firm grip. He was a bad boy and he was all hers!

Her touch seemed to galvanize him as he ran his fingers along the edge of the thong.

"Want me to take it off?" she offered tentatively.

"No. Leave it on. We'll work around it."

True to his promise he moved his fingers around the thong and inside of her. With a flick of his fingers he teased her clit before he thrusting his fingers inside of her heat.

"Oh," she clung to his cock, trying not to squeeze too hard.

She lost all of her concentration when McKee flicked, then thrust his fingers inside of her again.

Each time the rhythm picked up momentum. Each time she tried to resist.

Pushing back against his pressure.

Thinking she could analyze this feeling in just a second.

Until it swallowed her up. Then she sank helpless down to the edge of the bed, no longer able to stand, too full of sensation. So swollen from all of the stimulation, so revved, so helpless, she couldn't think.

McKee pulled her over his lap. Pushing her thighs apart. Kendall lay vulnerable, lost with her face pressed into the spread. While he kneaded, pressed, flicked, and thrust with his fingers. He ravaged her until she bucked under him then he grabbed her harder.

"Stop!" she ordered, frightened of the intensity.

Ignoring her, he thrust so hard his thumb slapped up against her pubic bone. It made her come in a screaming, thrashing pinnacle.

He held her tightly while she rode out the sensation.

When Kendall could move her arms and legs weakly, she realized she was still lying over McKee's lap. Naked and ass up. The thong was gone, and he was stroking her hair over her back.

"All of the different shades of brown, gold, and red, remind me of the light and shadows of desert canyons."

"Hmmmm?"

"All of these different colors." He gathered a couple of the long strands and used them like a paintbrush to tease the skin of her lower back. It gave her goose bumps.

Then he brushed lower.

Oh my.

He rubbed the silky stuff on her ass, just as she had always imagined a lover doing.

"Many of my people don't cut their hair."

"I like the way it feels," she confessed. Not going into any detail in case he found her too amusing.

"I like the way it feels too. Roll over."

She rolled and he shifted until she was looking up at him. He pulled her shirt up and then using the hair as a brush to tease her naked nipples. Back and forth he brushed the hair over her skin.

Patiently, he began rolling her nipples with his fingers, and then teased them with his lips, his teeth, until she arched upward crying out.

The bursting orgasm came as a surprise. No man had stimulated her nipples so skillfully.

"You're so responsive." He reached between her legs. "But you fight your responses. I can see it in your face. This time you're going to watch while I take away your control."

"The condom. Let's do this. I want you. You can feel how much."

"In a minute, little mustang. I want to know all of your secrets before I ride you."

He started stroking again, going from lighter to deeper pressure. She held her breath with each thrust, but she couldn't resist him anymore than she could have stopped the sun from rising. She came with a resounding intensity and found herself clutching him.

It took him only a moment to turn them both over on the bed. Then he rolled the condom on his cock before she could protest that she'd wanted to touch the long length of him first.

It seemed he'd run out of patience, and without any ceremony, he thrust forcefully inside of her. Slick from his foreplay, she sucked him deep inside of her, to a place she'd never been before.

When he began the rhythm, she was with him, pulling him closer, until there were no boundaries between them.

The rhythm faltered. His control seemed to shatter. He came as close as physically possible, and she held him there until there was no sense of who was riding whom.

Nothing existed but the ecstasy and the heat, which seared, and then shattered inside her.

As she came back to herself, separate, adrift, she clung to his physical heat, snuggling up to his strong waist and long legs. His arm came around her as she sighed.

She floated, soaking in his presence. Then she sank inside a dreamscape.

Chapter Four

Kendall dreamed she and McKee were in a desert canyon. They stood on the edge of a ravine where dark striations slashed the earthen walls like the decorative markings inside a red clay bowl.

A full moon illuminated every detail.

They stood close together beside a Quarter horse. A twisted thorn brush clung precariously in the soil near Kendall's cowboy boots and she was grateful she was wearing jeans.

McKee's hair was nearly as long as hers, only black and glossy under a black cowboy hat. He also wore boots, jeans and a dark button-down shirt, with the cuffs rolled up and there was a knife sheath at his waist outside of a leather vest.

"We're all decked out. Where are we going?"

His answering smile glowed in the moonlight, and his look was as tender as his touch as he pushed her loose hair out of her face as a light breeze teased the strands.

"Will you come with me?"

"Sure." She told him. She couldn't help staring.

There were no bruises on his face. There were no worry lines. Just crinkling smile lines around those amazing eyes.

And she felt good too. Happy. Wonderful.

And that was weird. Good thing she recognized she was only dreaming.

"You may have a vision." He warned.

Dreams were interesting. She'd have to take notes right when she woke up so she wouldn't forget...

Inside the dream, Kendall felt herself frown. She didn't believe in visions. But she could be respectful of McKee's cultural beliefs. "Okay."

"It's a not a decision to take lightly."

Dreams were weird; because she could feel the breeze growing stronger, she could also smell the horse, and McKee's vividly male scent.

"Okay, whatever you need." Here in the safety of the dream she'd give him anything, say anything, to have him smile at her again.

But he hesitated.

"Yes, I said yes." She wanted to see his eyes light up.

McKee put his hands around her waist and effortlessly lifted her up onto the horse. Then he swung up on the horse behind her, pulling her close, and they rode into a valley where people were sitting around a glowing campfire.

"That's not fire." The glow looked unnatural.

"It's a spirit fire."

"Okay." *What the hell is a spirit fire?*

They dismounted and joined the people around the fire; many of them appeared to be dresses in a mixture of Native American and Western apparel.

These are his people.

Segregated from the people sitting around the fire, there laid a slender, blonde woman. She lay broken, like discarded trash in the dirt.

At first Kendall thought the woman was dead, but then the woman's head swiveled in Kendall's direction, like the bones weren't quite connected to her neck anymore.

Her eyes were deep blue pools of agony.

"You have to help me." The crumpled woman's voice shrieked like the mounting storm in the canyon. "I'm lost. And I can't reach him."

Kendall looked at the others around the campfire but no one else seemed to hear the woman.

Although McKee's brow furrowed as if he could almost hear.

He looked like all the happiness had blown away. He looked like the one who was lost.

"Will you help me?" The woman's voice made Kendall's ears throb. In the dream she actually covered her ears as the voice strengthened, and then swept screaming around Kendall, like the wind from a storm.

"I don't believe in this shit." Kendall said under her breath. But she trembled because she knew the power of dreams, and visions, and how they might drive you to do things you should never do.

"Will you hear me?" the woman insisted. Those eyes welled up with tears flowing with such intensity the water began to swell and flowed into the low places all around them. From the distance Kendall could see the water surging in the ravine.

The woman's pain magnified until it became a stream in the desert, threatening to swallow up the camp and everyone in it.

"Okay. Okay. I'll hear you." The healer in Kendall couldn't deny such pain. "But, I really don't believe in this shit."

Suddenly the desert dried up.

The wind picked up and it sounded like women's voices wailing in agony.

What in the hell had she agreed to?

Chapter Five

Kendall jerked herself awake. She was shaking from her reaction to the vivid vision.

It was only a dream. A terrifying dream, but only a dream.

Time to go.

Way past time to go.

She was here to banish dreams, not add to them.

She rolled away from his warm body on the bed, grimacing at the sensation of loss.

She wasn't a lonely, kinda woman. Give her a novel, a textbook and a computer and she'd be comfortable. But this was different. There'd been no clinical distance; that had been the point.

However, she hadn't expected mere sex to send her over an edge. Making her long to curl up next to him and drift off, wanting to roll him over and demand more sex.

I'm on a higher mission, she told herself. When a professional went to bed with a criminal she doesn't stick around. It was dangerous.

It was also a temptation. She sucked in her breath.

"Are you feeling good, Babe?" His deep voice brushed intimately over her like smoke in the dark.

Babe? Why did he care? Why hadn't he rolled over and gone to sleep. He couldn't ruin everything now. Yet he'd already ruined her plan by giving her the most intense sexual interlude of her life.

"I should be going." She choked out.

"You could stick around…if you want." He sounded nonchalant.

"I could probably make you lose control again in a few minutes."

He's certainly arrogant. "Trust me. You weren't good enough for a repeat performance. I already got exactly what I wanted," She lied, as she stepped off the bed on legs weak and wobbly. Stiffening her resolve, she managed to straighten up.

A couple of steps took her to the pile of clothes, which were tangled on the floor near the door. It dawned on her that she should have been embarrassed to be walking around naked in front of a stranger but she couldn't manage to feel exposed.

She accidentally kicked something and his cowboy boot fell over. As she righted the boot, a dull glow of something white caught her attention. She reached down into the boot.

She wrapped her hand around smooth material, which seemed to flow into her palm. As she pulled it out a few inches, metal glinted, and a knife slid out of a sheath inside the boot.

How could she have been so reckless? But instead of being frightened, she felt an adrenaline rush again. She turned back to look at him and found him sprawled, tousled black hair and golden skin against the white sheets. Still, battered, cuts darkening, but looking like he could definitely go another round.

He was so sexy. Her outlaw.

Time to get outta here.

Perversely, she kept ahold of the weapon because she'd never held a real knife. It was odd that it felt so natural in her hand. The handle must have been made of some kind of bone, because it was almost body temperature.

The blade had been fitted so carefully she couldn't feel the seam. The light caught the metal of the blade and slung it back at her.

"Be careful with it. It's lethally sharp."

"It feels so funny. There's something about it…it's familiar somehow."

"Put it down."

"Where did you get it?" *What the hell are you thinking Kendall? It's a knife. Get the hell outta here.*

"You can't have seen one like it. My father made that knife the day I was born. It holds a piece of my spirit and his. It's been ritualized. It's…"

He broke off like he was embarrassed. "Please. Just set it down before you cut your hand off."

She put the knife back in the sheath. There was something else inside the boot, leather, more metal? What other fascinating items did he carry to hurt people?

She picked it up. The world spun in a different direction. The item in her hand made him more than a stranger. He was no longer part of a cure for what ailed her; He was just a guy she'd slept without any preliminaries. Oh, god, she'd acted like a whore!

She had no doubt who was guilty!

Turning toward the bed with the badge in her hand, she tilted it to where the emblem caught the ambient light and lit up in her hand. "You're with the violent crimes division?"

"Not tonight."

"Really? Can you take a night off from being a lawman? It sounds a little too convenient to me."

"I could take the rest of my life off from being a lawman if I want to." He rolled over to look at her. "You didn't exactly ask for my credentials in your rush to get me into bed with you."

"How dare you!?" She wouldn't give him the satisfaction of knowing Lacy had vouched for him.

"With pleasure, actually."

She could feel herself blushing and was grateful he couldn't see her clearly in the dim room. At the same time she tried to squash the little thrill his words gave her. Pleasure. It had been …"You're a mess." She accused, pushing her hair back from her face.

"I had a shower this morning."

"I thought you were a con. I even saw your mug shot. I had this all planned." *How could Lacy have left out this little detail? Not that I'd been listening. She remembered how she'd felt when she'd seen his mug shot. Like she'd been hit by lighting. Like tonight…*

No!

He looked up from his position on the bed and for a second she thought of a snake testing the air. Had she imagined he looked relaxed? What had she thought? One night with the amazing McKee would cure even the sickest mind? She'd been so stupendously stupid.

"I don't know why you're making such a fuss. Forget the badge. I'm not going to fingerprint you. I've something more carnal in mind."

Now he thinks I'm a con? "That's not possible. It's not going to happen again. This is crazy."

Looking suspiciously towards the door of the room, he asked, "Are we expecting a jealous husband? Boyfriend? Girlfriend?"

"Don't be ridiculous. I would never cheat."

"Then, what exactly's the problem?"

"I said I saw your mug shot. I thought I was having relations with the criminal element." Looking him over, she grimaced. "You certainly look the part."

Especially when a look of disdain came over his harsh features.

"What are you? An idiot? Some kind of violent offenders groupie? "

"No, actually I'm… yes. I'm an idiot." She went to drop the badge on the floor, thought better of it and tossed it on the bed.

Then without any prudish discomfort, she grabbed her skirt and proceeded to try to wriggle into it, tripping, until she grabbed onto the wall and steadied herself.

She didn't see the thong, didn't care. Being half naked with McKee didn't seem strange. Of course, she was just in shock because this whole event had gone so spectacularly wrong.

Zipping up the skirt she just wanted to get out of his room. Away from any reminder she's failed in her assignment. A lawman. If she'd wanted a good guy she could have found one at home.

Still, no one at home had ever made her feel as elemental as she'd felt in his arms. "Do you use some sort of Indian technique for heightening the senses during sex?"

Wouldn't that be an excellent research paper? Or help for couples looking to enhance their sexual relationship? Maybe she could salvage something from this experience.

"Did you use your brain?" He raised one eyebrow.

She smiled. No one had ever accused Kendall Waite, student extraordinaire, of not using her brain. It was kinda refreshing.

Picking her shirt off the floor, she had to untangle it from his tee shirt. It was hard to restrain herself from burying her face in his scent. *Of course she knew his pheromones only appealed because of genetics. Her body recognized the fundamentals.*

"You really thought I was a criminal?" He asked. It sounded like it was finally sinking in.

"Forget it."

"You could have gotten yourself killed. Raped. Abducted. Haven't you heard Robbie's incessant ranting about the two students missing from the college?"

Incessant. Big word. Of course. He'd have a degree in Law Enforcement and other credentials. The man was educated, experienced, and a fantastic lover. In other words he wasn't the one. She'd have to start all over again or go back home a failure. She sighed as she reached down to untangle her heels from his jeans.

"Did you hear me?"

She pulled her top over her breasts. "Yeah, I've got to go. Uh, thanks."

"What?"

"Thanks. For the…you know. It was pretty good. But I've got other stuff…" She gestured. How to explain the unexplainable?

"How are you getting home?"

"I'll call Tommy. He does the cab thing for Robbie's customers. Thanks." She put the strap of her little pocket purse over her shoulder.

"Stop thanking me. What's wrong with you?"

"Nothing, you're just not the one. I'm sorry."

He looked utterly stunned. "I'm not the one?"

She shook her head. And then she walked out of the door.

#

Jake McKee stared at the door that had just been shut in his face in utter disbelief. If not for the smell of her perfume, and the peach thong peeking out from under the sheets, he'd have thought he'd had a vision of amazing proportions.

He's had lots of experience with women but nothing like this had ever happened before. First, he'd had a mind blowing sexual experience. Then she'd blown him off like it hadn't meant squat to her. No awkward tries at attachment. She hadn't even asked for his cell phone number or tried to establish a common ground.

Hell, she'd rushed out of here like he was the devil himself. As if she knew he was a shadowed man. Shit, she'd certainly been the woman of desires.

That's why the prophetic shit drove him crazy. It was just too obscure. It could apply to any situation. And it might not apply to any situations at all.

I don't feel shut off from those stupid dreams. I'm glad I can't see the spirit world or sense a soul in trouble. No more spirit fires for me. I don't care about any of that shit. I'm glad to be normal. Why should I care about any of that?

A man found himself floundering unless he had something real to hang on too. Law Enforcement. Regulations, rules, laws, they often drove him crazy, but they also anchored him, except the mountains of bullshit paperwork.

Rolling over he tucked a pillow under his head. Regretting she wasn't here for a repeat performance. She had the most amazing little body, that silken hair which reminded him of the softest fur cape, and she responded with the gift of elemental passion.

He could imagine Kendall in a desert storm. She would probably revel in the violence of the rain, and the teasing of the lightning dancing through the valley. Then when she was sated, no doubt, she'd pack up her magic and move on.

Kendall hadn't even used his name; he doubted she'd remembered it. There was a graphic name for a woman like her. Only he was too polite to use it.

Chapter Six

"Sssss of a Whore."

Kendall looked up from her desk to find a flushed and sweating Sheriff Foley leaning heavily against the doorframe of his office bracing himself with both beefy arms on either side.

"Sheriff Foley's what's wrong?" She cried.

Pushing her rolling chair out from behind her desk, she jumped to her feet, racing to Foley's side just in time to support him as his knees bent and he started sliding downwards. She tried to wedge herself under his arm to keep him upright. His immense weight pressed on her, hurting, and she thought she heard him swear again.

More than anything his swearing scared her. Foley was Baptist to the bone and she'd never heard him say a dirty word.

"Greassssy breakfast." He mumbled, shaking his head slightly, and she could see how his normally florid completion had gone completely colorless.

"Doctor warned me. Hurts like a bitch…" He pressed against his chest with one large fist, listing to the right.

Kendall immediately grasped the seriousness of what was happening. "Do you have nitroglycerine pills? It's your heart."

He tried to pull himself upright. "Naw. Its jusssssss indigestion." But the effort seemed to exhaust him and he slumped over again clutching the frame of the door with all of his strength.

Knowing she couldn't hold him up, Kendall tried to push Foley down toward the floor, "Sit on the floor. I'm going to call for help."

But he hung on, feebly, swearing at her.

While, she didn't want Foley to hit his head on the cement floor, she knew he needed immediate medical attention, so she left him clinging to the doorway.

Muttering something to himself.

She hoped he was praying for both them.

Running back to her desk, she looked for her cell phone, but it wasn't anywhere her desk. "Where is it?" she cried. "Oh shit!"

But even as she cried out, she picked up the handset of the antique law enforcement telephone, and dialed 9 1 1.

"Damn it," The rotary dialing took so fricken' long…"This office is still in the stone age as far a some of the equipment…"

It began to ring.

The emergency dispatcher immediately came on the line.

Kendall kept her voice calm as she described Foley's condition to Imogene Jung, who also worked as nurse at the local, urgent care clinic.

"Yes. Imogene, I do know some of the basics. Yes, I'll keep him warm, and quiet. Just hurry. Send for the ambulance right now! He's got to go straight to the hospital in Lubbock." She slammed the handset down on the desk.

She looked over at Foley, he still struggled to hang on to the doorway but he looked shrunken, half of his usual size.

"I'm coming Sheriff, just a second."

Kendall grabbed her purse out of the drawer in her desk. She turned it upside down on top of her desk. Her cell phone fell out, of course, then her wallet, assorted other crap, and the small bottle where she kept pills.

When she had the bottle in hand, her hands shook so hard she wasn't sure she'd be able to get the childproof lid open.

She knew about aspirin therapy. If it were given at the onset of a heart attack it could help prevent some of the damage done to the heart muscle. But she couldn't remember if she had any regular aspirin in the bottle.

A thud and a moan alerted her to the fact Foley'd run outta of sheer stubborn, and hit the cement floor.

"I'm coming. I'm coming," she chanted.

Tears filled her eyes. She'd never imagined being alone and responsible for a heart attack patient. Even after her CPR certification. Had she been arrogant enough to think she was ready for clinical therapy?

The childproof cap spun in her hands clicking, and she felt the panic lodge in her throat.

"Stop."

Kendall heard an urgent voice inside her head.

"He needs you!"

"What?" she gulped back a sob.

She'd heard the same voice in her dreams before and after she'd left McKee late last night.

"Now I'm going insane," she almost sobbed, her sweaty hands slipping impotently on the childproof cap.

Foley made terrible sounds from the floor. "Fuck! Get it together, Kendall!"

She'd worry about this new trend of hearing voices later. Suddenly, as if she'd willed it to give up it's contents, the cap flew off of the bottle and several tablets spilled into her hand. There were three white tablets with B's on them that she knew were aspirin.

"Thank God. Thank God." She said, not inclined to question if there were a God at this particular moment.

Kendall grabbed a pen off of her desk and then turned and rushed to Foley's side. She went down on her knees beside him. His eyes were unfocused, and he was breathing harshly, almost snoring.

She crushed a tablet in the palm of her hand using the end of a pen like a pestle. Thinking Foley might choke if she presented the whole pill, although he needed as much aspirin as she could get in his system: because Foley had to weight nearly three hundred pounds.

She put the tip of her finger in the powder and experimentally poked it inside of his mouth.

He didn't bite.

A reluctant smile crossed her face and she shoved the powder deeper into his mouth, trying not to gag.

The powder seemed to dissolve and he hadn't choked on it, so she scooped up some more and put it inside of his mouth. Wondering if any of the aspirin powder was actually getting down his throat.

"You might be able to swallow it if we can get you sitting up."

Foley rolled his eyes but she couldn't tell if he'd heard her, and he was a huge, dead weight with his head nearly in her lap.

"This aspirin will help until the ambulance gets here. I can hear them coming down Main Street. Hang on. Can't you hear the sirens?"

He groaned.

"Please, try to swallow this, I know it tastes bitter but you've got to try. Help's coming. Right now! Just a couple more swallows until they get here. Sheriff? Can you understand me?"

Did he nod? She thought so. "Can you help me prop you up into a sitting position?"

"Ummm litttt...mmm"

"Okay. Don't try to talk." Kendall put some powder in his mouth and was glad to see him grimace at the taste. A bit of saliva pooled in the corner of his mouth. "I'm going to get under your arm and push until you're sitting up." It sounded good, in theory.

Kendall nudged his arm up and then tried pushing at his chest; she used her legs to push herself under his side. She dug in with her summer sandals but her heals slipped on the cement so she kicked them off and used her toes.

Foley tried to help, until his position was a little more upright and she got his head propped up, except she'd have to wriggle back around in order to get the aspirin anywhere close to his mouth. God, she needed help.

"What the hell?" McKee sauntered into the office and stopped just inside the door. "I know he's not a criminal so you can't be interested in..." McKee stopped abruptly, apparently assessing the situation, and then he moved in to take some of Foley's weight off of her.

"He's having a heart attack," she panted. "I've been trying to get him to sit up, so I could give him more aspirin."

"He's foaming like a dog." McKee sounded strange.

Thankfully he wedged Foley up against the door, anchored the sheriff with his body.

"I've never seen a heart attack victims foaming at the mouth. Do you know what you're doing? This isn't normal. Bad spirits...I mean symptoms."

Ah, she thought, this was obviously an example of how McKee's culture interpreting things differently.

However, she didn't have time to debate the proper course of action. Within seconds, she'd caught her breath, and turned around, and crushing the remainder of the aspirins in her palm. "Trust me," she admonished.

McKee grunted under the Sheriff's massive weight.

"It's the aspirin and saliva." She poked the powder as far into Foley's mouth as she dared. Then rushing over to her desk, she grabbed a napkin, and then rushed back to wipe Foley's mouth. He grimaced which she considered a good sign.

"I don't know how much he's getting." She almost wailed. "But I don't think it's enough. I thought I heard the sirens. This town has three streetlights. How long can it take and why the hell are they taking so long!?"

McKee ignored her. Saying something under his breath.

She didn't recognize the language. He almost sang, rather than spoke, the unfamiliar, beautiful words he chanted with such intensity. She knew he was asking for intervention from the spirit world.

The sound of the sirens got louder.

The ambulance pulled up right outside the building. "Thank god." She said reflectively.

"Which one?" He asked cryptically.

She smiled at him. No man had ever looked so good to her. She hoped it was because of his timely intervention.

Because she'd dreamed of him every night after she'd left him on Friday night. In those vivid dreams he'd made love to her endlessly, reaching deep inside her, touching her as no man had before.

Either way it wasn't the best news.

Chapter Seven

It took the EMS Technicians about fifteen minutes to get Foley on a gurney, then stick a bunch of nasty looking tubes into his arms. McKee watched with sympathy, noting that nothing humiliated a strong man like modern medical personnel and their paraphernalia.

Foley wasn't down and out yet. As they'd attempted to estimate how many aspirins Kendall had crunched up and fed to him, Foley actually seemed more aware of his surroundings.

"McKee, you're…in charge."

McKee nodded reluctantly. What else could he do? Foley seemed satisfied.

The sheriff was strong. His strength came from within. McKee's uncle would say Foley's tremendous weight represented the substance of his soul. The doc here just nagged about cholesterol and too many chicken fried steaks.

McKee thought of the lecture Foley had given him the other morning. When McKee'd been an unwilling *guest* in one of the cells. In a tone that could only be described as a roar, which had made McKee's already throbbing head ring, Foley had educated McKee on the consequences of not cleaning up his act, moving on, and getting over what ailed him.

McKee actually grinned at the memory. The old man was obviously way too ornery to die.

"Where's Chief Anderson?" McKee asked Kendall who sat on the corner of a desk like she had no strength left in her legs.

McKee had to admit she'd been incredible, if a bit unorthodox. After her abrupt departure the other night, he couldn't have imagined they would work so well together.

"He's in the hospital in Lubbock." She explained while wiping her face with a Kleenex. Then she pulled up her hair, twisting it ruthlessly, then securing it with a hair band.

McKee watched her twist up her glorious hair with some regret. He smiled when hunks of it fell back down to caress her neck. He could see her hands were shaking.

"Hernia surgery."

"What?"

"The Chief of Police had a hernia surgery with complications so he's not going to be riding to our rescue any time soon."

"Shit!"

"Deputy Nelson's in Florida, his mother's very ill."

McKee knew what was coming; like a storm on the horizon, and he was trapped in a canyon. "Fuck."

She tilted her head up, her golden-brown eyes wide in her pale face. "Could you control yourself? I think we could use a little leadership and stability around here after this morning."

"Aren't you on a high horse? I would have thought a stuck up, back east girl like you had heard it all."

"At least I didn't hear it when I was sleeping it off in a jail cell."

He noticed she chewed on her lower lip-looking none too confident. He thought about giving her a break until he noticed a paper that must have fallen on the floor during the crisis. It was Arranger's mug shot. "No, you were busy shopping the mug shots."

"You bastard. How can you be so rude!?"

"Honey, I call them like I see them."

"You aren't acting like a professional lawman. It's no wonder you landed in a jail."

"Isn't that why you picked me up in Robbie's bar? Because I'd been in jail?" He'd actually thought it had been mutual attraction, and his ego was stinging.

"Can you just go?" She asked pitifully.

The hurt in her pretty face made him suck in his breath. Turning away so he wouldn't have to see how he'd wounded her, he felt an unfamiliar frustration. Admiration warred with his instinctive wariness; she was a reckless force of nature, a power to be reckoned with.

He didn't have time for forces. He didn't have time to listen to his uncle or the spirits anymore—and he already regretted not heeding his uncle's warning.

He had to concentrate on his job with the Lubbock County Violent Offenders Task Force, and Last Chance *was* inside his jurisdiction.

He'd come to this town because his partner had been murdered and he needed to find her murderer and discover the whereabouts of the missing girls. He'd been drawn here looking for a clue or maybe he'd just exhausted all of his other options.

Most importantly, right now, he had to get his hands on and destroy the mug shot. With Foley in the hospital it might fall into the wrong hands—it obviously already had fallen into the wrong hands.

Not that he'd been thinking about his career these days but he wasn't exactly proud of what he'd done at Robbie's bar.

He looked inside Foley's office at the empty chair. He couldn't fill those extra wide boots, but he could stick around and keep an eye on Kendall. Keep her from shopping the mug shots and getting herself killed.

No one else should die.

He entered the office and carefully shut the door behind him. Once inside the Sheriff's office he looked around trying to figure how to get out of the situation. He ran a frustrated hand through his too-long hair. He needed a haircut. What was new?

Kendall had acted correctly-giving Foley the aspirin- but the pills were bitter medicine. They'd made him foam like a mad dog.

McKee fought a shudder. He had a phobia about rabies going back to his childhood.

He didn't need a dream to know there was an evil spirit here. Some bad shit was about to go down. He'd like to think like a white man and quell his superstition but he knew there were spiritual aspects to life which couldn't be ignored simply because he didn't want to acknowledge them. He sighed.

"Officer McKee don't you have somewhere you need to be?"

Even through the door, Kendall sounded uptight. "No."

Why did she rattle him?

"Are there any phone numbers or files you need?" She yelled.

"No, damn it!"

"Foley had a list of emergency numbers. You might want to call his wife." Kendall's voice tapered off like she was sniffing, maybe crying. "I can call Janice, or the hospital can notify her, and then we can offer to pick her up and take her to the hospital so she has someone with her…"

"I'll take care of it."

It would be easier to get rid of Kendall if she would just dissolved into female hysterics. Why did she feel she had to be a heroic? And why didn't he want to give her credit?

Probably because she slept with me and then walked away without a backward glance.

He actually felt trapped in Foley's office with Kendall standing outside the door.

"I'd be happy to help. It's my job. Plus, I've got to call Lacy anyway and then…" Kendall was still yelling through the door.

McKee eyed the Joe's Diner coffee cup on Foley's desk. It was empty of all but a drop or two of coffee residue.

"McKee? Do you hear me?"

He picked up the mug and then let it fall from his fingers to shatter on the cement floor into a million shards of white ceramic.

There was blessed silence from the other side of the door. He felt better.

"What the hell are you doing in there?"

"Breaking a pattern."

Kendall shut up. Then he heard the sound of the doorknob turning, and the creak of the door opening

"Why did you do that?"

He kept his back to her and the door. "Because it felt good."

"Oh. I usually need a good reason, in triplicate, before I do something." Her voice trailed off.

"Including what we did Friday night?"

"You'd never understand."

He let it go. He didn't want to understand or care, but he was finding it difficult not to ask. "I'm probably going to stay here until either the Sheriff or the Chief get back on their feet, since I'm in this area anyway. My partner will be joining us. We'll be doing actual police work." He ground a piece of the mug on the floor under his boot.

"I can help you."

"Yes. Get out."

"I mean I can really help you."

"By shopping the mug shots?"

"How dare you?!"

"How dare you pick up a stranger in the bar, you thought was a criminal?"

She was breathing hard but she didn't answer.

"Bring me the mug shot."

She didn't ask which one. Instead she spun around and went into the other room. She returned with the mug shot and thrust it at him. He grabbed it without looking at it and shoved it in the drawer of the desk shutting it firmly.

"I'd like to help." She said almost meekly.

He spun around to look at her. "What makes you think I need your help?"

"I've been here for a month and I know the routine, and there's Lacy. We'll get you settled." She sounded more confident.

"I don't need you."

She smiled. "We'll see."

Then she sauntered into the reception office. For the first time since the crisis with Foley he noticed she was in bare feet, with pretty pearl polish. He hated the way she'd tamed her hair.

"We need a dress code." He muttered. Her feet were too sexy.

"We have a dress code."

"You seem to be barefooted."

She paused as if considering his comment. "Are you always this difficult to get along with?"

"Yes. In fact, I'll need your employment folder."

"Are you questioning my credentials? This town was lucky to get someone like me. I received my PhD. With honors." She told him smugly.

He didn't want her here: tempting him with her brave spirit and her reckless femininity.

"I need someone who doesn't sleep with the inmates."

Her face flamed. Those eyes snapped. "What I do on my time off is my business!"

"If I'm the boss, it's definitely my business."

"Oh! It would serve you right if I left."

Obviously furious, she hesitated, as if she didn't want to leave. What was a woman like Kendall doing in Last Chance?

It didn't matter he had to get rid of her. She was a distraction he couldn't afford.

She got up and slipped behind the desk, as if it would protect her from his wrath. "If you fire me, Foley's will chew you up and spit you out. Watch and see. He's tough. In a few days he'll be strong enough to send you packing."

McKee leaned against the doorjamb. Kendall was so passionate it was exhausting. Too bad, she wasn't using the passion for a more enjoyable type of exhaustion. "Not if I tell him that your sexual preferences run to criminals," he smirked. Now he had the upper hand. She'd turn tail and run.

The look on her face made him wonder.

"Look at me?" she twisted the pearl stud in her perfect ear.

"What?" He had a real bad feeling about what was coming.

"I'll tell Foley I knew you were a lawman all along, and I'll tell him I trusted you not to take advantage of me, even though I'd obviously had too much to drink." She gave McKee a smile full of guile as she settled into the part, putting her hand to her face, and fluttering her lashes.

"Oh Sheriff Foley, I'm not used to drinking hard liquor. I'm a debutant. A good girl. I wear pearl studs to the office." She said in a voice full of little girl innocence.

She stopped fiddling with her earring and gave McKee a sly smile. "He'll come down on you with all three hundred pounds." She examined her nails as if they were discussing the color of her manicure.

McKee knew her dramatic performance would have exactly the effect she suggested, on both Janice and Sheriff Foley. Foley actually believed women needed to be protected.

Who'll protect me? "So, you would lie?"

"Like a rug." Her smile was pure innocence.

"You think you have everything in your life under control?"

"Sure."

He winced. "So you expect me to work with you as if nothing ever happened?"

"Yep."

"Do you promise not to look for another criminal to pick up at Robbie's bar?"

"It's none of your business what I do when I'm off duty."

"Why'd you do it?"

She pushed a stack of colored post-it notes across the desk at him.

There was a phone number written there.

"I suggest we keep our conversations professional. Perhaps you should call Janice Foley?"

Wanting to strangle Kendall with her own hair, he chose the more mature path and walked away with the phone number tucked in his pocket. He settled in the Sheriff's chair and called the number.

Janice answered immediately, from her cell phone. She reminded him that in a small town, news was the only thing that traveled faster than emergency vehicles. She told him she and the Sheriff were waiting for the emergency helicopter to come and transport Foley to the heart hospital in Lubbock.

By the time McKee hung up the phone he felt calmer. Convincing himself that he could tolerate a couple weeks with Miss Debutante.

"Fricken, frick, fuck!"

McKee was on his feet before he knew it, then he was through the door. "What's wrong?"

"My foot." She raised tear stained eyes to tell him. "It's on fire. It's one of those damn things!"

He moved in to help but hesitated to put his hands on her again. It had been combustible the first time around.

"Oh! shit!"

A scorpion curled its tail upward there under her desk.

Kendall moaned, lifting her foot to examine two angry bites under her big toe. "It hurts so much. I hate those things. Is there anything in this stupid state that doesn't bite or sting?"

"Are you asking me?" He resisted the urge to reach down and brush the tears off of her flushed cheeks.

"I already know you sting."

McKee smiled as he ground the scorpion under his boot "What are you smirking at?"

"Nothin'"

"Go away. You, you,…bastard."

"Naw, I think I'll stick around in case you swell up and swallow that dirty tongue."

"You're horrible!" She looked him right in the eye. "I hate you."

"You could quit. Go home and save us both a lot of grief."

"No." There was a stubborn line between her eyes. "You can't make me. The Texas critters can't make me. I'm staying." She fished a piece of ice out of a cup on her desk, and then rubbed it on the biggest of the bites. "I don't quit anything."

"You sound like a sullen teenager and I'm supposed to trust you to run the office?" He hoped he didn't sound as weary as he felt.

"Get out. I don't need your help; in fact I'd rather die than have your hands anywhere on me!"

He leaned forward so she wouldn't miss what he said next. "That wasn't the impression I got Friday night."

"Oh!"

He put his fingers under her chin, lifted it slightly, and then looked directly in those stormy eyes. "Just remember you haven't got everything under control."

"I know what I'm doing!"

He nodded. "I think you'll live. This time. I can't vouch for the next time you do something stupid."

Pulling away from her was almost physically difficult. Her passion drew him in dangerous ways. The golden light in her eyes, her glorious untamed hair, her beautiful curves and most importantly the lightning in her soul was electrifying.

Desert lighting could easily kill a man.

"In fact, I'm rather glad you didn't die. You wouldn't believe how much paperwork is required when reporting an accidental death." He winked and walked out of the office.

A heartbeat later he couldn't help but grin, when he heard the sound of glass breaking against the door he'd pulled shut behind him.

Apparently, she'd be breaking some patterns of her own. Only she didn't know it yet. The great spirits were tricky bastards. McKee might enjoy watching what they had in store for feisty Kendall Waite, if he hadn't already planned to stay the hell outta the way.

Chapter Eight

Around ten o'clock Tuesday morning, McKee made it into the office, and Kendall thought he definitely looked rough around the edges.

Unfortunately, her libido appreciated his unshaven, scruffy look combined with his unofficial, worn-out jeans because her heart stumbled and then accelerated as she recalled the way he'd looked minus those jeans.

"Good morning." She gave him the brightest smile she could manage so he wouldn't guess the dirty thoughts running through her usually ordered mind.

Lacy added a quick hello.

"I'll be helping out in this office," McKee growled. "Until collective law enforcement gets back on its feet. My partner will be joining us soon." He looked like he'd rather be in a jail cell.

Pointed at Kendall, he admonished. "I'm going to be watching you." Then he stalked into Foley's office and slammed the door.

"I hate him." Kendall muttered. Lacy smirked. "He was *that* good?"

"As I've told you repeatedly, it's none of your business."

"I was floored when you left the bar with him. I didn't know you were the impulsive type. Getting carried away by your hormones and everything."

Should she blame it on hormones? Or stupidity? Surely there was something. "I'm not impulsive. I always have a plan, and right now I plan to drive him right up the wall."

"I plan to pamper him." Lacy sauntered over to the coffee pot and poured a large cup of coffee. "He's cute."

Then Lacy went over to rap sharply on Foley's office.

"What the hell do you want?" McKee barked through the door.

Lacy jumped, sending coffee sloshing over the edge of the cup to puddle on the floor. "Oops."

"What do you want?" He repeated, his voice loud and impatient. Kendall grinned, wondering if Lacy had the courage to go through with her errand.

"It's me. Lacy." She answered apologetically from outside the door. "I thought you could use some coffee."

"Come in."

Kendall got up to get some paper towels to wipe the trail of coffee from the floor. She smirked when Lacy came right back out of the office as if she'd been summarily ejected.

"I'm sorry about the floor." Lacy offered. Looking harried.

"It's industrial strength cement, so don't worry." Kendall sat back on her heels. "Please explain to me why you want to pamper that incredibly rude man?"

Lacy grinned. "Because he's beautiful."

"So?"

"And because he's been through so much pain in the name of a woman. It can't help but break your heart."

"God you're such an incurable romantic." Climbing up off of the floor, Kendall motioned Lacy toward the kitchenette in the front corner of the building. "Tell me everything you know about him."

"His partner was killed almost exactly one year ago. That's why he broke up Robbie's bar the other day. Because he hasn't been able to figure out why she was killed or catch the killer."

"He just informed us that his partner was coming." Kendall didn't intend to feel any sympathy for the man.

Lacy shook her head. "His former partner was a woman named Anne. She was a little firecracker with an attitude and a gun. I really liked her a lot."

Kendall fiddled with her earring. "I wish Foley had stopped eating all of those chicken fried steaks when I told him. Surely his doctor explained that his cholesterol was too high."

"Well, I'm eating healthy." Lacy got a yogurt container out of the little refrigerator. "You're a little short in experience. Chicken fried steak is as Texas as rodeos, and longhorns. You couldn't make Foley change his diet with good advice. And I'm sure he'll be fine."

Her voice trailed off as if she were really afraid Foley wouldn't be fine. "Janice told us Foley's condition is stable. He's too strong willed to die."

"Are all the men in Texas as stubborn as Foley?" Kendall asked, considering the man in the inner office."

"No, McKee's worse.

"Great."

"And he's special. He's got some Native American blood."

Kendall refilled her coffee cup, trying to act as if she wasn't curious about McKee. "What tribe?" She asked as if she didn't really care. Not that she'd know one tribe from another. But it certainly explained some things; McKee was different, fascinating, and dangerous, like the knife she's found in his boot.

"It's the Jumano Nde tribe, which means Red Mud Painted People." His uncle's the Shaman and he's determined to get the tribe recognized by the Federal government. McKee's partner is Rider Blue Storm, his cousin, and another member of the tribe. Rider says McKee was in line to be the Shaman because they believe he can contact the spirit world."

Kendall nodded politely even though she didn't believe in spirits. "I wonder how they speak to the spirit world."

"Prophetic dreams. I had a few dreams that seemed to come true. And I hear… I mean…dream about spirits." McKee interrupted their conversation, leaning arrogantly against the counter just outside of the little kitchen nook. "You want to know anything else?"

"We didn't hear you come in," Lacy stammered.

"We're having a private conversation." Kendall pointed out to him.

"Private? About me?"

He ignored Kendall. "Lacy will you please go over to the post office and see if there's a package for me?"

"Sure," Lacy stammered.

"Now."

Lacy shot Kendall a wide-eyed look, set her yogurt container down on the counter, and then rushed out of the door.

"That's crap! Couldn't you come up with a more plausible excuse?"

"Does it really matter?" He stepped right inside the small kitchen nook crowding her.

She grabbed a donut off of the table; to give her hands and mouth something to do that wouldn't get her into trouble. She took a large bit.

She could almost feel him staring at her mouth as she chewed.

"Is there anything else you wanted to know about me?" He asked casually.

Shaking her head she said inanely, "These donuts are dangerous for your health." She found a spot of chocolate icing on the knuckle of one of her fingers and without thinking; she touched the glaze with the tip of her tongue.

His gaze burned. "Like you."

The temperature rose a couple of degrees. Kendall wondered how sturdy the little table would be if he laid her down on top of it. She chewed vigorously; she'd never admit what she was thinking. Not to him. Not to anyone. "I'm a pretty straight-forward woman." She lied.

"Then you're not particularly honest with yourself."

"Like you were *real* honest with me the other night."

"I had no idea you'd object to sleeping with a lawman; from now on I'll be sure to whip out my badge."

"You were quick enough to whip out something else." Kendall muttered. "And that's where I would suggest you pin your badge."

"I'll bet you never spoke to Foley like that."

Absently she took another bite of the donut. She'd like to know what it would feel like if he licked the chocolate icing off of her nipples.

Where was Lacy?

How long did it take to go to the post office? "Shouldn't we get to work?" She urged.

"I thought you had some questions for me? Why don't we get them out of the way?" He took a step closer.

She couldn't think of anything. She could barely think. "What's with the knife?" Kendall blurted out. "It's not standard law enforcement issue."

He took another step closer and put his hand on her shoulder. She tried not to react.

Breathe, one, two, and three.

Time to chase him away before she gave herself away. "Didn't you get the message? I'm not into lawmen."

"You smell sexy. Even though you look so prim in those khaki pants and that prissy white blouse. It makes me want to mess you up." He stroked her hair. "Besides, I'm not only a lawman. You shouldn't try to compartmentalize. Accept all the different pieces of your heart."

"You sound like a philosopher."

Sighing, he let his hand fall to his side. "Naw."

She waited for him to elaborate and instead, he just leaned there looking incredibly decedent. "Is there anything important you want to tell me? If not, I'll just speculate." She asked tartly. "It might be entertaining to enquire around town. It's a small town."

"My uncle tells me the path of one's destiny will eventually be laid out by the great spirits. Or some such shit." He pushed his hair back from his face. "So, I'd be careful of thinking you're in control, it'll come back to bite you on your pretty ass."

She was in control. She'd definitely taken charge. Look how bold she'd been the other night. So what, if she'd had a little setback in the shape of his badge. "So you'll be a Shaman?" Kendall asked. "How fascinating. Do you really have visions? What does that mean exactly?"

She didn't dare mention her own dreams; or that his face had been featured inside those dreams for as long as she could remember. She felt goosebumps on the back of her neck at the thought. Coincidence. Nothing more.

McKee raked a hand through his hair as if embarrassed. "I haven't had a dream in a year."

"Oh."

"But when I did dream, I dreamt of spirit fires and sometimes the dead would speak to me."

Kendall sucked in her breath. Her legs wobbled. Wow. She really didn't want to know anymore.

"It's okay. I'm sure that's personal information. We should, uh, get back to work." She didn't want to talk about her old dreams. Nor admit she'd been having new dreams since they'd been intimate, about spirit fires and a dead woman. And she wouldn't even acknowledge the voice she'd been hearing when she was awake.

I'm not going crazy.

"I thought you wanted to know stuff about me. Isn't that why you were pumping Lacy for details?"

"I'm not interested in the that stuff." She pulled away.

"You don't believe in prophetic dreams?"

"In counseling, we tell our patients to pay attention to their dreams. I wonder if any of the symbolism transfers across cultures like common mythology symbols, the whole universal myth theory."

"Myths? Are you hiding behind some theory?"

Exactly. That's exactly what I'm doing because the alternative's too weird.

"What do you do besides work as a clerk for the distinguished law enforcement agency of Last Chance?" He sounded almost angry.

"I majored in Psychology." She braced herself, knowing he would ridicule her career choice. "I'm taking my boards soon, to become a counselor."

"Sexual obsessions, fixations and other weird shit?"

"Absolutely not. Why would you ask me that?" She felt incredibly vulnerable. Hadn't he enjoyed the sex? He'd taken her somewhere she'd never been before. And unfortunately, she really wanted him to do it again.

He shook his head. "Most counselors are looking to cure themselves."

The thought had occurred to her, though she didn't appreciate it coming from him.

"Is that supposed to be a revelation?" Why wouldn't he stay out of her head? Didn't she have enough problems? She hated him.

She desired him.

And to be fair, he had every reason to be incredulous of her credentials after her behavior the other night. "At least I didn't get myself immortalized in a mug shot."

"Why don't you two take a break?" Lacy suggested, interrupting them from the doorway, sounding slightly breathless from the speed of her errand. "Agent McKee, there wasn't a package, but they said they'd call our office if one arrived." She looked from McKee to Kendall. "In the meantime can we help you settle into the office? Do you need anything?"

McKee shook his head as he moved away from Kendall. "I'm going out to the car to get my files and my laptop."

Lacy nodded.

Kendall sagged against the counter, bracing her weak knees. That man was dangerous to her equilibrium. She'd never been so distracted by anyone's sexuality.

The outside door slammed behind him

"Wow. I knew you must have had fantastic sex, but now you've got to tell me all of the sizzling detail."

"If you were paying attention to more than your active imagination, you'd see we're not exactly getting along."

"Yeah," Lacy fanned her face. "That's why the temperature's about ten degrees hotter than it was before he sent me on a goose chase to the post office."

"Why don't we pretend the other night never happened?" Not that Kendall believed it was even a possibility.

Lacy grinned as she shook her head. "Come on, this's a boring town. We thrive on speculation and innuendo."

The outside door banged open as McKee blew back inside with a stack of boxes in his arms. One box slipped off of the top, and fell, the contents exploding all over the floor.

McKee cursed, but he didn't look back at the mess, as he trudged past the women, into the inner office.

Lacy looked at Kendall. "Should we grab those?"

Curiosity getting the best of her, Kendall nodded. Together they scrambled around, picking up file-folders, pages, and pictures off of the floor.

One small red-leather book attracted Kendall's attention. She reached for it, touching it, and then pulling back as if the book burned her fingers.

It's my imagination.

This is probably McKee's version of a little black book and subconsciously I think it's probably smoking hot.

And I would never lower myself to snoop. Never.

She sat frozen in place with her hand hovering ridiculously over the book.

"Grab it," a voice commanded. "That's my journal."

What the hell? No way. Kendall shook her head as if she could shake the voice from her head.

"Do it," the voice insisted.

Furtively, Kendall looked up to see if Lacy had noticed anything. No, she was busy stacking the contents of one particular folder that had come apart leaving a pile of pages strewn all over.

"Lacy, did you hear anything?"

"Huh? No. I'm trying to get these into some kind of order."

"I thought I heard something. Or someone." Kendall said cautiously.

"No, I didn't hear anything." Lacy didn't even look up from her task.

No. I'm absolutely not taking orders from some random voice inside my head. It's not professional, it's stealing, and it would be the end of my career if anyone ever found out.

"Get over yourself and grab my journal," the unfamiliar, but compelling voice demanded.

"Oh, damn." Lacy said.

Kendall looked up from where she squatted over the book to see Lacy chasing a single sheet of paper as the fan sent it blowing across the cement floor.

While Lacy had her back turned, Kendall nudged the book under the closest desk--her desk.

This voice thing's probably just an excuse for more questionable behavior. But I guess looking through his book is probably no worse than sleeping with him.

Just then, the man in question stomped out of the inner office, pushing the outside door hard enough that it thumped against the wall. "Just stack those inside my office. I've got an errand to run."

Kendall jumped. Had he seen her lift the book?

See voice, you're going to get me in trouble.

Of course, the voice didn't answer.

Where was an imaginary voice when you needed it?

Apparently, McKee hadn't seen anything, before he'd gone thundering out of the front door.

Kendall climbed to her feet, feeling wobbly, jittery.

She told herself she could merely leave the book on the floor under her desk, until someone else noticed it, and brought it to her attention. She'd pretend to be surprised. No one would ever suspect she'd snooped.

I didn't snoop. I won't.

"I think it's going to be a little more exciting with McKee in charge." Lacy declared with glee. Stacking the remaining stuff haphazardly in a box.

Kendall felt pretty sure Lacy hadn't noticed her snagging the book. "Yeah, about as exciting as a blustering Texas thunderstorm."

But Kendall couldn't stop thinking about the consequences of stealing McKee's book—which was a definite change in her personality and ethics.

Her mother would be proud of her ingenuity. She'd totally go for the voice being real.

Her mentor would have a lot to say about mental illness, and how such conditions were often hereditary, and could manifest at any time in a person's life.

Am I seriously going crazy or what?

Chapter Nine

Kendall headed for the coffee pot in her little house, lured by the delicious aroma, and the added bonus of homemade cinnamon rolls dripping with cream cheese icing sitting temptingly on the counter beside her coffee pot.

She seriously needed a caffeine and sugar fix.

It was impossible to sleep. Every time she dozed off, she had vivid nightmares filled with haunting voices-one haunting voice in particular.

She grabbed a piece of cinnamon roll and stuffed it into her mouth so she wouldn't think about it.

The majority of activity at the law enforcement building had been inquiries about Foley's progress, and folks delivering comforting home-baked goods, like the delicious cinnamon roll she was enjoying.

Janice Foley had stayed at her husband's side, calling in to give Kendall an occasional task of filing paper work or sending a message along to one of the police stations in Lubbock.

McKee was hiding out in Foley's office, when he wasn't avoiding the office altogether.

Kendall finished the roll, and then checking her tile floor for any unwelcome pests, she stepped forward in her bare feet. She wouldn't make the same mistake twice. It was amazing Texans hadn't eradicated scorpions from the landscape. Couldn't they use pesticides? Napalm? A-bombs?

This state was a downright dangerous place. From one hundred and two degrees in the shade the thermometer had recorded yesterday, to any number of obnoxious critters.

Like McKee.

Precious meowed from her perch on the counter and Kendall patted the Persian absently. "Yeah, Precious, I'll feed you."

The cat meowed again.

No one would know it, but the prissy Persian had an unexpected wild streak, and had likely run away from her previous owner before Kendall had rescued her from the animal shelter.

Wild. Thoughtless. Like sleeping with a stranger.

Are these dreams a way to deal with my guilt? I don't feel guilty. I just feel like tracking him down and having sex with him again. Is my subconscious trying to warn me away from dangerous behavior? Make me want to get away from Last Chance and…everything? Especially McKee.

The cat meowed.

"Okay. Okay. I'm getting the food. And I'm not really hearing voices. It's only my imagination."

Precious meowed encouragingly as Kendall got out a can of cat food. "I'm just emotional. Foley almost died in my arms and I had unusually great sex with a lawman and then embarrassed myself. I'm just trying to deal with the shock of all this stuff subconsciously."

Kendall slammed the can of cat food down on the counter. "Shit! I didn't come all the way to Texas to end up crazier than when I started out!"

Precious leaped off of the counter and then moved over to hover at the edge of the doorway.

"Sorry." Kendall said to the empty room. "I'm used to talking to myself but I'm not used to hearing other people's voices in my head."

The cat bolted for the other room.

She hadn't read the little red book. She'd left the book under her desk; and the next morning she found it sitting inside her top drawer.

No ghost puts a book inside a desk. The janitor probably did it.

Kendall remembered arguing with the blue-eyed, broken woman last night in her dream. "I'm not reading that book," Kendall had insisted.

"Yes, you're going to read my journal." The broken woman had informed her.

"No offense, but you can't make me."

"You sound pretty childish." The voice had taunted her. "Read the journal and there's a good chance I'll leave you alone. At least one of us will sleep in peace."

"I don't care about either one of you," Kendall had told her earnestly.

"Like hell." The broken woman informed her. "You're gone on McKee. I know I was gone on him."

"You were his lover?"

"His partner. Not his lover, mores the pity. You know who I am. Even though you're pretending to be crazy rather than admit it. I'm Anne."

Kendall had awakened, heart thudding, head pounding. Wondering at the way her subconscious was working. Nothing about the situation felt rational. Least of all her reaction to McKee, those feelings scared her more than her conversations with a dead woman.

The voice I'm absolutely not hearing when I'm awake.

The sound of her Beethoven phone ring tone interrupted her thoughts. Relieved to have something else to think about, Kendall grabbed the phone off of the charger. Assuming she knew who was calling her so early. "How do you know I'm up? I might still be half asleep or getting my coffee."

"How did you sleep?" Lacy asked.

"Fine," Kendall lied.

"I didn't see you at Robbie's last night."

"I had some studying to do." Kendall lied again.

"What are you doing today?"

"All kinds of exciting things," Kendall said sarcastically.

"Well, you won't be complaining about the lack of entertainment tonight because you're going to have to put on your cowboy boots. It's fair weekend."

"Fair?"

"People have been talking about it all week and town's been unusually empty since everyone was setting up down at the fairgrounds. Doesn't any of this sound familiar? Oldest fair in the county, midway, livestock, funnel cakes, and a cowboy band that's going to knock your socks off. We even get some folks all the way from Lubbock."

"My socks *are* off." Kendall wiggled her toes.

"I'll pick you up around two this afternoon. I'll bring you some boots to wear."

"Why so early? It's going to be hot. Really hot."

"Because there are events all day long. I've got to be there for the stock show: my niece's showing a calf. There's gonna be BBQ, rides, and beer. It's going to be a whole day of fun...and I even got a table so I can showcase my jewelry because you've been nagging me."

Kendall gave a little yip of pleasure. "Wow. You're going to sell some of your jewelry?"

"Yes. You have to be there in case I crash and burn. You can hold me through my storm of weeping."

"I'm there. And there's no chance of crash and burn." "Don't expect too much."

"Then we'll do a website and…"

"Okay, Kendall. I'm nervous enough and I haven't even told you about the dance. We're going to finish off the night by dancing with cowboys."

"You're engaged."

"I've got lots of old friends and relatives standing in line to dance." Kendall thought about a long day of doing nothing but thinking in her house, thinking about the voice and…McKee. "A calf could be fun. A fuzzy little calf might be sweet."

"Fuzzy little calf? They usually come in close to a thousand pounds."

"Okay, so I won't touch the calf. I'll still go."

"Good girl. You've got spunk. It's too bad you're too old for the greased pig contest."

"Thanks, for small favors. Bye." Kendall set her cell phone on the counter and then scarffed down a rather large piece of the gooey roll. Since she was planning on dancing later, she could afford a few extra calories now.

Then she spent an overachiever kinda morning cleaning everything in her house with the music blaring loud enough to drown out any voices.

Wishing she could clean out whatever was wrong with her mind as easily as she cleaned the dust outta the corners.

Chapter Ten

Kendall was never more grateful for the distraction of Lacy's knock at the door.

"Oh boy, am I glad to see you. I've never been so bored." She had to push the cat out of the doorway as Lacy came inside.

"Why aren't you studying for your boards?"

"I was taking a break. I've been a little distracted lately."

"Are you finally going to tell me what happened on your date with McKee?"

"Shut up and hand me those cowboy boots before I kill you."

Lacy waved a pair of tan cowboy boots. "No details, no boots."

"Nothing happened." Kendall crossed her fingers behind her back. "We took a little ride on the Harley and then he took me home."

"McKee took you home without putting his hands on your body? I doubt it. He's been looking at you all week long like you were tastier than any of those cinnamon rolls."

"Would you believe a kiss?"

"No, way! That man had more than a little taste, if his present state of distraction is any indication."

"If you'll let go of the boots, I'll tell you on the way." Kendall coaxed. "I've got to get out of this place."

"Okay." Lacy handed her the boots.

"I'll need some reciprocal information." Kendall said as she sat down on the couch and tried to pull on the boots.

"Like what?" Lacy made herself comfortable on the arm of the couch.

"I'd like to know more about McKee. The inside info as to how a special taskforce officer gets himself slapped in jail for the night."

It was a more honest way to get information than reading someone's secrets from their private journal.

"And I want to know more about Anne."

"I've got it all, Baby. I'm information central."

"Why did Foley put a special taskforce officer in jail?" The boots were surprisingly comfy.

"Probably, because the Arranger boys play rough. I get the vibe Foley thinks the brother's dirty, despite the fact that James Arranger's in the highway patrol. The brothers might have gone after McKee later that night, or the next day when he was vulnerable, sleeping it off."

Kendall stood up and walked around the room. "I wish someone had told me McKee was in law enforcement. It would have saved me a lot of grief."

"I told you, but you were totally fixated on that mug shot."

"Why take a mug shot of a law officer?"

Lacy shook her head. "I think Foley was so angry that he wanted to show McKee what a fool he'd made of himself. You know make him feel ashamed enough to straighten up."

"These boots feel pretty good."

"I think you're changing the subject. But it's okay. Here. Put this on."

It turned out that Lacy had brought more than the boots. Kendall obligingly squeezed into a little jean skirt and tight tank top. Then there was the fabulous necklace draped fetchingly over her cleavage. Let McKee drool. It wouldn't bother her at all. She even let her hair fall down her back in a ponytail.

It didn't take long to drive out to the edge of town where a huge field had been cleared for the fair. Midway rides were set up in a large circle teaming with people of all ages.

Kendall and Lacy walked over and were soon swallowed by the crowd of hot, but happy, humanity. They wandered around the field being hailed by everyone. It felt small and intimate to be greeted by so many friendly townspeople. It gave Kendall a warm feeling.

Of course it could be the soul-sucking heat. Standing in line, in the Texas sun, for yet another lemonade, flavored with the sweat dripping off of her nose, Kendall dared to asked more questions about McKee. "Why would a law-man get himself busted?"

"You heard he's all broken up because he lost his partner. That night was the anniversary of Anne's death. She was shot execution style, left in the desert, and no one knows why." Lacy nibbled on a plate of gooey nachos loaded with jalapenos and melted cheese.

A thousand questions crowded Kendall's busy mind. She took a bite of fried bread dough dusted with powdered sugar, called a funnel cake, and tried to organize her thoughts. "His partner, Anne."

"Yeah. His new partner is also his cousin, Rider Blue Storm. I imagine Rider'll be showing up soon."

"You mention him a lot."

"No, I'm just expecting him. You know, Partners stick together."

Kendall nodded, though she wasn't convinced. "Okay, another Indian agent. Is he as cute as McKee?"

"Honey, Rider's too-hot-to-handle. The man's pure player. I would never take him seriously. He's left broken hearts strung across the entire territory."

"McKee hasn't?"

"McKee's the brooding type. He doesn't play often. Rider can charm the pants off of a cowgirl in record time. He's fascinating. He's amazing. Worse of all, he knows exactly what he does to a woman's blood pressure. You just can't seem to help yourself."

Lacy sighed and touched the small diamond ring on her left hand. "At least until now."

"Okay. About the former partner, Anne, it sounded like they were romantically involved? Is that why he's so broken up?"

Is that why she's so sad? So alone in the dark?

Kendall waited to hear the voice but it was silent.

"Let's sit in the shade." Lacy suggested as she handed Kendall cold lemonade. "You look like you're wilting and I need a hit on my inhaler."

Kendall settled thankfully under a circus-type tent that at least kept the sun off. Fanning her heated cheeks, she wondered if she was getting sun burned despite all of the sunscreen Lacy had sprayed on her. "Thanks. How can you people take this heat?"

"It's a dry heat."

"Yeah. I've heard that." Kendall watched the colorful crowd eating and moving around through the thin haze of summer dust stirring under their boots. "What was Anne like?"

"She was fierce and beautiful. I don't think they were romantically involved; but he sure took her death hard. He hasn't been the same since. He used to be quite a hero around these parts, even saved Robbie's life during a knife fight, but he's changed since Anne died."

Kendall tried not to feel sorry for the brooding agent but she couldn't seem to help it. She tried to get into his head, understand how he must be feeling. "He's supposed to balance the scales for strangers, yet he can't even do it for a friend- possible lover. Nor can he escape his past, which is usually a compelling underlying compulsion. In McKee's case it probably includes a cultural disassociation."

Lacy looked over at her in surprise. "Wow. Deep. I guess that's why you're the professional."

"Did you go to college?"

"For three fun-filled semesters. I went to Texas Tech."

"Isn't that where the missing students disappeared from?"

Lacy shuddered. "Yes. They went missing during different semesters. No one knows anything."

"And Anne was found in the desert."

"Yeah, but there's no apparent connection."

"Nothing?"

"They were all petite and blonde, as Robbie keeps pointing out. Just like Anne. It makes me feel like a possible target. It's eerie."

"Don't think about it. College kids do any number of crazy things. They might still show up alive and well." Kendall hoped she sounded more positive than she felt.

Lacy looked down at her watch. "We've got to go. It's time for the chili cook-off."

"Great. You Texans like your food as uncivilized as the rest of the state."

"Hot. We like our state hot."

Kendall wiped her forehead. "Yeah. That's an understatement."

"Just concentrate on the cowboys. The heat they'll generate will definitely make-up for any discomfort you may be feeling at this moment."

Kendall thought about McKee. Hot. Okay. She could definitely handle things hot. "Lead the way."

They wandered toward the tent where the merchandise was being set up, stopping at the chili cook-off tables along the way. There were numer-

ous samples, which Kendall decided to avoid altogether. "You get some."
She told Lacy.

"I'm feeling a little queasy." "Its just nerves."

"If you say so."

They entered the merchandise area and got assigned to a table. Lacy
took several lengths of velvet in different colors out of a bag. "I thought
these would compliment the pieces I've chosen."

"Your eye for color's amazing." Kendall wouldn't have noticed the
stones Lacy'd chosen contained so many colors until they were nestled
artistically against the different colors of velvet. "This looks great."

Lacy bit her lip. "Are you sure?"

"Yes, I've never noticed all of the striations in turquoise until now.
Your star cut topaz is really beautiful."

"Do you think these will sell?"

"You'll run out of merchandise in an hour." Kendall predicted.

They were so busy Kendall barely felt the heat until there was a lull in
the women gathered around.

A couple of girls came up to the booth. One of them stopped to look
at the earrings. "Oh, my friend Amee would love these earrings." The dark-
haired girl exclaimed.

"Yeah. I kinda like them myself," said the girl beside her. "Whatever
happened to Amee anyway? I heard she transferred out?"

The dark-haired girl frowned and put the earrings down. "I don't
know, JayLynn. I can't seem to get a straight answer outta anyone at Tech."

"Wow, this bracelet's great. They can't give out information at Tech?"

"I can't get anyone within the university to give me any information.
The professor who was willing to talk to me didn't make any sense-he said
she had a serious boyfriend and they went off to Mexico."

"Amee's probably back in Texas by now. She wouldn't move to Mexico
indefinitely."

"I don't know where she is." The dark-haired girl looked at Kendall.
"My friend would love, absolutely love, these stones." She grabbed the cell
phone out of her purse, hit a couple of buttons, and then she held it up for
Kendall. "This is Amee's picture. Have you ever seen her before? Maybe she
came by to look at the jewelry?"

Lacy looked at the photo of the small blond girl, shaking her head. But
she felt all the little hairs stand up on the back of her neck.

Weird. Kendall got an image of a dried up riverbed with the same striations and sparkles that set off the golden druzy stones Lacy had used to make the earrings.

What was happening to her? More importantly, what had happened to Amee?

"Ask questions," Anne's voice prompted her.

Get outta my head. You don't exist. This is just a sympathetic reaction to finding out McKee probably loved you—or something.

Kendall shook her head to clear it. "No. Sorry. I haven't seen Amee, but you can leave your cell phone number and I'll give you a call if she comes by to look at the jewelry."

The girl nodded. "Thanks. It's so not like Amee to just disappear. I know her mother's got a webpage describing her and pleading for help and it's linked everywhere at Tech but no one seems to know anything"

"Ask more questions." Insisted Anne's voice.

If you know everything, why can't you just tell me? Not that I believe in you or that I'd believe you...

There was no answer from Anne's ghostly voice.

But Kendall felt she had to try. Even if the voice only existed in her subconscious. "When did Amee go missing?" Kendall asked curiously.

"Well, she really didn't actually go missing from Tech, she quit. I guess. It just felt weird. She left without saying goodbye. And she would never do that."

"You mean she left owing you five hundred bucks." JayLynn said dryly.

"No, she would've called me. And she was hardly ever mad at her folks."

"Except when they wouldn't give her money for books after she gambled her text book money in Vegas."

"I still don't think she'd just disappear."

"She'll show up. She just has a new guy and she's busy."

"I think she's in trouble. I just have this feeling."

The girls turned away from the table, still arguing about their missing friend.

Kendall allowed herself be distracted by the sales activity because it beat wondering if she had a future outside of the mental ward.

Chapter Eleven

Sunset snuck up on them, setting the evening sky on fire. If the temperature had cooled at all, the cowboys drifting in from the midway definitely heated it back up. Kendall had mellowed because of all the cold Texas beer she'd consumed.

Kendall and Lacy waited in line for another beer while admiring the parade of men in black and white cowboy hats. "How do they decide what color hat they want?" Kendall mused aloud. "It must certainly say something about how they perceive themselves, heroes or rebels." She didn't confess how much more the men in the black hats appealed to her.

"I'll keep that in mind." Lacy laughed. She'd pulled a pretty red cowboy hat over her hair. "But try to look at them as a woman, instead of a counselor, or you aren't going to have a good time."

Kendall nodded. "I'm definitely looking at them as a woman." There was something about a man in a cowboy hat and boots sure to send the female pulse skipping along at a heady rate. She wrapped her hands around her cold beer and sighed.

Okay, maybe Texas had its pleasures after all.

One cowboy stood out, especially from the back where his jeans hung lovingly to his tight ass; giving her a jolt right down to her toes, until he turned, noticed her, glowering at her from the edge of the crowd. "Of course, he's chosen a black hat."

"I guess I know which cowboy you're fixated on." Lacy laughed.

"I'm not fixated."

"Let's go talk to him." Before Kendall could protest, Lacy took off through the crowd toward McKee-dragging Kendall along by the arm through the crowd.

Kendall didn't want to loose Lacy in the crowd, so she went along. Eventually, they got closer.

Kendall noticed an island of space around McKee. Was it a dangerous aura that alienated him?

"Hey, McKee, I'm glad to see you here." Lacey gushed. "Can you keep Kendall company for a few minutes? I've got to find someone." She blurted out, before rushing off into the crowd.

"Damn." Kendall muttered almost under her breath. McKee's smile was slow and sexy.

"Why are you so happy? We don't even like each other."

"We don't have to like each other to give each other pleasure."

Kendall shook her head tightly; she really wished he wouldn't smile like that because it did dangerous things to her heart rate. "How did Lacey convince you to come out to the fair?"

"She wanted me to help sell her jewelry."

"Are you still looking to fuck the local bad guys? You'll get hurt if you're not careful. Hurt bad."

She didn't flinch at his use of the curse word-in fact it hovered between them. The word, the possibilities, and oh, she wanted him to do that to her, again, take her outta here right now. And it must have shown on her face.

"Are you crazy?" He asked.

Maybe. But not in the way you're thinking. "I can handle myself. I'm a big girl."

"You certainly give this event extra dimensions." He complimented her with a heavy-lidded expression and an admiring glace at her cleavage.

She wanted him to run his hands over her bare skin. She wanted it so badly. It was so easy for him to set her on fire.

"Are you here as the local law enforcement?" She gave him a parody of a smile. She couldn't let him think he could seduce her again. "Are we stuck with you here in Last Chance? Or will they be sending someone else to keep the peace? We didn't see much of you this week."

"I'm surprised you'd want to see me."

She tilted her head trying to see his expression from under the black hat. "Is that an apology?"

"I don't think what you did was wise. But if I can't convince you to go on home, then I think we should keep things cordial between us. Keep the peace."

"Thank you."

"I still want you to steer clear of anyone you might see in a mug shot." She felt the heat in her face. He didn't know much about keeping the peace.

"I'm not the one who ended up in a cell."

"Hard-headed to the end."

"You have no idea."

Lacy bounded over with a gorgeous dark haired guy on her arm. "Look who I found in the crowd, Rider Blue Storm."

"McKee."

The men nodded at each other.

Rider's smile flashed under a tan cowboy hat. A matching suede vest covered his shirt.

"Oh, you've already had words?" Lacy asked Kendall.

"Of course not. No. He actually found some class and apologized."

"I did not."

"Did you proposition her?" Lacy asked McKee avidly.

"Can someone please catch me up?" Rider Blue Storm asked. "I seemed to have missed a few steps."

Glad of the interruption, Kendall stuck out her hand to the cowboy in the tan cowboy hat. "Hello, I'm Kendall Waite, I'm sorry Lacy's too busy being indiscrete to introduce us. And McKee's just being an ass."

His smile was mischievous. "Hello. And aren't you one to tell the whole truth and nothing but."

Kendall felt a smile tugging on her lips.

"Kendall, this is the other half of our violent crime team, Rider Blue Storm. They're cousins, and no matter what he says Rider has a similar effect on women. Except for me of course," Lacy explained.

Rider's smile shone like a full moon. His spirit was obviously brighter than his cousin's. The man was devastating good looking, but he didn't affect Kendall's pulse rate the way dark and dangerous Jake McKee did. "I'm pleased to finally meet you. Lacy's been telling me all about you."

Impishly, Rider tipped Lacy's cowboy hat until it threatened to tumble off of her pretty hair. "It's always nice to be appreciated by a beautiful woman. Especially, if she's saved me a dance."

"I'd love to dance, just remember your manners." She pushed the hat firmly over her hair.

Kendall looked over Rider's shoulder. Arranger, the man from one of the mug shots, strutted right through the center of the dance floor.

"Uh oh."

Rider turned to appraise the situation.

Having been a witness to many bar fights, Kendall scouted out a long table where it might be safe to hide if a fight broke out.

"Don't worry, Kendall, Lacy." Rider reassured them. "It's too early for anyone to take him on. They aren't drunk enough. We'll have him tucked away in a cell before he becomes a problem." He started toward Arranger and McKee.

Kendall and Lacy followed in Rider's wake.

Arranger approached McKee with a cocky, menacing stride. "Hey, Injun, you and me got a score to settle," Arranger hollered.

"Shit." Rider said. "I didn't figure on him gunning specifically for McKee."

"You know that stuff you missed," Lacy told him. "Well it included a little argument with McKee at Robbie's bar."

"Get lost, Arranger, and I'll forget you ever showed up here tonight." McKee told the man calmly.

They all waited to see if the man would be wise enough to take advantage of the opportunity McKee was offering.

Unfortunately, Arranger stood there bristling. He grabbed a beer can from a nearby table and guzzled it down, despite the protests of the man to whom the beer obviously belonged.

Rider hurried forward. Kendall and Lacy followed blindly, with Kendall wondering what the hell she was doing.

"Don't think a tin badge is gonna save you." Arranger barked. "It wouldn't if you were some big shot secret agent," he sneered. "I'm gonna take you down even further than I did before. Shithead."

"You'd better go and sleep it off before I teach you a lesson." Retorted McKee.

"Naw, I've a few more things to say." Arranger scratched his chin.

"I don't believe we've met. I'm his partner and I'm also metaphorically wearing a badge." Rider spoke up from where they stood beside McKee.

"That mean you got his back?" Arranger looked them over with cruel blue eyes. "You and the pussies?"

"The man's brilliant." McKee taunted.

"I've not only got his back, I'm fixin' to come down on you like a rock-slide unless you leave right now. We got a lot of good folk out here having a nice evening."

Arranger leaned toward McKee. "I don't wanna take on anyone, but you." He gestured toward Rider. "McKee, you go a round with me and this pretty boy don't get hurt."

"No." Rider said abruptly. "We're a team."

"Sure." McKee contradicted.

Arranger rubbed his hands in apparent anticipation.

"But we've got to take it outside of the crowd. You want to go over to the livestock barn?" McKee nodded towards the stockyard.

"What? You got a bunch of additional pussies out there? What are they? Sheep? I'll bet you don't care what you fuck."

"Just a few of your close relatives."

"I'm gonna show you what kinda shit you're made of, chicken shit."

"McKee, this guy isn't worth loosing your badge. Especially after the incident in the bar." Lacy warned.

McKee just nodded towards the barns.

"I mean it McKee. You aren't going to waste yourself on this asshole." Rider closed in on Arranger.

McKee stepped between them. "Rider, you stay here and keep an eye on things."

"Don't." Rider warned. "He's a worthless piece of shit.

Arranger looked from McKee to Rider.

Kendall watched, fascinated. McKee was all business, but the threat of controlled violence resonated in his voice. His shoulders where tight while his arms rested ready at his sides. She knew the signs of a man ready to fight and he demonstrated all of them.

Meeting McKee's gaze, Kendall shivered with the excitement of the moment. Not because she wanted to see McKee in danger, but because the man was so sexy when he was puffed up on testosterone.

Like the champion bull they'd seen earlier in the day: heavily-muscled, docile, beautiful, with great big calm eyes, eating his hay in his stall, but everytime he moved those muscles rippled.

"McKee," she wanted to say something but her head was so full of contradictions she couldn't find the words.

"McKee." Rider, on the other hand, crowded Arranger.

It looked like Rider was trying to make himself the target. Then McKee could just take Arranger to jail. Kendall half hoped it would work. Unfortunately, Arranger seemed to have fixated on McKee.

"Rider. I need you to get my back." McKee said.

The statement had a galvanizing effect on Rider. He stopped trying to rile Arranger, allowing the men to walk by.

Rider stood ridged. Probably frustrated and angry, but he stayed.

"Aren't you going to help him?" Lacy asked wide-eyed.

"I can't."

"It's like a code." Kendall hypothesized, torn between going with McKee and staying with Lacy. "It means he really needs Rider to do this for him. It's a trust thing. It probably goes back to their childhood."

"I'd rather be kicking Arranger's ass." Rider said tightly neither denying nor confirming her guess. "I can't believe McKee's risking his career on that scumbag."

"We could follow and see if he's okay. I could scream if it gets outta hand and McKee needs help. You'd have an excuse to come running. No one could blame you." Lacy offered.

"He'd be furious."

"Not if we go in the side door; he'll never see us."

Rider looked undecided.

"The last time he fought this guy McKee got knocked out. Arranger doesn't fight fair." Lacy said staunchly. "That's why we should go."

Kendall had to admit she felt afraid for McKee. Yet the possibility of seeing him fight thrilled her. What was wrong with her?

"You both stay right here where I can keep an eye on you." Rider ordered. "McKee can take care of himself. I don't need you girls to get into trouble."

"Yeah." Kendall said as she turned to walk towards the barns.

"Of course." Lacy hurried after Kendall, pointing for her to turn to the left. They went through a series of smaller buildings housing chickens and rabbits before entering the largest metal building housing the arena. The smell of animal waste permeated the still hot air. The crisp hay mixture muffled the sound of her boot heels on the cement floor.

Arranger's angry voice reverberated through the barn. Some of the animals moved restlessly in the small enclosures where they were penned for the stock show.

Kendall looked toward the voices of the men, in time to see McKee toss his badge heedlessly into the straw.

Her heart sank. Would he really throw it all away? Just like that? It was surprising how much she ached for this man who'd obviously worked so hard at being a lawman, then casually tossed away his self-respect. She knew exactly how it felt to be on the verge of fulfilling your goals and then wondering if it would all slip away.

"Why do you want to fight inside a horse trailer?" Arranger asked. "You a fuckin' coward."

"Because if anyone sees us fight, I'm done. Foley's got no patience for me making trouble in his town." McKee unbuttoned his shirt, and then he hung it on the edge of the trailer. "Unless you've changed your mind? Ape-man?" McKee unbolted the back doors of a large horse trailer, and the doors swung open with a thin whining sound.

Arranger leaned forward to take a look inside, before turning to look back at his enemy.

McKee stood, his golden skin gleaming in the fading light. Bare-chested, with beautiful sculptured muscles, and gloriously handsome from the waistband of his black jeans to the tousled black hair on his head. Exotic tattoos marked him. He looked like a warrior who had stepped out of time.

Several magnificent scars marred the perfection of his shoulders, one on his abdomen. Kendall's heart pounded. The man was incredible, all proud, masculine male. It made her mouth water.

"Right here. Right here, out in the open." Arranger demanded. Motioning toward the central arena.

Lacy sucked in an audible breath.

"What? Isn't there enough room in the trailer? You can't throw a punch unless you got some room? Or are you afraid of a little shit? Big hairy coward. You're yellow, even with a belly full of beer," McKee grabbed his shirt and drug it over his shoulder. "What a waste of my time."

Kendall breathed. She simply didn't know if she wanted them to fight or not. She just wanted to run her hands over every inch of McKee's body. Sexual tension tightened her nipples. God, she wanted to jump him.

"You want to fight in the trailer so no one sees you get the shit kicked out of you? Then we'll fight in the trailer." This time, Arranger stuck his head in the door of the trailer, sniffing like a wary animal. "It stinks like hell in there."

Kendall held her breath. Would Arranger go into the trailer? Would McKee pound him against those bars? Her own nostrils flared as if she were a horse scenting the air. All of the little hairs on her arms stood at attention, alerted by anticipation and adrenaline.

Lacy made a soft moaning sound.

Kendall patted her shoulder. Lacy obviously felt the tension as well; it hung in the air like the ozone of an impending storm.

Arranger tentatively stuck his head a little further into the huge trailer where the bull had been.

Kendall felt like urging Arranger inside.

She'd never seen such massive animals in action as the bulls she'd seen today; sheer testosterone on the hoof. Several thousand pounds of sculpted muscles, and barely leashed power. One toss of a massive bull's head had sent a handler hurtling into the ground.

McKee stood there behind Arranger-with the same kind of restrained visceral power-about to kick Arranger's ass all over the trailer. Kendall actually held her breath in anticipation.

"You go first," Arranger declared. "Sure." McKee elbowed him aside.

Arranger moved ahead of McKee, putting one foot on the edge of the trailer ramp, then another—his expression like that of a stubborn, wary pig.

With a move so fast she could barely follow it, McKee spun around and planted his foot in the middle of Arranger's ass.

The man flew off balance, going head first into the trailer with a thin scream and then a muffled thump.

Kendall muffled a victory shriek.

McKee guarded the doorway to the trailer. Kendall wanted him to stand over her like that. He could conquer her anytime. She was so aroused by this stuff. The veneer of civilization just seemed thinner here in Texas.

"How you feeling, Arranger?" McKee asked casually. "That manure taste pretty good?"

"I'll kill you McKee." Arranger choked out, struggling to get his feet under him and then slipping on the slimy manure to land on his fat face.

"You won't kill me today." McKee slid the metal bolt closed, securing the trailer just as Arranger finally made it to the door. Arranger bounced off of the aluminum, cursed, slid down, and then landed with a shuddering thud that shook the whole trailer.

"I guess you won't kill me tomorrow, either," McKee told him. "Since it sounds like you'll be nursing a concussion."

Lacy sighed.

McKee spun around so fast Kendall had to bite back a thin scream. "Who's there?"

Kendall was at a total loss. What to say? If he saw her now, he'd know she was aroused; she took an immediate step backward.

Lacy took a shaky step forward into the light. "It's only us. We wanted to make sure you were all right." She admitted. "Should I go tell Rider what happened?"

McKee nodded. "We need to get Arranger outta here before he starts yelling. People will notice."

Lacy nodded, then turned, and sprinted away. Kendall couldn't take her eyes off of McKee.

"Why don't you step out of those shadows and see what kind of man you seem to want."

She shook her head, knowing McKee couldn't see her clearly from where he stood.

"Are you frightened? I knew you were foolhardy, but the woman who handled the Sheriff's heart attack wouldn't be afraid."

"I'm not afraid." Her voice trembled, as did her hands, and her heart. She'd discovered a new obsession. One she really couldn't afford.

"See what inevitably happens to a piece of shit."

"Yes." She murmured.

"I hope you're thinking."

I'm thinking hopelessly inappropriate thoughts. About dragging you out in one of those piles of hay and giving us an outlet for all this adrenaline. She'd seen him angry-- almost violent, now she'd witnessed the power of his restraint. The man was magnificent. Unfortunately, he thought as little of her as he did Arranger.

She gasped as he came around the corner, silent as a shadow.

"Are you wasting yourself wanting that Neanderthal?" He demanded. His breath felt hot on her cheek.

He'd moved in so close she couldn't breathe without the engorged tips of her beasts brushing his warrior chest.

"So you want a man with darkness in his soul?"

"Yes." The admission came from that place deep inside of her, a place she hadn't dared to admit to anyone else.

She looked up into his face knowing he'd see the naked pleading in her eyes. Perhaps he'd misinterpret her hunger and use it against her, but she couldn't explain how much she wanted him. She couldn't explain it was safer to want a criminal than a complicated man like McKee.

Pheromones or something else, she wanted him.

As if compelled by her urgency, he leaned down and took her mouth. The conflagration swept through them, wild, hot, and all consuming.

Kendall leaned into him: plastering breast, hip, and leg, against the long length of him.

McKee lifted her skirt to expose her female flesh over her silken thong. The onslaught weakened her knees so she clung to his naked shoulders to stay upright.

She reached for his cock fondling the straining hardness through his jeans. Craving him with shocking intensity. The thought of being taken by this tough cowboy: his hard, rough edges, melding with her softer ones, made her shudder to a mini climax, drenching the thong.

After a deep breath she reached for the snap on his jeans. All thought of sexual preliminaries vanished as she struggled to open his zipper and free his cock.

All the while his mouth ravaged hers.

His hips thrust against her pelvis. The tip of his penis was firm and hot. Running her hungry hands over his erection, she moaned. She wriggled, putting the cradle of her hips against him. He pushed back against her, coming closer, coming…he stopped, and abruptly pulled her skirt down.

"McKee?" She sobbed. Bereft. Her knees wobbling and her flesh aching, she wondered, how could he pull away at this stage of the game?

McKee was zipping his zipper when she heard the sound of boot steps coming up behind them. The heavy footwear crunched on small gravel between the metal buildings.

"The posse." McKee said flatly. "Riding to the rescue."

She barked out a laugh.

She couldn't help it. There was an incredible irony in the fact she'd come to Texas to solve one problem, and had become enamored with a much taller, bigger problem.

She barely recognized the person she was becoming. She had to wonder whom would the posse be rescuing?

Chapter Twelve

Inside Kendall's dream she saw Jake waiting for her at the top of a desert pass between weathered boulders. He sat on a black horse with a fiery sunset behind him, his long black hair blowing in the cool breeze and he wore a fringed, Indian style jacket.

I'm sure I've seen that outfit in a TV Western. I'm sure that's the reason for the sense of recognition.

A cold wind blew over Kendall's vulnerable, bare flesh.

It's so cold inside this dreamscape, and I'm afraid it represents the cold of the grave...

As she got close enough to see his face, McKee's bleak expression tugged at her heart, so Kendall urged her horse forward with a touch of her heels.

"Why are we here?" she asked with trepidation. "I don't want to be here."

"She's here somewhere." He said looking outward over the dry creek bed. "I've been looking for her for so long. I have to find her."

"Are we talking about one of the students from the college?"

Or, are we talking about Anne? I certainly don't want to open that can... or grave of worms.

He looked at her with terrible pain in his eyes. "I can't help her but maybe you can."

"I don't want to go down there. I'm not really qualified, for huh, this aspect of law enforcement and I don't think I can face retrieving a body." *Or talk to a spirit...thing.*

I can't listen to her anymore. She's not real.

"Will you help me?"

She could see it was tearing him up to ask for help. Hot tears of sympathy wet her cheeks, stinging in the cool wind. "I don't have any training for this."

"You helped Foley. That took a lot of courage."

"Foley was alive. I don't even believe in this afterlife shit. I don't. I won't!"

"I shouldn't expect you to accept this place." He sounded resigned. "Perhaps this is what my uncle means about marrying in the faith. My people see the world very differently and most of them couldn't accept."

His voice became harsh, "So why can't I fucking see this myself!"

Guilt gnawed at her heart.

It's just a nightmare, she reminded herself. Funny how she knew she was sleeping even though she could feel the wind in her loose hair. She could smell the familiar horse smell and she knew she rode Tommy, her horse from home.

Perversely, she could feel her nipples, swollen and erect because McKee was so near and she wanted him to touch her so badly.

She shifted on the horse as the core of her heated up. Was this just a 'wet' dream? That kind of dream she understood.

McKee smiled at her as if he could hear her internal dialogue. "Dreams connect people."

"We almost connected at the fair. Want to try again?" she offered.

"We're sharing this experience on a divine level."

"No, that's not how it works. I've studied dreams."

"We're connected."

"The meaning of a sex dream's obvious." *And safe.*

His smile didn't reach his magnificent eyes. "You're resisting the real message."

"That I've dreamt of you for years? You merely resemble some actor from a TV Western I used to watch when I was a kid."

Except, I can feel your pain, your sense of being wronged. I thought I dreamt of a bad man, a wounded man...and you're hurting, so I have to help you. Just not in the way I thought. And I desire you so much.

He turned to her with hollow eyes. "Kendall, I care enough about you to let you go. Go home and be safe."

"I want to help, only…" She couldn't refuse him. Hadn't she waited for years to help heal him? "Can't we somehow call for help? Get a helicopter or something."

"You have to go to her. Acknowledge her. But you also have to accept that her spirit still lingers."

"I talked to her and now she's talking to me!" She moaned. "I don't know about this stuff."

"She won't talk to me. My life's been fucked up since she died. And I guess since she's still here, its no picnic for Anne either."

Kendall looked around and there was nowhere to go in the weird twilight, so she reluctantly nudged Tommy forward, more afraid of losing McKee than anything else. "You could at least acknowledge what I'm trying to tell you. I know all about Anne. And I have her journal."

He didn't answer. He rode his horse forward.

"It's getting colder," Kendall shivered. "And I don't want to be here."

"Come on. There's a fire up ahead. This is the place of joining." He promptly disappeared around a huge boulder.

What's this? Stonehenge in the desert? "Great," she sighed.

Kendall rode around the huge boulder to find McKee dismounted and standing over a ghostly fire.

Illuminated by the light of the weird fire lay Anne. Her legs were splayed obscenely, half buried in the ground and her shredded clothing and bright hair was dusted with fine red sand. Her bluish, swollen skin had dark circles around deep wounded eyes.

Anne looked directly at Kendall. "I don't want to be here," she said plaintively.

"We'll get you home." Kendall said. Even though Kendall knew Anne would never be going home.

"I'm so lost."

Kendall's heart broke for Anne. "What can we do for her?" she appealed to McKee.

He looked down as if he couldn't see the body. "I can do nothing."

He can't hear her. "Don't you hear anything? Try."

McKee looked at Kendall blankly. "Why do you ask me?"

"Because you're the one with gifts. I'm a scientist."

"So maybe all you hear is the wind crying. It can play tricks on you."

"It's not the wind. Believe me. I can see her and I can hear her and she's dead!" Kendall's voice rose as she tried to convince him.

"I'm not crazy." *Now she was trying to convince herself.*

"What does Anne want?"

"How am I supposed to know? I don't council ghosts!"

He shook his head as if he were disappointed in her answer. Then he took a few steps away from the eerie fire.

"Don't walk away! Answer me!"

He turned back. "You have to listen with your instincts. You have to acknowledge all the little parts of yourself."

"This isn't about me!"

McKee turned away and disappeared like a ghost. Kendall stood mesmerized above Anne's body.

Tears sprinkled Anne's face, little droplets catching the firelight. "I couldn't breath."

Kendall shook her head. "I don't understand. And I hate a problem I can't solve."

"There's more of us."

"What?"

"It's colder."

Kendall looked over at the fire. Someone sat there in the dim light chanting.

She felt as if she were only seeing his shadow or spirit. "Go over to the fire. Maybe the Shaman can show you the way into the…ah, light."

"No one's listening! Why aren't you listening? I'm telling you the answer."

Kendall gasped. The pain and fear the spirit exuded seemed to stab into Kendall's heart. "I'll do something for you. I promise."

"Do it for McKee." Anne cried.

"Why can't you talk to him?"

"I don't know. He won't hear me."

"Just tell me who did this to you."

"I told you but you're not listening."

"You love him."

"He's promised."

"You love him."

"You love him too. Will you end up like this?"

"I don't love him. I only had sex with him to get the bad boy thing outta my system. I never counted on feeling anything for him. I also never imagined I'd be trying to help a ghost."

Anne smiled and there was blood on her teeth.

Kendall shivered. The bright blood on those gleaming skull teeth, those deep, shadowed eye sockets, and that macabre grimace was the most terrifying sight she'd ever seen.

"Be careful, Kendall, or you'll end up lying here beside me."

Chapter Thirteen

Kendall woke up in a cold sweat, pinned to the bed by a dead weight. "Oh, oh."

Precious blinked at her from her spot between Kendall's legs where she lay stretched out.

"I'm okay, just in case you wanted to know." Kendall struggled to get her pillow under her head when she could hardly move from the waist down without dislodging the cat.

Precious shifted, a little, then settled back in her warm spot, where she blinked big, golden eyes that were the same color as the dawn light coming in the window.

"Did I thrash around a bit? Wake you up? So sorry." The cat didn't answer. Thankfully.

"Here kitty kitty kitty."

Precious just looked at Kendall.

"Come here and comfort me, you dumb cat." The cat just blinked, apparently still sleepy.

"You could come and earn your kibble. Purr for me. Calm me down. After all these nightmares are shattering my sleep. I'm horny as hell. I'm talking to a dead woman who can't seem to give me any helpful information, and I'm exhibiting classic symptoms of more than one mental illness."

Precious just licked her paw.

"But don't worry, I still know how to open a can of cat food."

Precious rose, stretched, and then leapt off of the bed.

Kendall pushed her summer weight comforter off of her legs and then climbed of the bed. She ran her hands through her hair that was a tangled mess.

"I just need to talk to someone who's alive and real. Lacy will at least be sympathetic."

Precious meowed from the kitchen. "I'm coming."

Kendall fed the cat.

Then she pulled on jeans, a tee shirt, raked her hair into order, then pulled it up into a ponytail. For once she skipped her coffee ritual to rush over to the office where there were real flesh and blood people to talk to, or at least there would be people in the office in a few hours.

I really just needed a change of scenery.

At the office she let herself in with her key and then made coffee. While it was brewing she sat down at her desk to consider her options.

I should quit. Stash the little red book. Pack. And drive away. Why wouldn't I go? I don't need to be here, especially, given all the terrifying things happening.

That dream was the last straw! Had Anne been threatening her or warning her?

Kendall opened her desk and looked at the red book like it was a particularly venomous variety of Texas snake.

"I'm put it on McKee's desk. He'll find it when he comes in to work today and I'll be long gone."

She picked up the book, gingerly, between her fingers.

The book seemed to jump out of her hands where it fell to the floor, spine down, pages open and vulnerable like Anne's body had been in the desert.

Kendall felt a touch of panic at the thought. Anne's dead. She can't talk to me. She can't influence me. And if she warned me it's only my subconscious warning me.

Kendall reached down to retrieve the book, only to see the handwriting on the pages was small and precise.

Curiosity and urgency burned inside of her.

Kendall scooped up the book and then sat down at her desk. She took a deep fortifying breath, as she prepared to set aside what was left of her morals.

I'm so scared.
I'm scared of my own shadow.
I'm scared McKee will get tired of me.
He must know how I feel about him. It's in my expression.
It's in the way my body leans towards his
In the cruiser, my thoughts are less than professional.
I want him. In so many ways. In so many places.
I'm inappropriate and pathetic. I know.

Kendall turned the page, her hands shaking.

This sounds like it could be my dairy. My thoughts. My pathetic need…
Does he know? Does he care?
Rider tells me that he's sworn to marry a woman of the blood.
It's a tribal responsibility.
Rider's father claims him. Because of his prophetic dreams.
He's the lineage of the next Shaman. So, even if he loves me,
He betrays his heritage.
My poor McKee.
Driven, broken by his dual demands. As I am.
I've thought of putting us both out of this misery
I need to ask for a new assignment.
But I'm having the dreams again. I'm afraid.
I'm afraid
I'm afraid
I'm lost.

Kendall noted Anne had written the sentence over a number of pages.

There was a description of Anne's dream, but Kendall skipped over the entry to near the end of the book, she wasn't ready to discover if she and Anne were sharing the same dream. Because Anne was dead and that would make the threat more immediate and real…

In the back of the book, Kendall found what she'd unconsciously been looking for all along.

McKee's the only one who can save me
Although, I hope I can show him how brave
I am and save myself.

Will that make him love me?

Kendall slammed the book closed. Anne had loved McKee, and he might have loved her back given how deeply he appeared to be grieving.

Either way, Anne's death would have hurt him deeply, especially in light of her last statement. Had she gone into a deadly situation to make McKee love her? It was a real possibility and probably put a load of guilt on the man.

What had frightened Anne? Was it tied to the missing girls from the University?

Kendall buried the book deep in the bottom drawer of the file cabinet. She couldn't give it up now. But she couldn't read it until she had some time to think.

Her heart ached for Anne. For McKee.

No wonder he was in such pain. She wished she could help. But she didn't have a clue. Obviously, McKee hadn't found any useful information in Anne's ramblings of unrequited love, or he would have found the murderer by now.

What had Kendall expected to find? The name of the murderer? Redemption in McKee's eyes? The key to his soul? She didn't know. She only knew she should leave town, but she couldn't go. Not yet.

She wanted to check something out first.

She accessed the law enforcement computer where Foley's ID was saved to the database. Kendall had only to look up his personnel file on paper (surprisingly, the office still had files on paper) and take a guess at his security questions to reset his password. It wasn't hard; everyone knew where he'd gone to high school, and who had been his first girlfriend.

She felt guilty about breaking the law. But she couldn't seem to deny the urgent message from her dream. Besides, it was easier to break the law than to read Anne's journal.

Once in the database, she began researching, focusing on the disappearances of young women from the university campus.

She didn't find many. The information seemed to be mostly about Melissa, and some things about Carrie, who'd been missing since winter semester.

Then she remembered the worried look on the faces of the young students as they spoke of Amee's disappearance at the fair. One of the girls had said Amee's mother was online talking about her daughter's disappearance.

Kendall began going through Tech's Facebook, twitter, and Instagram, sites to find out what the parents were communicating about.

There were also parent support websites, with both current and archived articles.

Kendall focused her orderly mind on absorbing the information.

The archived parent websites had a few notices from the parents of young women who'd apparently dropped out of Tech, and then disappeared.

There were heart wrenching pictures and pleas for information.

Kendall got up, stretched and then headed for the coffee pot. Students, who officially dropped out of their classes, before they left Texas Tech then disappeared, would be in a different category than those who just vanished like Melissa and Carrie.

Kendall poured herself a large cup of black coffee, while she mulled over the information.

Students signed up for classes via the computer. They dropped classes the same way. What if someone capable of hacking into the college database had taken them? A staff member at the college could just make it look like the girls had dropped out of school, and then they just disappeared. A serial killer might be at work in Lubbock County.

Kendall suddenly felt a wave of cold flow over her, like she'd stepped into a refrigerator. She rubbed the goose bumps on her arm.

Amee had most likely ended up discarded in the desert.

And because of Anne's warning, or more likely because of my subconscious making me think I'm talking to Anne, I didn't believe they're the only ones missing.

I can't research every young woman who dropped out of Tech and went home. It's impossible. Some of the other parents may not have made the connection. They might believe their daughter left school and went away with a friend or a boyfriend.

There has to be a commonality. How to discover it?

And if Kendall believed there was a predator in the desert, targeting young women, then she had to believe the warning...that Kendal herself might become a victim.

Chapter Fourteen

McKee came in the law enforcement office when the ancient phone was ringing shrilly. Kendall pointed at the antique phone in an effort to communicate that he should answer it, as she was taking instructions for some follow-up work for Janice Foley, who had called Kendall's cell phone promptly at nine o'clock.

Of course, Kendall didn't mention her early morning undercover work to her supervisor.

McKee gave Kendall a look, which indicated he didn't want to answer, and then picked up the phone, when it just kept ringing and ringing.

It's such an obnoxious sound that you can't help but pick it up, that's probably why Foley keeps that ancient phone around. And it's about time McKee did some work around here anyway.

Kendall surreptitiously shut down the police database she'd been accessing, and leaned back to concentrate on the list she'd been complying of the duties Janice needed her to complete.

"Yes, I faxed a copy of that file to the Lubbock office. No, nobody's called. Yes, the information on the Burrow's case is all filled in and filed. How's the Sheriff? Fine. Good. No, you don't need to come to the office. Don't worry. If we need anyone we've got backup."

At the moment, the back up in question was bent over scribbling a note on the desk, gorgeous backside in the air.

Kendall felt a real sense of connection to Anne and her dilemma.

The man was killer gorgeous.

Kendall had to slap a hand over her mouth to keep the hysterical giggle inside after the research she'd just completed. The serial killer was probably gorgeous too. The college students hadn't known what was underneath the charm.

I don't know much about McKee either. Other than he's dangerous.

The other night they'd been about to engage in wild, uninhibited sex at the stockyard, and today he seemed unfathomable and unapproachable.

He obviously regretted everything and I should too.

"Okay," she told Janice. "I'll call you at 4 p.m. Tell Sheriff Foley I said hello."

Kendall set her phone down then looked up at McKee hoping he couldn't see she'd been thinking about him. "Thanks for getting the other line. Who was it?"

"Some lady, named Mrs. Sultemier, who's frightened the town's going to hell because the Sheriff's injured. She says she's got her gun loaded. You might want to check up on her later."

I think everyone in town has a loaded gun." Kendall babbled. "Apparently it's a Texas thing."

"Kendall, I need you."

Her heart nearly stopped.

"I've got to go out on a call and I want you to come with me."

"Why me?" Kendall knew she sounded almost frantic. "I've got some filing to do. Go through the mug shots. Look for another criminal so I can get the hell out of this place." She taunted him so he'd get mad. He wouldn't expect her to go with him if he was furious with her.

What would he think if she jumped him in the squad car? She wanted to put her hands on him so badly.

"So, it was Arranger you were hot for the other night? You want me to give you the key to his cell? You can pay him a little visit?"

"Go to hell."

"I expect you to behave, and be serious. This is law enforcement not a game. Some people actually count on the law to save them from the bad guys. Not use criminals for sexual entertainment."

"Are you kidding? I'm always serious. I'm the most serious person I know. You just don't understand me. I'm deadly serious. If I don't get this right I've got six years as good as down the drain." It felt better to be angry than vulnerable.

"If you're not careful you'll be dead."

Hadn't Anne said the same thing?

"I can handle myself."

He gave her a cold look.

She never knew dark eyes could be so glacial. It hurt. His condemnation. And it would get worse if he knew how much she wanted him. She shouldn't care. "You feel something. That's what really burns you."

"I feel nothing but a sense of responsibility that comes with the job. You've got a dangerous hobby. Think about those missing girls. I'm sure they were just out looking for a thrill."

"Then why aren't you out looking for those girls?"

Instead of obsessing over your partner. She didn't say it. She couldn't. But she did wonder if he felt something more for Anne than just remorse. A vicious pain went through the middle of her. Had they become lovers after that entry in the diary?

"You know better than anyone else why I'm stuck here." He ran a hand though his hair, looking flustered. "I'm still trying to figure out why you're here."

What would he think if he knew his face had been the one in her fantasies? "I truly have no idea." But it seemed to be fated.

A fate I can't seem to escape.

"Then what're you angry about? Do I owe you an apology or something? For the way I manhandled you the other night? I didn't hurt you did I?"

She couldn't let him feel guilty. "No. I wanted, uh, what happened … almost happened."

He seemed to relax a tiny bit.

"Is there anything else you want to clear up?" She asked.

Do you want to start up where we left off?

Did he look hopeful?

Was he aware Lacy had called to say she was going to take a stack of get-well cards to Sheriff Foley before she came in to the office, and they were alone?

Long enough to…

"No, nothing else." He said abruptly.

He obviously had no interest in taking up where they'd left off last night.

And it was all she could think about. She'd had a hard time deciding if she preferred that he penetrate her up against the wall or push her down on top of her desk.

Then she'd decided she really wanted to push him down on her desk and just climb on top of him and take full advantage of his glorious cock.

"Kendall? I wasn't kidding, I want you with me." His words hit her like ice water.

OMG What was she thinking!?

She shrugged. Her nipples felt heavy and swollen. She crossed her legs, which had gone weak. "I really don't think it's a good idea. To want me. I mean. To want me with you…" She babbled.

McKee grabbed her gently, but insistently by the arm. "I can't trust you with Arranger down the hall."

She hadn't even remembered Arranger was in the cellblock until McKee reminder her. Apparently, only one particular man did it for her now.

At the last minute she scooped up a notebook to use as a shield. She placed between her breasts and her lap. She kept her legs firmly together.

"This won't take long." He escorted her to the cruiser as if afraid she'd run.

She gave him a tight smile. How to tell him all of the equipment on the dash, and the security grate between the seats had her imagining several sexual sceneries? In fact it felt so much like police business it gave her a dangerous shiver. She had to get out of this before she did something even more dangerous than the amazing sexual encounter in the barn. She needed to think of Anne's pathetic need for McKee and the tragic ending.

"I've got the utmost confidence in you, McKee. I don't know why a big, bad, violent crime lawman needs any help. Just let me stay and do some filing. It'll be safer for both of us." She reached for the handle on the door.

"Guess you got your spunk back." He grinned as he locked the door with a click. "All we've got is a small errand. Then, we have to investigate a missing tractor, but don't worry; I'll be sure and point when we actually see a tractor, since you've probably never seen one in person."

Apparently, he'd missed her warning. Too bad. "Very amusing. My family just happens to have a farm in Virginia. I've even done a little tractor racing with my cousins."

"Great. Then you should be a lot of help in the field." He sounded less than enthusiastic as he started up the car.

Why couldn't he respect her? Everyone else did. She glanced into the back seat. Hmmmm, maybe it was because she was having very unprofessional thoughts.

I'm crazy. It's the only explanation. Kendall crossed her legs and then uncrossed them.

But the image wouldn't go away. She could vividly imagine what it would be like if he'd dragged her to the car with the intensity he'd demonstrated last night. In her fantasy McKee would press her against the door, while she bucked against his hard, strong body. He subdued her, and then locked the handcuffs on her wrists.

Back in the real world, Kendall tried counting the telephone poles along the road. Anything to stop the movie running in her dirty mind, knowing it was headed towards un-rate-able.

The radio in the car crackled as McKee searched the lonely airwaves until he found an old rock and roll station.

In her mental movie, she could see them frame, by erotic frame. He had her by the arms, her breasts pressed tightly against his chest. Then he turned her around, the heat of his hip close enough that she could feel his gun digging into her hip. His gun and his cock.

Roughly, he'd push her into the back seat of the police car. Where he would secure one cuff to one end of the grate. This would stretch out her arms, leaving her vulnerable. He could see straight down her blouse. She'd hang there from the grate, spine curved, breasts heaving, her legs spread on the seat as she tried to get them underneath her weight.

In her imagination, he'd smirk at her, those damn black eyes flashing. Desire like a storm between them; but she wouldn't let him see the violence of her raging emotions.

Get control of yourself. Kendall jiggled her legs hard enough to rock the car. Surely they'd arrive at the stupid ranch soon.

Picking up her notebook and pen she opened it to a blank page.

She doodled. Then she started writing in earnest.

The satisfying thing was she knew even in her cheesy B-movie, she'd be defiant, spitting in his face, when he pressed it close to her breasts. Wanting to take a bite of him, like a wild woman.

Anne had probably been a nice girl.

But Kendall was coming to discover she had an edge and was finding it intriguing. If McKee didn't give her everything she needed; she could imagine herself taking a very intimate bite of his cock.

Oh, man, McKee would laugh if he knew how much she desired every long hard inch of him. It would amuse him to know everything she imagined in her mind.

She wrote about how…handcuffed in the back, she'd spit defiantly in his face. And then he'd lean down to unbutton her blouse, baring her breasts to his hungry gaze and scraping her nipples roughly with his teeth.

Stop Kendall!

She slapped the notebook closed.

Then she looked over to see if McKee had noticed her writing a porn novel. There was nothing like engaging in a full-fledged sexual story when they were on official police business. This was exactly the behavior Kendall had worried about!

McKee just stared out of the windshield as if he were alone.

Time to start going through the mug shots with a vengeance. Anyone was safer than McKee.

They drove over super-heated asphalt; the Texas highway was already hot enough the tires seemed to suck at the road; it was as if the road and the tires were on the verge of melting into one another.

Like lovers.

Dust and heat made the road ahead shimmer like a mirage. Everything felt as if it weren't exactly real, especially Kendall's recent preoccupation.

Maybe I'm still dreaming. A wet dream. Women have them. We're just more discrete about it.

There wasn't a living thing taller than knee high out on the side of the road, certainly nothing big enough to distract her from her x-rated thoughts, other than a buzzard flying in a lazy circle over the landscape.

Okay, so it's a nightmare.

There wasn't a soul within miles to see them if they got naked in the car on the side of the road.

She opened the notebook again and started writing furiously.

Out here in nowhere-ville they could do anything to each other. She wrote about him turning off the police siren on the way to some fictional emergency because he needed her more than duty, or pride. His hands would be shaking on the steering wheel. He'd have a glazed look in his eyes. Then he'd come around to the back of the car where she'd be open to him. Vulnerable.

He'd confess he couldn't drive, couldn't think, with her behind him. He'd admit her scent was driving him crazy. He'd nuzzled her neck. His hands would wander over the silky material of her bra-her nipples were so hard they'd ache.

Kinda like they did now.

Kendall tried to bring her wicked imagination under control. They were going out on police business to find out what had happened to a valuable piece of machinery—she chanted to herself. The job was important. She needed the correct mindset.

It wasn't appropriate. She pushed the notebook to her aching chest. But the movie inside her mind wouldn't just shut off--just because she wanted it to. The fantasy was a conflagration. A fire. She was out of control.

Would he whip out his weapon? Even in her wet dreams McKee kept her guessing. She wanted to beg him to pull her skirt up then run those clever fingers over her engorged clit. He could have her so easily. That kinda police brutality appealed to her. She was so wet.

Kendall rubbed her legs together. Fidgeting. Anticipating.

"Kendall?"

"What?"

"Are you okay? You seem kinda nervous."

"I'm not nervous," she protested. Sounding strained.

"This isn't going to be a difficult call. Routine. I wouldn't put you in danger."

Because you put Anne in danger?

But she wanted him to put her in the most basic danger. Intimate danger.

"Kendall?" He tentatively touched her hand.

All of her nerve endings lit up. Kendall sucked in a breath. She turned to look at him knowing her eyes must be wide with everything she was feeling.

He took one look, then jerked his hand away as if she'd bitten him, muttering. "Ah hell."

"What?" She tried to sound innocent.

"Nothing." But he kept his eyes firmly focused on the road.

"Is the big, strong officer feeling nervous?" She taunted.

"Just concentrate on the task at hand. Please." Did he sound vulnerable?

In the real world, Kendall set the notebook down at her feet. Sitting back she unbuttoned the top button of her blouse, then ran her fingers down the deep vee. "It's hot."

McKee sucked in his breath in an audible hiss.

She leaned toward him on the seat. "You seem to be a bit overheated yourself, Officer." She could see sweat beading up on his forehead along his hairline, despite the air-conditioning going full throttle.

Goose bumps climbed her arms. She reached out to stroke a silky strand of hair lying on his forehead. This time it wasn't just a fantasy. His hair felt slightly damp and silky. "We both know you're dutifully concentrating on the task at hand."

He jerked away from her touch. "If you weren't so damn obvious."

"Whatever are you talking about?" She stayed within touching distance just to make him squirm. Or maybe she just couldn't resist.

"You know."

"Enlighten me."

"I can see what you're thinking. Your eyes are glistening and your nipples are…"

"What?" Was he blushing? Could the big bad lawman be blushing? "Erect? Aching?" She ran a finger over one tightly beaded nipple. "They *could* use some attention."

"Stop it. Kendall. Behave."

"We could stop. I promise it would be pleasurable. You could push me down on the hood, then pull my jeans down, and have me. Finish what we started the other night. No one would see us."

"You'd get burned," he replied, "laying on the hot metal, in more ways than one."

She rolled the firm nipple around in her fingertips. "This would feel better if you did it for me. McKee, I think you want me as much as I want you."

"Wouldn't you rather do it in the back of the cruiser so we can fulfill some sick fantasy you have about sleeping with a criminal?"

That hit a nerve. But she ignored the twinge. "Sure." She almost panted. Would he really fulfill her needs right here?

"We're here. So you'll just have to put a lid on that fantasy." He turned off of the highway on to a dirt road. The cruiser lurched in and out of the deep ruts until they reached an ancient doublewide trailer. Kendall held on to the door handle to keep from being thrown against her seat belt.

If she hadn't felt so frustrated, Kendall might have been amused, because she obviously made him nervous enough to mistreat the cruiser.

"What are we doing here?" She asked. "These people don't look like they can afford a tractor."

"They couldn't. How nice of you to stick your nose in the air because your relatives could afford a tractor."

"I didn't mean it that way." She wasn't a snob. As a young child, before the State had taken her from her mother and sent her to live at her aunt's house, this place would have felt like a palace.

"I'm running an errand. Picking up a friend and taking her to her daughter's house to baby-sit."

Maggie came out of the door of the double wide with a little girl of about seven years old clinging to her hand.

Kendall felt a deep sense of unease. The sight of the two of them, hand in hand, took her back to days she'd tried like hell to forget. "Why didn't you tell me it was Maggie's errand?"

"I know what you think of her." He waved them over to the car.

"I never said anything specific," Kendall protested.

Maggie opened the door, helped the child into the car, and then climbed into the backseat of the cruiser. The girl looked at them with wide eyes.

"Summer's sure growing." McKee said.

Maggie's probably is struggling to feed her regularly.

"Yeah, she's getting big and she's smart too. She's first in her class." Maggie said proudly.

You probably can't help her with her homework. When you can get her to school at all. Any minute the State will yank her out of your arms and give her to well meaning strangers where she'll cry herself to sleep for months.

Kendall sat up straight in her seat. Had she really ever thought of her aunt as a stranger? Had she grieved for her mom? Why couldn't she remember?

"Are you teaching Summer to sing?" McKee spoke animatedly to Maggie.

"Yes. She's wonderful."

Summer looked down as if she were embarrassed.

Kendall's mother wasn't a great singer, but she'd sung along with rock and roll, and she'd loved to dance. They'd danced all over whenever they'd played the radio, twirling each other and laughing. But eventually, the dancing and practically everything else about her mother had made Kendall feel ashamed.

"Summer sings in the church choir.

"What songs do you know, Summer?" he asked. He obviously saw value in a tired old woman who held Maggie's hand like she would never willingly let go.

All of a sudden, Kendall remembered how they'd had to drag her physically, screming from her mother's arms. Kendall remembered the frantic terror in her mother's face, and the way her mother had also shouted and cried. Kendall realized she probably hadn't been the only one who'd cried herself to sleep after that terrible day.

Why didn't I ever think about it from Mom's perspective? Because I hurt so much? Or because I needed someone to blame?

Summer sang an old hymn; about saving grace...the soothing melody eased the constriction in Kendall's chest.

"I love that song," McKee said. Summer smiled shyly at him. McKee had certainly charmed her.

Kendall knew how that felt. He'd put a spell on her as well. Unfortunately, it had been a short liaison.

In a few minutes the cruiser pulled up to another doublewide trailer where flowers bloomed valiantly in the heat.

"Thanks for the ride, Jake and Kendall." Maggie smiled at them. "We really appreciate it. Rhonda's sick and the kids are running her ragged. I figured I'd help out for a little while."

Maggie and Summer climbed out of the cruiser. They joined hands as they walked toward the door.

Kendall watched. "Is that her daughter? She's kinda old to have a daughter that age."

"Summer's her niece's kid. Seems the mother ran off. Maggie said a wild gene runs in the family and she took Summer in until her mother finds her way home."

Kendall wondered if someone could find her way home after such a long absence. Was it possible? What did home look like?

Could it be a cowboy lawman with a wild streak? Or had she gotten crazier since she'd come to Last Chance? Especially, considering the cowboy had most likely been in love with his former partner and was also committed to marry a woman of Native American blood.

And the dead partner was ordering Kendall around. Talk about impossible relationships!

McKee wasn't anyone's safe haven or home.

But he was something.

Jeeze. She was crazy. She sat wondering how she'd gone from one crazy, but possible, obsession to be totally derailed by another, impossible obsession.

Stubbornly silent, McKee drove them further out into the desolate West Texas desert.

Eventually, he turned off the main highway. Bumping along a road, if you could call it a road, where the dirt in the air became so thick it felt like they were in a cocoon of dust.

Suddenly, the cruiser lurched; throwing Kendall up against the restraint of her seatbelt so hard she came outta of her daze to protest, "Damn, McKee, can you please slow down?"

"I'm sorry. It's a dry creek."

"What the hell's a dry creek?"

"It's a low spot where the water runs off in a rainstorm. It can swell up until the creek's several feet high and wide. The force of the water can carry people and animals downstream. It can be deadly."

"Flowing water? Here?" She couldn't even imagine enough rainfall out here to make a dangerous creek where there was nothing but dust, and a tumble of broken boulders and debris.

"Remember the storm we had a couple of weeks ago? This part of the road swelled up with about four feet of water. The current carried that stuff into the road. The rancher probably drives a big truck so he didn't notice. Gotta get a crew out here to clear this roadway."

They pulled up to a house. It looked slightly faded from the extreme heat. Kendall could sympathize as she got out of the cool cruiser then stepped out into the full force of the sun.

Kendall drew her hand back from the vines that crisscrossed the pillars that held up the porch as she climbed the stairs to the front door. Everything in Texas seemed to sting or bite.

"Morning Glories. My wife loves blue." The man who spoke from the porch swing looked sheepish. "They look nice and fresh in the morning no matter how hot the summer gets."

Kendall fell in love with the lean rancher at that moment. It didn't matter that he had arms like brown tree limbs sticking out of a tee-shirt covered by faded overalls. He pushed the squeaky swing back and forth with his oversized boots. He was definitely safer than McKee. "I'll bet the Morning Glories are lovely."

McKee scowled. "Did you report a tractor missing?"

The man took off a denim ball cap and then wiped his snow-white forehead with it. "You a deputy?"

McKee nodded. "I've been authorized until Foley gets back on his feet. I was here with the West Texas Violent Offenders Task Force."

"Looking for those poor girls?"

McKee just looked grim.

"I hear Foley's gonna be fine." The rancher said.

"He's a strong man. He'll live." McKee said.

Kendall knew McKee meant Foley's spirit was strong. Somehow McKee's faith in Foley made her choke up. "Sheriff Foley's already complaining about being stuck in the hospital. In the meantime we've come out to take down some information about your missing tractor." She opened her notebook.

"You folks come in outta the heat where you can breathe." The rancher got up from the porch swing and then headed toward the front door.

McKee followed the rancher into the house.

Bemused, Kendall followed the men, grateful for the air-conditioning. The rancher and McKee began exchanging information with their heads together. Looked like the territorial dance was done, and they'd moved on to male bonding

Kendall looked around curiously. She was drawn toward a whole wall of memorabilia. There was a framed photograph of the house take from the air with lots of land around it.

"How many acres do you have?" She asked absently. No one would come all the way out to this desolate place to steal a tractor.

"A half section." The farmer replied.

McKee shot her a male look saying she shouldn't interfere with his manly, lawman business.

"Just asking," she shrugged.

"Would you like a glass of sweet tea?" The rancher offered solicitously getting out of his seat then heading to the refrigerator.

Kendall nodded, knowing that drinking sweet tea was a Texas ritual. No way to hurry the rancher if he wanted to drink tea. She turned back to the wall of pictures.

"When did your tractor go missing?" McKee asked as he watched the rancher pour three tall glasses of tea.

"Last night I guess. It was there yesterday when I finished the plowing."

"Did you leave the key in the ignition?"

"Didn't think so at the time, but I must have forgotten it because the key was gone from the hook this morning." He said, gesturing towards a rack with hooks and keys by the back door. "Though I have to admit we don't lock doors around here. Not much call to."

Exactly. These people didn't lock their doors because no one came out here. Kendall zeroed in on a family picture. There was the rancher grinning with two tall teenage boys on either side of him in football uniforms. "Are these your boys?"

"Yeah. We're hoping to go to the playoffs this year." He handed her a huge glass of iced tea.

Kendall nodded. "They're in high school?"

"Let's go out to the site." McKee suggested. "I'm sure it would be more informative than looking at family pictures."

Kendall buried her frustration in the tea glass, drinking fast enough to keep her mouth busy.

"Sure," the rancher nodded.

McKee probably would have caught on to what was going on with the tractor, if he weren't so intent on discrediting Kendall. Impatience and anger surged through her, more familiar and more comfortable than sexual desire. Now she only desired to kill the man.

"Why should we go out to the site?" She demanded impatiently, taking a breather from the tea.

"Why not?" The men asked.

"Because it's obvious your sons and their friends probably took the tractor out for a joy ride and all you have to do is find out where they ditched it."

Neither McKee, nor the rancher looked surprised at her suggestion, nor did they look galvanized.

How to move them along? What was it about the people in Texas? Was it the heat that made them move so blasted slow?

"When we were in high school we were always high-jacking the farm equipment. Your sons had a motive, and I presume they also had access to the keys. I'm sure they just had a tractor race before running the tractor into a ditch. Maybe one of them just wanted to take a girl for a ride and the other's not telling. You'll have to ask them where it got stuck."

The men looked at her like she'd spoken a foreign language. "Well?" She prompted them to action.

The rancher wiped his brow again. "That's a possibility. The kids get riled up during fair weekend."

"So?"

"We'll go out to where you had the tractor last and take a look." McKee gave the man an almost friendly look.

The rancher nodded.

They'd obviously closed ranks but she didn't have to waste her time. "Fine. I'll take the cruiser and go back to the office."

McKee glared at her. "You can't drive the cruiser. I'll take you back if you're in an all fired hurry."

"I thought you had to go out to the field?"

"I think Mr. Schuster should double check with his sons as to the whereabouts of the tractor. If they didn't take the equipment, then I'll come back and we'll look for it."

Kendall drank more tea in order to keep her mouth busy.

Mr. Schuster immediately pulled out his cell phone and hit a button. In a minute he had someone on the phone. "Grant, did you and your brother take the tractor last night? No? Mind if I send Agent McKee over to talk to you about my missing tractor?" There was a pause and Mr. Schuster grinned at them.

"What? You might have taken it over to the dry creek and gotten it stuck in the mud? Just wait until you get home! You're gonna dig that tractor outta the mud with your bare hands."

Mr. Schuster tucked his cell phone in his pocket then told her earnestly, "You solved it little lady. I guess you musta drove your daddy plum crazy."

"Only a little crazy." She grinned. Wishing she'd had a father. Someone who might threaten to make her dig with her bare hands, then grin at her.

Kendall took a last deep gulp of the tea, wanting to please the rancher, even if she already felt uncomfortably full. It must have been twenty or more ounces.

"So, we've solved the mystery," she rubbed her hands together. "It's time to get back to the office to see if Lacy's had any emergencies. I'm sure there've been tons of calls for us."

McKee followed her out of the house, too docilely.

They climbed into the cruiser silently. He took it easier on the dirt road. In fact, he seemed to be crawling along.

She'd been in such a hurry to leave the ranch that she hadn't realized she had to pee until she was sitting in the cruiser. Oh no.

All that sweet tea was putting pressing on her bladder and it would take at least twenty minutes to get back to the office.

"I guess you feel pretty smug."

"No." *I feel the urge to go.*

"You don't belong out here. Rich girls think they're immune to bad things, but you're going to get hurt."

"I'm not really a rich girl, more of a poor relation. I lived on my aunt and uncle's farm. I didn't have a father. My mother literally has no idea who fathered me. Really. It's true."

He laughed shortly. "Only a rich girl would have a tractor at her disposal to play games on. On our ranch we'd be lucky if we had one sorry tractor slapped together and we'd spend so much time wearing out our britches on the stupid thing trying to scrape up food, we'd never risk such a valuable piece of equipment for fun."

Crossing her legs against the uncomfortable feeling, she tried to concentrate. "I'm sorry. I know it can be hard. My mother used to have me look for change in the couch cushions so we could get a dollar hamburger." Kendall made it sound like she hadn't actually been hungry at the time. Like it had been a game. And she shivered. Not only from the urgent demand of her bladder.

"I don't need your sympathy. I need you outta my hair so I can concentrate." He raked a hand through his hair just as the car hit a pothole.

"Could you please take it easy?" She growled from between clenched teeth. Completely consumed by her need to pee.

"Are you going to tell me how to do my job?"

"No."

He glanced in her direction. "What, no elaboration?"

"You knew when we got out there in the middle of nowhere that no one had driven off with his tractor. He's got what? A couple of hundred acres? Where would a thief take a tractor?"

His chuckle surprised her. "That *was* a problem."

It was amazing how many beautiful white teeth he had when he bothered to smile.

But it didn't matter when all she could think about was the pressure on her bladder, "Can we please pull over?" She cried.

His smile shut down. "What? My driving again?"

"Now!"

Obediently, he slowed down and then he pulled over to a stop on the side of the long empty road.

"I've got to find a bush or a shrub." Looking around frantically, Kendall couldn't find anything brush tall and wide enough to hide behind. She curled into a sort of fetal position on the seat and bore down. "God." It was a prayer.

"See, I'm not always smart," she panted.

"Didn't anticipate the tea overflow." She grabbed the door handle and all but fell out of the cruiser. "Be a gentleman and keep your face forward." Although at this point she didn't care. Her body screamed for release.

There was literally nothing taller than scraggly desert grass available as a shield. Wandering into the dust on the side of the road, she fumbled with the button on her jeans, in agony.

"Don't look." Her voice came out shrill.

"Don't worry, I've seen it all before."

"How could you joke at a time like this?" She danced as she struggled to find a place where the grass wouldn't touch her, squatted, and started breathing again as she yanked the thong to the side.

She darted a look at the cruiser and saw McKee sitting at attention with his head forward. Turned out, he could be a gentleman, after all.

She felt a spurt of relief.

Her eyes practically crossed in relief as the pressure left her bladder. The warm scent and dampness spilled from her grateful body into the dust.

Now, just a little jiggle to dry off; no way she was going to use any of this grass as toilet paper. She wasn't a complete idiot. She'd done this before on long road trips with her mother.

"Aren't you finished, yet?"

"I said not to look!" Her jeans slipped from her fingers and pooled around her ankle into the dirt. "Oh shit!" The thong snapped into place like a slingshot getting damp in the process. "Awh!"

He leaned over. "Are you okay? Did you have a run in with another scorpion? Don't use any of the grass; you might get a sticker bush."

"Are you kidding?" Kendall frantically tugged at the jeans while keeping her eyes focused on the back of his head. With everything but her dignity firmly in its place she sauntered up to the cruiser as if she hadn't just suffered the most embarrassing event of her life.

"Everything taken care of?" He inquired solicitously.

"Of course, I can handle myself."

"Okay, Babe." He smiled again.

She felt all warm and gooey inside. Stupid how such a little thing like a pet named loosened her up.

Kendall opened the door to the cruiser and then she felt a little itchy stingy sensation on her left hip. She scratched that hip, then felt another burning prickle down near the edge of her thong. She desperately wanted to scratch, but McKee was looking at her with those sexy, dark eyes.

"You okay?"

The stingy sensation became fiery; she could feel her eyes bugging out with the intensity of the burn. "Oh, no!" she wailed. "What's the matter with me?" She scratched and danced. She'd never felt anything like it before.

"God, it's burning me!"

McKee grabbed her around the waist. He reached down into the waistband of her jeans then plucking something off her back. "Looks like you got into some fire ants."

"What? What the hell are fire ants?" Scratching like mad, she tugged on the button of her jeans, more anxious to get them off than before. "What do I do?" She cried.

McKee helped her out of the jeans. Kendall was too miserable to protest. He laid her down on the seat of the cruiser where he began brushing at the offending demons on her skin.

Kendall cupped her hands over her crimson thong shaking with vulnerability and trepidation as he helped her picked off the small fiendish ants that burned like fire. She swept her head back and forth on the leather seat, which smelled like fermented laundry.

"It hurts so much," She moaned. Undone by misery and the embarrassment.

"Does it sting under the thong?" He demanded.

"I don't care. Leave me alone now. Just let me be."

Her fingers tightened on the thong where her sensitive flesh burned.

He brushed her hands, and the thong to the side, and picked ant off her most intimate flesh. She pushed his hand away. But he wouldn't stop. She closed her eyes in mortification.

When she opened her eyes, his expression was as gentle as his touch. "It's okay. Kendall."

"No, it's not." humiliated, hurting, and even perversely aroused by his touch, she didn't know what to feel as he got the last of the ants.

"Hey, I think I've got them all now."

She felt his touch as he eased her thong back into position.

"Oh, thank God." She knew her emotions were as bare as her ass.

"Don't be embarrassed. These things can kill."

McKee moved a few feet away from her, and then he picked her jeans up off the ground and shook them out briskly.

Probably to give her some needed privacy. Bless him. "What do you mean those tiny little ants can kill?" Asking questions gave her something to focus on besides her near nudity.

"They've been known to kill a fawn or a calf if it's weak or injured."

"What a horrible, horrible death." Kendall said with feeling. "I think I'd rather be eaten by a killer shark. At least it would be quick. Next summer I'm going to California."

He handed her the jeans. She folded them. Then shoved them on the floorboard. No way was she going to risk putting them back on.

"Can you take me home so I can get some clothes and put some ointment on the bites? I'm not putting these back on even if I have to walk down Main Street in my thong."

"There's an image." He said drolly. "If Foley hadn't already had a heart attack that might do it."

Chapter Fifteen

The bathroom in her house had felt roomy, until he stood there looming, larger than life.

"Kendall, what're you doing? Why don't you strip your clothes off and just get into the water I ran in the tub."

"I don't know why you insist I take a bath."

"Because you were squirming all over the seat on the ride home."

"It burns."

She wished he'd said he wanted to join her in the bath or that he wanted to see her naked again: anything but this matter of fact stuff. It was embarrassing. "We should just go back to the office."

"Lacy's got the office covered."

"Okay, I'll get into the bathtub," she said miserably.

"Call me when you're nake…ready."

"You can go now. I'm going to be awhile. If I have to take a bath, I might as well try to relax."

"I'll stick around in case you need anything."

"I can handle it." She told him tartly. If he thought getting her naked would do him any good at this particular time, he had to be crazy.

"Do you have to have everything perfect?"

She grabbed her lavender bath beads. "The shock of the bites wasn't just physical. I've been attacked in a very vulnerable, intimate way. If I were the patient, I'd suggest relaxation techniques." Couldn't he go away before she went to pieces?

"That fancy stuff won't help. Don't you have any baking soda? That smelly shit might actually burn those bites." He crossed his arms like he was a resident expert.

She wanted to slap him, maybe because he had a point. Mostly, because she'd expected him to be an ass, and instead he'd been wonderful and tender.

"You can get out now, so I can get undressed." She sniffed. *Get a hold of yourself, Kendall. You've had a few shocks.*

"I'll get the baking soda from the kitchen." He shut the door firmly behind him.

To keep her hands and mind busy, she bent down to retrieve a box of matches, then she lit the candles she kept around the edge of the large tub.

Why did she always feel sexual tension when he was near? It was infatuation. She didn't even know much about him. She couldn't love him. She couldn't.

I think I've gone and lost my mind.

"Why are you lighting candles in broad daylight?" From the doorway he sounded almost as aggravated as she felt.

"They give off a relaxing fragrance. It's called aromatherapy. I know Native Americans have similar rituals. So, you must know it works." She snapped at him.

"Great. Aromatherapy. Do counselors charge for this shit?"

"I'm not a counselor. Yet." She sighed.

"I haven't passed any of my boards," she told him long-sufferingly. "I'm not even sure I'll do well in my job interviews. I guess it doesn't surprise you, since you have such a low opinion of me." She confided with a sniffle.

Let him think she cried from stress. She'd maintained her perfect facade until she'd been attacked by the Texas beasties, including McKee, and then undone by his tender rescue.

He didn't say anything, just looked at her, those dark eyes inscrutable.

"I have my reasons for everything. They may not be good reasons, maybe not logical reasons, but they made sense at the time."

Except falling for you.

"Want to explain those reasons to me?"

"No. Just go away. I don't know why you're still here. You already assured me that I'd live."

He stood, shifting from large foot to the other large foot as if he didn't know himself why he stood in her home fidgeting.

She shuddered. The bites throbbed in earnest now. It was an awkward place to have throbbing unless you wanted someone to intensify that throbbing. Then bring it to a climax…jeeze, she was certifiable.

"Go!" She started to pull her shirt off of her shoulder, and then realized he still hovered, taking up all the air in the room. "I really don't need you for this part." She assured him.

"What do you need me for?" The look he shot her increased the temperature in the room by several degrees. Then, as if uncomfortable by his question he went out, slamming the door behind him with a vengeance.

Kendall undressed in record time. Tentatively, inch-by-inch, she settled into the water. Clenching her jaw when the water began to cover the bite area. She could feel them swelling. McKee'd never want to have sex when she looked like a swelled up freak, even if her body couldn't seem to get the no-sex message.

"How're you doing in there?" His deep voice came straight through the door.

"Don't come in here." Her voice rose to a strident screech as the doorknob turned. She tried to cover her breasts with an impossibly small washcloth.

"I've seen it all before," he assured her as he strode into the bathroom.

Precious sashayed behind him.

"I told you to get out." She screeched.

"I was out."

She reached up and pulled her hair band loose, to allow her hair to cascade down around her shoulders and over her breasts. Then Kendall laid the cloth over her lap. Didn't McKee or Precious understand she'd like to be alone?

Apparently not, because his wicked grin washed over her flesh, as if he were more turned on by what she'd done with her hair than her original nudity. She immediately felt the heat of more than the bath water.

"Trial by fire." She said more to herself than her audience "Fire burns."

Don't I know it? "Just go away. I don't think there's anything else you can do for me. I can take it from here."

"You must be feeling better. You've got your bite back." His grin was pure devilry.

"Please just leave me to my misery."

"Let me see."

"Go away!"

"Ant bits get little white blisters on them. It's not big deal unless you scratch them, then they'll get infected."

Precious jumped up on the edge of the tub and walked along the edge, weaving in and out of the candles as she often did.

"Damn, prissy cat." He muttered. Sitting down on top of the commode.

"She just looks prissy, she's actually pretty tough. She was a rescue animal. What do you have against cats?"

"She's getting in the way of the view."

Kendall could feel herself flush. "You're insane."

"Yes, that happens a lot when I'm with you. You make me feel alive again. You're like a force of nature."

"Yeah, I'm just a natural disaster."

"You're certainly a lot of trouble."

"Then arrest me."

"I could, but you know what we'd end up doing."

Kendall couldn't respond. The thought of having him in a cell was too to close to her fantasies.

"Unless you'd prefer Arranger?"

Either he'd misunderstood her silence, or he was being mean. "You know it has nothing to do with wanting that disgusting man. Did you have to go and ruin it? Please, leave before *I* call the police." She barley held back the tears of stress and disappointment.

Does he really despise me?

"Fact is, for the moment, I am the police." He winked and looked smug. "You could sue for harassment."

"I hate you."

"I don't like you much either." His tone was tense.

"Then why were you so nice to me out there?" She sniffed.

"I wasn't. Not really. Why don't you go home to Virginia? Save us both from this situation. Aren't there any bad guys out there?"

"I told you, I was attracted to you. I was stupid enough to assume it was mutual." She sniffed.

His look was probing.

"That night, I wasn't as rash as you seem to think. Lacy vouched for you. So it wasn't exactly a random encounter with a guy who could have been a dangerous convict. I just didn't listen when she told me the part about you being a lawman."

Kendall didn't admit the part where she'd been mesmerized by his mug shot and hadn't heard a word Lacy had said after Kendall has seen his picture and recognized him as *her* man. The man from her dreams.

Did those stiff shoulders relax just a little?

They looked at each other with the sensual heat stretching between them so strongly she could practically smell smoke.

"Your cat's on fire."

"What?" She asked dreamily.

"The cat's on fire."

"Huh?"

McKee lunged at her from the commode, scooping up the cat, then he promptly dumped Precious into the tub on top of Kendall.

"Oh my God!" Precious immediately started to paddle, yowling pitifully. Kendall tried to grab her but suddenly the cat was all claws.

"Precious," Kendall cried out. "Calm down. Kitty, kitty, kitty." The cat howled.

Kendall grabbed a towel, and wrapping it around her arm, she tired to scoop the cat up out of the water but the cat just kept struggling.

McKee laughed.

Kendall couldn't stop to strangle him but it was tempting.

Finally, Precious got tired and limp enough to allow Kendall to give her a boost, so Precious could scramble out of the tub, looking as foolish and wretched as Kendall felt.

Kendall stood up in the tub, embarrassment entirely forgotten in her anger at McKee's mistreatment of her cat. "Why the hell did you dump my poor cat in the tub!?" She screamed at him while crossing her arms over her breasts. "She hates water."

"She was on fire."

"What?" Kendall shook out the hair clinging to her face.

"It doesn't take a detective to see the stupid cat's tail caught on fire from one of your relaxation candles. I told you not to light those candles."

"But..." She looked over to see the cat licking the charred fur on her tail.

"I thought I smelled smoke," she muttered.

"Yes. Smoke. I saved that stupid animal."

Kendall sank back into the tub, defeated. "Oh my god," she hid her face in her hands. "I'm such a horrible mess when you're around."

"Yes, you are. But a rather beautiful mess."

She looked at him with wonder. After every humiliating thing that had happened today he still thought she was beautiful. He'd been tender and sweet as he picked the ants off her most intimate places. He'd taken care of her and then he'd saved the damn stupid cat. At that moment, the obsession became something else, something deep and terrifying.

She wrapped her arms around herself and rocked back and forth. "I'm afraid this isn't good timing for me."

He nodded. He even smiled. The man had a killer smile.

"I'll catch you later."

Kendall nodded. But as she curled there in the cooling tub she thought it might be better if he didn't catch her later. She knew she was likely to get as burned as poor Precious.

Chapter Sixteen

That night Kendall took another dream ride in the desert. Tommy, her gelding, seemed to know where they were going, but she could only look around for McKee.

Where is he? I don't want to be here by myself.

She couldn't find him. He hadn't been back to the law enforcement office the next day or the next. She'd been left alone to do her research whenever Lacy ran an errand out of the office.

Kendall couldn't believe it had already been ten days since Foley had had his heart attack.

At first, Kendall felt relieved that McKee had been too busy to spend time at the office. But now the sting of the bites and embarrassment were fading. So where was the stupid man?

She wanted to tell him that she'd found another girl who'd gone missing several years ago. Frantic parents had posted messages about Rhonda Mettles in the parent magazine for Texas Tech and they'd posted again recently on the anniversary of her disappearance.

In Kendall's dream the wind began screaming as if to regain her attention. Only it wasn't the wind; it was a woman's heart wrenching screams filling the empty land.

Kendall raced the horse over the red ground leaping over cracks in the dry earth. In her heart she knew she was running away from the screams.

I'm a coward.

It seemed as if she rode for hours until she came to a spirit fire and the shadow of a man chanting. She slid off the horse and walked over to sit by the fire.

"I'm cold." She said to the shadow man. The fire writhed and crackled but gave no warmth.

The man didn't answer.

"I'm trying to figure this stuff out." She complained. "Why me? I've no spiritual background, except the crap my mother tried to feed me."

There was no answer from the man in the shadow, and Kendall felt like she'd never connect with him. He couldn't approve.

"Hey, I'm trying here."

The shadow man looked up. For a second, she thought she saw an older version of McKee, sitting there, and then nothing.

Lightning flashed and it rained so hard that the pressure of the rain eroded the earth beside her until it exposed Anne's body.

"You're back," Anne said.

"Believe me, I didn't want to come back."

"Stop whining, and read the journal." Anne ordered her. "You've woken the spirits of the girls he's taken and they're demanding that you help them. He'll take another if he can. And then the river of tears is going to run again."

"Who is he? You saw him. Who is it?"

"It's colder."

Kendall rubbed at goose bumps as large as bee stings on her arms. "Yes, it's cold. But what does that have to do with anything?"

Anne tried to say something else but lightning cracked.

#

Abruptly, Kendall sat up in her bed. She was shaking but awake. Safe. Sorta.

Anne was gone, dead of a bullet wound.

And certainly not able to speak to Kendall.

Only, Anne's essence was sitting in the desert beside a spirit fire.

It's just my subconscious trying to help me solve the crimes.

But my subconscious didn't know anything about these crimes. Originally, I thought the red book was McKee's book. How can it be my subconscious?

I'm going crazy here.

Still trembling from the intensity of the dream, Kendall wiped the dampness off of her cheeks. Reaching for her cell phone, the lighted dial told her it was three a.m.

"No time like the present. I'll never go back to sleep anyway. Not with these nightmares."

She pulled the journal out from under her pillow, opening it, reverently, and respectfully, knowing how tragically this story ended.

Unfortunately, her love story seemed destined to end up the same way. But Anne's warning was there in her head. That she might end up lying beside the dead woman in the desert. Helpless.

Covered with millions of stinging, voracious ants.

Chapter Seventeen

Someone called out to Kendall; the insistent wailing seemed to come out of her nightmare, the anxiety overwhelming her.

Anne was calling out. Anne cried and cried.

Kendall woke with her heart beating hard in her chest and her eyes full of tears.

These days, she felt driven by Anne's pain.

Precious walked across her face, purring and drooling, and as Kendall pushed Precious away, she realized it wasn't a ghost calling at all, but her cell phone buzzing insistently on the nightstand by her bed.

Reached for the phone, Kendall felt fuzzy headed from the sleeping pills she'd taken last night after reading only about half of the heartbreaking pages of Anne's journal. Unfortunately, the sleeping pills hadn't kept the dreams at bay.

Nothing really kept the nightmares at bay, but doing the research to find the answer gave her something else to focus on.

I should admit to McKee that I've used the police database.

She hadn't actually spoken to McKee since her accident with the ants.

The cell phone buzzed again.

She saw Lacy was calling.

It was broad daylight and probably already ninety degrees outside. Her phone told her it was after nine a.m. She picked up the phone feeling guilty for oversleeping.

"Hello?" She croaked into the phone.

Oh hell, the sleeping pills had seemed like a good idea at the time. She had never taken sleeping pills before but wasn't safe to dream…

"Where are you? Are you okay?" Lacy asked her breathlessly. "You're never late to work. And this isn't a good day to be late. I need you to come into the law enforcement building, right now."

"What," Kendall rubbed her face with her hand, trying to clear her head and make sense of Lacy's call.

"What's wrong with you? Are you okay?" Lacy asked.

"I had a rough night."

"Were you with McKee? Please tell me you were with McKee, and I'll cover for you for being late…"

"You'd cover for me anyway. It's not as if there's anyone else in the office nowadays."

"McKee didn't spend the night?"

"Sorry."

"Then get your ass in here. What are you doing anyway?"

"I couldn't sleep. I took a sleeping pill. Are you okay? You sound like you're having trouble breathing."

"Just a little nervous. You've got to come to the office. Okay?"

"Yeah. Let me grab a shower. Do you need anything?"

"No, but hurry okay? You won't need a shower where we're going."

"Can you give me a hint?"

"Just hurry."

Kendall skipped the shower. It would have taken too long to blow dry her hair, and she was worried Lacy may be on the verge of an asthma attack.

Feeling nervous and outta control, Kendall used two pony tail holders to wind her hair into an extra tight knot.

Stepping outside into intense sunlight, hurt her head and her eyes, she gulped a breath of air so hot it burned going down her throat.

Gotta love Texas-it's either burning, stinging, or biting.

Fortunately, her old Honda Civic was parked under the carport, so the metal handle didn't quite blister her finger as she pulled it open to climb inside the stuffy car. Driving the two blocks to the station, she thought she knew why Lacy was upset.

Hadn't Anne said that they'd awoken one of the girls? There had been dreams last night faded, disjointed dreams of a young woman lost and afraid.

If there's some sort of afterlife shouldn't it be a happy place? Shouldn't those innocent girls be at peace? Is this why McKee's angry all the time? He's dealing with the knowledge that the crimes cause suffering in life, as well as in death. How do you bring peace to the dead?

Kendall shook her head. She didn't understand any of it. What was she supposed to do next? Running home to Virginia seemed like a good choice.

"I could give my notice to Janice today. Go by the Foley's house and drop it off. Very official. They don't really need me here right now anyway. It's too hot for anyone to commit a crime."

Spoken aloud, it sounded lame and cowardly.

"How is it I remember these dreams so clearly? Nightmares about shades rising outta the desert, walking on bones for legs. And the ants. Oh God, the ants."

She shivered.

"I don't want to remember. But I can't stop. And what exactly am I supposed to do? Anyway?"

There was no answer. Where was the ghostly voice when you needed one?

Once she was downtown, Kendall parked on the empty street then rushed inside the law enforcement building. "Lacy, what's going on? I could hear you struggling to breathe on the phone. You need to calm down or you'll have a major attack."

"They might have found one of the girls." Lacy said in between puffs on her inhaler.

"I figured it might be something like that."

"Why aren't you asking me if she's alive?"

I know she's dead.

"Okay, Just calm down."

"You know the call you made with McKee? The one where you figured out the teenagers had taken the tractor for a little ride?"

"How'd you know?"

"I typed the report. McKee gave you all the credit."

"Did you see him? Where's he been?" Kendall demanded.

"I don't know any more than you do."

"Why didn't he give it to me to type? I type."

Lacy shrugged. "He left a handwritten report on my desk."

"What exactly did he put in the report?" *Had he mentioned her humiliating experience with the ants?*

"Don't worry, the report was disappointingly G rated."

"What does the tractor case have to do with it?"

"Well, when those boys dug a rather sizeable hole in the dry creek around the front tractor tire, with their father breathing down their neck, they found an empty purse matching the description of Melissa's purse."

"Oh, no."

Lacy nodded. "Yesterday, a helicopter searched along the creek. The pilot reported seeing something suspicious. I called the guys. Today they're going to take some saddle horses to the scene to check it out. I don't know if I'm going to be able to go."

"What did the pilot report?" Kendall asked. Wondering if her dreams had been accurate. Afraid of what it meant if those dreams were real. "Maybe I should go too."

Of course my dream's not accurate. It's a dream. It's not surprising the body got buried in the desert. I probably watched some random movie about a serial killer and that idea got into my dreams.

"The pilot saw some sort of cloth, a rounded...item...which could be a skull, some lines, possibly leg bones buried under the silt after this last rain."

"Oh, okay. Let's be clinical about it." Kendall felt her knees buckle and she grabbed hold of the table. "Was it by some big boulders?"

"No, nothing like that. There's only a deep indentation of mud and sand. There's not even a bush, because it's the dry creek. You know dry creeks only fill up when it rains like hell. Then the water washes away everything in its path"

Including purses. It's not like my dream. My dreams aren't real.

"She's dead. She's really dead." Lacy's voice came out sounding strangled.

"Stop. Getting upset is not helping." Kendall knew she had to get it together or Lacy would need an ambulance. Her kind of asthma could actually be life threatening. It must be terrified to be afflicted with an illness that could literally steal your breath away.

As if to demonstrate, Lacy started wheezing.

"Hey Lacy. I got the call." Rider came into the law enforcement office looking nearly as handsome as McKee. "I hear we're going for a ride today."

"She's not going anywhere." Kendall turned back to Lacy, "Lacy breathe." She admonished.

"I'm fine." Lacy gasped.

"Where's McKee?"

Kendall shrugged. Why did everyone want to ask her where the agent was spending his time? He obviously wasn't inclined to spend it with her. And that hurt.

"I call…ed…him t…oo."

"Be still," Rider admonished the girl. Putting a large hand on her shoulder. He looked over at Kendall with apprehension. "What's wrong? What can we do for her?"

"Just keep her calm. She needs to wait a minute for the meds to kick in."

Her friend was trying desperately to breathe in a paralyzed respiratory system. "Lacy you'll have to go to the clinic for O2 if you don't calm down."

Lacy took another hit off of her inhaler. Then she took a long slow breath.

"Better." Kendall admonished. "Stay still. It'll be better in a few minutes." Kendall hoped she sounded more reassuring than she felt.

Lacy nodded again.

Feeling tight in her own chest, Kendall took a few deep breaths. Sympathy pain, she told herself, don't be silly. Still, it was funny how much Lacy had come to mean to her.

"Is she going to be all right?" Rider hovered.

Lacy found the energy to give him a wink.

Kendall relaxed. "She's going to be fine. She just likes to push the envelope. Our Lacy doesn't let anything slow her down."

With wide eyes, Lacy gestured toward Rider with her chin. Her breathing seemed to ease just a hint.

"Are you flirting or do you have something important to say?" Kendall asked her with a grin.

"I know what she's upset about." Rider took off his cowboy hat, and then pushed at the hair clinging to his damp brow. "It's okay, Lacy. I'm going riding with McKee. Stop fighting the attack. Just relax."

"Riding?" Kendall's ears perked up. She hadn't actually ridden a horse since she got to Texas.

"I meant horses." Rider said apologetically. "It's slower, but it's easier to see where you're going, and we won't risk messing up the uh…scene. Plus some of this area is eco-sensitive. Desert plants sometimes take years to grow and seed so we don't want to be driving over the terrain."

Lacy tensed. She ended up having to take another hit off of the inhaler. Rider put a hand on her shoulder as if he understood her distress.

"Even though the pilot reported the possibility of human remains, it's just as likely to be trash. It's happened before. Don't worry about it. It's routine to check everything out."

Lacy shook her head emphatically.

Rider put his hand up. "Stop. You'll start wheezing again. We'll go. It's not a big deal. You stay here and take care of yourself. You did a great job of finding the horses and getting the map of the area while McKee was out wasting time."

"I'll go with Rider." Kendall reassured Lacy. Both of them looked at her.

"What? You think only Texans ride horses?" Kendall inquired sharply. "Don't worry. It's going to be nothing. Just a horseback ride with a handsome man."

"It will be quicker if I go alone."

Kendall was getting pissed off. Why where Texans so arrogant? Apparently it was a natural failing. She ought to write a paper on it. She had enough evidence from dealing with McKee. "What? Do you think I'll slow you down?"

"I reckon you would. It's rough country." His Texas accent bled through his usually precise speech.

"I'm from Virginia. Where we have large farms and lots of horses. I've been riding since I was a teenager."

Since I got relocated to Virginia.

"What did you say?"

Kendall gasped, and Lacy sucked in a shallow breath as McKee spoke up from the doorway. Her heart jumped. The man's jeans hung on his slender hips courtesy of a black belt. His black shirt emphasized his amazing coloring. Even the perspiration that dampened his shirt, just made her want to strip him down and ride on him awhile.

"McKee, you scared us." Lacy nodded emphatically.

Rider grinned as if McKee were cool.

Men. They never grow up.

"Keep still." Kendall ordered Lacy, as she tried to resist the effect McKee had on her while concentrating on his arrogant question. "I said I could go riding with Rider, because I've been riding all of my life. The farm I grew up on was a horse farm, and I helped exercise some potential racing stock."

"Why didn't you tell me?"

"I told you about my aunt in Virginia and the tractors" "You didn't tell me that you ride horses."

"You make assumptions about me. Why should I tell you anything?" "I have my reason."

She shook her head. "Not since the first time. And that was obviously a mistake."

Rider watched them with apparent fascination, as did Lacy. Kendall decided to change the subject.

"Lacy's had a little asthmatic episode but she's going to be fine. Keep her still for a few minutes. Sit on her if you have to. I'm going to get my riding boots so I can go with Rider. I assume we're going to be riding western style."

She concentrated on Rider. It was safer. Though just as devastatingly handsome as McKee, he didn't affect her the way McKee did. "I hope you've got decent mounts."

"Yeah, we've got a couple of quarter horses we've ridden before."

"Good, because I'm going to leave you in the dust." She rubbed her hands together, excited by the prospect. She'd show these cowboys what a Virginia girl could do.

Both Rider and McKee were shaking their heads. "I'll go." McKee said with flat finality.

Kendall put her hands on her hips. Damn if he was going to ruin her chances. "I told you, I can ride. Don't you believe in me?"

He grabbed her and gently pulled her by the arm into Foley's office before closed the connecting door. He loomed over her in the middle of the room.

"You shock me." He said with raw intensity.

"That's because you don't see me clearly. You're still looking at me though some filter of my presumed background. You won't let your guard down enough to see me for myself."

"I'm looking at you as a woman. Trust me."

She shook her head so hard her hair came partially loose. "I still want to go." She insisted. "I'm qualified."

"I'll go."

She opened her mouth to protest, but he put his hand up and absently loosened her hair, smoothing it down around her shoulders.

"The ground in the canyon looks like this, all of the colors of the earth, layers of bronze, reds, and browns with glints of gold-to someone who knows how to look at the beauty of the desert. I wish I could see you ride a horse with your glorious hair flying like a banner in the canyon."

"In your dreams."

"I don't dream anymore." He touched her face.

"I can ride. Maybe I can help. Please."

She wouldn't be distracted from the mission, no matter how amazing his touch made her feel.

"If it's one of the missing girls out there she won't be pure or beautiful anymore. You don't want to see what we're going to find. She's been missing for weeks. The creek and the critters will have been at her. The sight of her remains will haunt you like nothing has ever haunted you. Remember the ants?"

"Oh God." Even the memory of the ants made her shudder.

He removed his hand from her face, and then he rubbed his arm as if he were feeling a chill.

"Do you have to go?" Her heart ached for him. She'd never realized this job would be so personal for a lawman. He wasn't thinking of the young woman as a potential body. He was thinking of her as a human being. A person.

"Better get it done. We may need as much daylight as we can get." His tone was hard.

Kendall mourned for him as he walked out of the office with an unfamiliar slump to his shoulders. As best she could, she controlled her facial expression before following him into the outer office. They were speaking quietly as she approached when Rider looked up with a toothy smile.

"I was looking forward to that ride into the sunset."

Rider was a stunningly handsome man; but she only had eyes for McKee. She approached him cautiously. Not sure of her reception, since the man was preoccupied with a terrible mission. She stood on her tiptoes to kiss him. She intended to buss him on the cheek, but he turned into the kiss, and with an aching tenderness tasted her mouth.

Kendall leaned into the embrace. Burrowing into his chest. Wanting to warm him with her love. Wishing it could shield him from the impossible ordeal ahead. Knowing it could not.

When he let her go, she leaned over McKee's arm and kissed Rider on the cheek. "Good luck and God bless."

"*Vio Con Dieous*," Rider murmured.

"Take care of each other." Lacy managed to whisper, which immediately taxed her.

McKee reached out to give Kendall one more rough kiss before sweeping out the door with Rider on his heels. Both men held their hats in their hands.

Cowboys.

Still, they go as if the hounds of hell were riding with them.

Lacy gave a little cough and gained Kendall's immediate attention. "Aren't you feeling better?" Kendall scolded. "You won't be able to breathe if you don't relax."

Lacy shook her head. "You try...to relax. . now."

Kendall sank into the chair. "No, way." She patted Lacy's jean clad leg.

Chapter Eighteen

Waves of heat and dust lapped at him as he guided the horse with his legs. The familiar rhythm soothed McKee despite the uncertainties he faced. He never forgot how much he loved riding-making that elemental connection to the physical world. How exciting to think Kendall shared his love of horses.

The dry creek they followed cut its way forcibly through the desert landscape, a twisted, tortured bed of brown and cream mud with a cracking crust. Water ran over this part of the country with violence. When it came at all. Creating temporarily swollen streams of swift moving currents, and debris, before drying up utterly. Until the next downpour. Alternating waves of life and death, love and loss. In this part of the country there were only extremes.

What Kendall couldn't understand was that he had nothing more to offer her than this empty streambed. There was nothing gentle or dependable about his nature. He'd sweep through and steal her heart, leaving her broken. Like Anne. Though he'd never meant to hurt his partner.

Kendall couldn't count on him. No woman could. And she wasn't of the blood. He couldn't bear to disappoint his uncle again.

Though Kendall had proven hardier than he's suspected. And she rode horses. The thought was arousing. She'd be magnificent with her hair flying behind her. She kept surprising him, his lady of desire.

As Rider and McKee approached the target area, they slowed down, perhaps, unconsciously, afraid of what they might find.

Rider spoke for the first time in over an hour. "Too bad we didn't bring the girls. It looks like it's going to be a romantic sunset. I could use a nice picnic basket about now. Do you think Kendall can fry chicken?"

McKee smiled, this was safe territory. Rider liked to lighten the moment. "A guy could certainly go for a picnic basket after a long ride. And sweet tea. I could really use some tea."

"With a pound of sugar. You have such a sweet tooth." Rider grinned like a fiend.

"I do not."

"You do, too. Like a woman."

McKee shook his head at Riders foolery. Though it felt good to act as boys again. It helped them find their courage.

He slowed his horse to navigate through a deep wound in the gorge where white limestone rocks cluttered the ground like bleached bones. Then he came up beside Rider.

"Are you going to ride, or moon over the sunset? Lacy's got a guy in the military. Too bad you've no woman to fry chicken for you."

"I was surprised to discover our city girl can ride horses. Not that your ugly horse, Hellraiser, could compete with Thoroughbreds. She'll wonder why you bother to feed his mangy hide."

"I don't want to talk about Kendall." *Any more than you want to talk about how you feel about Lacy.*

"You care about her." Rider's tone was almost gleeful. "And you met because Foley took a mug shot of you. He'd never do that. You have to admit other forces are at work here."

"I burned that fucking mug shot. Who told you? Lacy?"

Rider grinned, like a kid. "You can't hide from your destiny, boy," he said, parroting one of the Shaman's favorite phrases.

No, he could hide. Just ride away, go home and lose himself on the land. And lately he'd been so tempted. "Foley was just so fucking pissed off. He almost had a heart attack that night he was so furious. He did it outta anger, and possibly illness."

"It was still outta character. And the photo drew Kendall to you. Lacy said it mesmerized her."

"Bullshit."

"You know what the Shaman would say."

McKee thought of the postcard. Pretty much everything about his 'lady of desire' had been a disaster, yet there was something about Kendall that was as elemental as this desert when she let it shine though all the academic bullshit she thought she knew…

The dreams were coming back. The focus was strange, like he was hitching a ride with someone else, and he was afraid he knew who was actually doing the dreaming when they were curled up together after…they'd been intimate.

"It's…it's not what you think." He stammered.

"So she's gonna be available after your done fucking her…?"

"Shut up, you filthy, fucking ugly Indian." McKee snapped. Anger as hot a lightning raced through him at the thought of Rider picking up Kendall at Robbie's bar. He thought about Rider stroking her desert colored hair and McKee's hands gripped the saddle horn so hard they ached.

Rider just laughed. "Why? Because you're a stupid, blind, mangy son of a horse trader who can't see what's in front of him?"

McKee started breathing again, nearly as loud as the horse underneath him. Of course Rider would never do that. *Shit. I've got it bad.*

"Oh Cuz, you've got it bad." Rider said, then he shook his head.

"Lousy blanket ass." McKee muttered. "Have to stir up trouble with your mouth because you can't reach up here and punch me like a man."

"I'll punch you. Mess up your ugly face some more, so Kendall comes running to me. I'm not stupid enough to let someone that fine get away. I'm not the antisocial asshole who gets along better with an ugly horse."

McKee wiped at the sweat trickling down his forehead from under his hat. "Don't call my damn horse ugly just because he bucked you off a few times."

"A few?" Rider adjusted his own hat. "He's as hell hound ornery as you are. Stupid prick."

McKee grunted.

They just looked at each other, then they grinned, silly boyish grins, strange how the old insults sent them back to their youth.

"What do you think the chances are that this sighting's the missing girl? It's probably debris."

McKee hoped Rider was right. But his gut said otherwise.

"What about Kendall? Will you be bringing her home?" Rider prodded.

"Don't ask." McKee said menacingly. "Just leave it alone."

"You have feelings for her."

McKee didn't bother to deny it. "We both know I have other obligations."

Rider snorted. "What? To the blood? When it comes down to it a man's only obligation's to himself."

"You don't sound much like your father, the Shaman."

"Not me. Remember, you're the one with all the gifts."

Did Rider look pensive? Had he missed the attention his father had lavished on another boy? McKee had tried to be a brother to Rider in return for the gift of a surrogate father. Had it been enough? How could it have been?

"I don't have a gift." McKee growled utterly tired of obligation hanging like a noose around his neck. At the same time, he knew Melissa was up ahead. He could hear the whisper of her voice in the light wind blowing toward him. He could hear her protest at lying out here all alone. She expected him to give her rest.

Peace.

"I can't even give peace to myself." He protested.

I'm damned if I have the gift.

Listening to things on the wind that a man shouldn't be able to hear.

And I feel like I'm living in hell, cut off from half of myself, if I don't have the gift.

I am contrary as my old horse after all.

"What?" Rider asked. But he knew. He sniffed the dusty breeze.

"Nothin'."

"A woman like Kendall has a way of healing a man with troubles."

"She doesn't know anything. She's clueless. First day, I was here she stepped on a scorpion while waltzing around barefooted. Next week she tangled with some fire ants. No way she fits here." McKee gestured around the harsh countryside. Trying to push the image of Kendall with her trembling thighs trustingly open to him while he collected the ants from her soft, vulnerable flesh.

"She sunburns, she's soft, and Texas is a tough bitch. This place will chew her up and spit her out."

"I hear they've got some pretty land in Virginia." Rider urged his horse into a low spot, then up the other side of the creek bed. "But you gotta admire a girl who sticks it out after getting stung by fire ants. She's got guts."

"It only proves how unfit she is for this part of the country."

Rider took off his hat. He wiped his brow with a blue bandana. "I don't know. Lots of the folks who came to this country didn't seem to fit, but they stuck like damn burrs no matter how our ancestors tried to run them off."

"And my obligations?" McKee said distracted by something in the wind, tugging at him, trying to hurry him, unhappy to have been discarded like trash.

"You're using your gifts. Just not the way Shaman Blue Storm might have expected. But he's mellowing."

"Yah, I got another postcard. Something about a sunlight woman who seeks, and saves, blah, blah, blah. Why can't he just say what he means? Find an Indian woman; have a kid he can play grandpa with? And what woman of the fucking blood is blonde? What's she going to do to save me? I don't need saving. You're his son. You should be the one getting the postcards."

"I don't know what he means by a sunlight woman. Lacy's got that sunlight hair. You know, German heritage."

"No offense but Lacy can't even breath."

"Lacy's tough."

"You'd better watch out, you admire that woman too much."

Rider looked over at McKee almost bleakly, he didn't say anything.

They rode in silence for a while. With no trees to block the view the sky looked impossibly big.

"He calls me nowadays."

McKee looked over at Rider. "No shit? You and your dad are talking now?"

Rider nodded. "You'd be surprised what a brush with mortality can do. That prostate cancer scare re-arranged his priorities. If you asked him now, the Shaman would say he never expected you to follow through on your promise. He's already let it go. Now you should do the same."

McKee shook his head. Listening to the wind as it blew obligation all around him. "I can't let it go."

It wouldn't let him go.

"You are such a damn fool. And I think you're hiding behind that stupid promise. Keeps you from having to commit to anyone. Like Kendall."

"Shut up." McKee was trying to hear it.

"Blue Storm never wanted to tie you down to anything you didn't believe in. He just sensed your prophetic abilities might win him the validation he needed for himself and the tribe."

"Validation." It echoed in McKee's head. "She needs someone to see her. She needs to go home."

"The girl's body is up ahead, isn't she? You've got that damn spooky look on your face."

"She is, and we're going to take care of her."

"Well shit."

They rode in strained silence.

The smell hit them, mild, but definitely the smell of decay, before they actually found her pitiful remains half buried in the dry creek.

McKee looked at Melissa's body grimly, thankful he'd kept Kendall from coming out here to witness this. It would just add to the nightmares he suspected she was having. Vivid nightmares. His nightmares.

"It looks like she's been here all along." Rider said quietly.

"Yes." The young woman's tangled hair covered most of her grisly skull and the inside of her quilt patterned, cloth jacket had been exposed, surprisingly, bright red. The pilot had mentioned the red color.

McKee couldn't help but think of Anne. How he missed her. How he'd failed her. "Call it in. Tell them we'll need a helicopter with a full team."

"It's going to be a long night." Rider said.

"Yeah."

Chapter Nineteen

A long scalding shower only washed away the filth he'd dug through, in a vain attempt to find a shred of evidence pointing to the killer, but couldn't wash away his sense of impotence.

He'd been too late. Way too late. Again.

McKee stumbled out of the bathroom and into the motel room.

The dark was easier on his eyes after the harsh lights at the crime scene. His memory was brutally branded by the visual of the body. So, when he touched the shape of another body lying under the sheet. He nearly cried out in horror.

"McKee?" Her sleepy voice inquired fretfully. "Damn it Kendall, I wasn't expecting company."

"I'm not company. Think of me as a giant teddy bear, here to keep any nightmares at bay."

He wanted to argue, but he needed her so badly. Needed something. "I should make you go." He said as he slid into the bed beside her and brushed up against soft, smooth skin.

"You're naked." He accused.

"It's hot as hell tonight and that cheap air-conditioning unit's ancient. It's a miracle it's still chugging along, rather loudly, I might add."

She rolled over baring herself to him.

"And it's close to ninety in this room. So I'm naked....I wanted to comfort you. I don't expect...

To seduce him? To tempt him? The position of her beautiful body said otherwise, stretching, thrusting her breasts out with those tight little nipples erect, just waiting to be petted.

"How the hell did you get into my motel room anyway?"

"Small town, and we both work for law enforcement, so people trust us. It doesn't hurt that Lacy's cousin owns the motel. And her aunt's more informative than the weekly newspaper. Like I said, small town."

Kendall rubbed up against him.

McKee wanted to push her away, but he allowed her to wrap her arms around him and lay her head on his chest.

I don't want to hurt her feelings.

After a moment, he even allowed himself to stroke her silky hair, and breathe in her essence--so different than the sights and smells of this horrific night.

Settling in with a sweet sigh, she asked nothing from him, giving her comfort without qualification, even though he knew she must have been dying to ask about what they'd done at the scene. Kendall had an inquiring mind.

He tried to will the images away. But like a child's kaleidoscope they crowed together.

Kendall's arms tightened as if she could sense his pain.

He tried to control his reaction. No need to share the discomfort. He was strong enough to handle this. He'd handled it before; solving violent crimes was what he did for a living.

His eyes ached fiercely.

Suddenly he felt moisture on his chest. With a start he realized that Kendall was crying. Silently, without moving she began weeping the tears he couldn't shed himself.

Slowly, the poison inside of him seemed to leach out in the cleansing river of her tears.

McKee pulled her up beside him then he stroked her wet cheeks to feel the gift of the tears she'd given him.

Then slowly, inch by tantalizing inch; his fingers followed her silken hair where it caressed the sweet curves of her tender, naked flesh. The firm bud of her nipple contrasted with the softness of her breast. He couldn't help but tweak that bud, and pinching gently. Rolling it between his fingers until it was fully engorged.

Kendall sighed softly at first, like the soft breeze teases the desert sand.

Then she whimpered under his hands.

He continued his exploration downward: to the smooth skin of her belly, then her hips, which led to the female fur between her legs. Each stroke within the valley between her legs made her curve sensually against him, begging without words, for fulfillment.

The low sounds she made were reminiscent of a desert breeze increasing intensity, stirring the sands, promising something more powerful was blowing into the desert…something which brought moisture and release… With a few strokes, moisture seeped into the silken surfaces as he fondled her clit.

He increased the intensity of his touch. Enjoying the stirring of her desire, the small helpless cries, and little frantic motions as she tried to evade the intensity of his touch.

His erection was painful. He ignored his own discomfort. Holding her down. Taking her all the way to the edge.

Like a storm in the desert, Kendall didn't hold back her passion; she reached for more, opening herself with utter abandon to his caress, clinging to him as he slid teased, stroked, and then penetrated her with his fingers.

She cried again, this time overwhelmed with pleasure.

Unrelenting, he slid his fingers in and out of her body until she threw herself against him and then cried out. He grasped her waist and her curvy little ass as she rode out the orgasm.

Sexual urgency soon overtook his good intentions. He couldn't seem to keep his hands from wandering hungrily over the territory of her flesh--especially when she whimpered and writhed beneath the onslaught of his desperate need.

Every stroke seemed to ignite a similar passion in Kendall. They were back in the midst of the sensual storm they created whenever they touched.

Her eager response turned him on until he could hardly breathe. McKee tried to be gentle, treating her like a lady this time, even as she grabbed his arms and thrust herself urgently against him.

Her hands cupped, rubbed, and fondled his cock until it was poised between her legs. Then she rubbed up against him until he thought he'd explode.

He grasped her hips and thrust, until his cock was so deeply seated inside her warmth, up against the walls of her womb.

They were so close.

He grabbed her ass, holding on to the dizzying feeling. He tried to keep something back. But she wriggled even closer, grasping him, sucking him into herself with all of her feminine muscles.

She held nothing back. Crying out against him. Pulling his hair, gasping, and crying fresh tears as she writhed against him in a dance of ecstasy.

McKee couldn't deny himself any longer. He pulled back slightly, and then pounded into her, each thrust was violent and primal, proprietary.

Kendall screamed, held his hips, pulling him closer, and tighter, until they were both embraced by the lighting.

Chapter Twenty

The next morning Kendall made her way into the law enforcement building a few minutes late. Not that anyone noticed.

According to the impersonal note left on her desk; something else had been needed from the crime scene,

Damn him for being professional at a time like this! He could have at least made the note a little warmer, considering she'd awakened alone in his bed, feeling abandoned after making a fool of herself by crying on his chest the night before.

So why had she gone to him last night? It made her feel incredibly vulnerable.

McKee hadn't even woken up randy. Lordy, the man had to think she was the biggest fool in the world for offering herself to him for comfort and whatever else he needed.

Apparently he didn't need her.

Coffee. She had to make some coffee so she'd have something to bury her red, embarrassed face into when McKee came back out into the office.

Would solving the mystery of Anne's death finally quiet the demons howling within McKee's mind? Would it give them a chance to find out if there was anything besides great sex between them?

Kendall was determined to find out.

Lacy had taken time off to collect stones for making her jewelry. Kendall wondered if Lacy was subconsciously looking for the body of the other lost woman, Carrie.

#

Kendall did a similar thing, looking for the missing young women. Shamelessly using the police database and the Internet to gather the information she needed. Normally, this opportunity for this sort of uninterrupted research would have appealed to her.

Kendall had a theory. She thought Amee and others might be victims of what she'd started calling the college killer.

According to the police reports, the girls weren't considered missing from the college because they'd officially dropped out of their classes. They'd packed and cleaned out their dorm rooms. Notes had been left for friends. A witness claimed she'd seen Amee in El Paso on her way over the boarder with her boyfriend.

It had been different with Melissa and Carrie. They'd disappeared from the college abruptly, without dropping out of school. Carrie had disappeared during the winter semester, and then Melissa had disappeared during spring break. And now they've found Melissa's body.

Carrie's body's out in the desert too.

It's the same killer. I know it. He just didn't cover his tracks as com-pletely. Maybe killing Anne messed him up. Changed his MO. Or he's accelerating.

He's got access to the college computers. He can move around on cam-pus. It's probably someone with student assistants who are unknowingly helping him cover his tracks.

However the college killer hadn't counted on the Internet. The grief-stricken families were networking on parent support sites, and constantly posting their pain at the loss of their little girls. There were pictures of the girls, mostly blondes. But dark haired girls changed their hair color, didn't they?

One of those girls, named Irene Helm, hadn't been heard from for eight years and she looked so similar to the recently missing Melissa that Kendall didn't think it was a coincidence.

Those girls hadn't quit school and run off with boyfriends. They were in the desert. One by one they entered her dreamscape.

She pushed her hair off of her face.

But I'm no expert. I need to get enough data to run it by McKee.

But Kendall knew she hadn't yet discovered the common thread link-ing the victims, besides that they were all attending the University and they were blonde.

She got up to stretch.

McKee had made himself so scare; Kendall actually hoped he'd find out about her hacking into the police database. They'd have a big fight.

Make up.

Have make up sex?

But he kept his distance, except in her dreams.

#

Late Thursday afternoon, the old fashioned phone rang; shrilly, incessantly, until Lacy finally picked it up.

Kendall looked over. Was it bad news? Had they found another body?

Subdued, Lacy spoke to whoever it was on the other end. She picked up a pencil, and made notes.

Sighing, Kendall took a sip of her water. Law enforcement felt like a morgue. They all appeared to be grieving in their own ways.

Lacy put the receiver down on the phone.

"We have to radio the agents. It's Frank Grobe. He's a scumbag who likes to beat on his weaker relatives. Word is that he knifed his cousin."

Kendall turned around, desperate to have something to distract her from her grim thoughts, and even grimmer research. "What are they going to do?"

"Grobe's crazy. He's been fighting with his cousin since high school. There're even rumors they're sometimes lovers." Lacy shrugged.

"Wow, in such a small town?"

"Trust me. Strange things happen in all towns."

"Okay."

"So they'll go pick up Frank, put him in a cell and let him cool off. I just hope he's not so liquored up that he shoots at them. I hope Rider's okay." Lacy twisted the engagement ring on her finger round and round.

Kendall wondered if Lacy was aware that she had feelings for Rider? Probably not. She positively glowed when she spoke about her fiancé and the impending marriage. Kendall wondered if she loved her fiancé, as much as the idea of being married. Lacy seemed to have taken playing house very seriously as a little girl, and apparently couldn't wait to get started.

Another call came into the police station, an hour later. Kendall jumped up to grab it. McKee was very short on the phone. He reported that they had Frank in custody and were indeed taking him over to the jail.

Kendall hadn't realized she'd been worried, until she put the phone down, and said with relief, "They're okay. They've got Grobe in custody. Did you get the paperwork ready?"

"Are you kidding? I've got it done in triplicate. I'll take it over to them." Kendall reached for the file, "May I take it?"

Lacy gave her a knowing smile. "Sure. I'm sure you'd like to see McKee in action. I know I'd be anxious too if I weren't otherwise committed. Have a good time." Lacy winked.

I shouldn't do this. I'm so hot for him.

Lacy had no idea what Kendall had in mind: to seduce McKee right there in the jail, in one of the cells.

McKee would probably be disgusted. He'd never understand.

He couldn't know Kendall was working to free him from one kind of prison-by finding the killer.

Even as she imagined him in another. Naked.

She wanted to give herself into McKee's custody. She imagined herself vulnerable, handcuffed, and at his mercy in every way.

Chapter Twenty-One

Kendall arrived at the jail just in time to open the door for Rider as he dragged a wiry, bearded man into the law enforcement building. Obviously, resentful at being held in custody, the prisoner cursed and struggled with his hands securely handcuffed behind him.

McKee followed, unfazed until he saw Kendall watching their prisoner, Frank, with obvious fascination. She even licked her pink lips until they were slick and glistening. McKee looked at the prisoner, wondering what a woman like Kendall saw in a man so gross.

McKee wanted to shake her. Didn't she understand that her fascination with criminals could eventually get her killed?

"Fuck you. Fuck you idiots. She's just a cunt. Let me go. Let me the fucking hell go. You're not even a Sheriff. You can't arrest me." Spittle flew from Frank's mouth and stuck to his whiskers.

McKee controlled his urge to shudder at what he imagined a man like this would do to Kendall.

McKee decided to point out a few eye-opening facts to Kendall, in case she was paying attention. "Well, Frank, she might be a cunt, but you're the one who slept with her, then knifed her husband when he objected. The man claims you've gotten a couple of kids on her."

McKee hoped he'd let Kendall know exactly what kind of scum she was drooling over.

"Piece of shit."

"He might be a piece of shit but he's lucid enough to press charges." McKee said mildly. Watching Kendall's every move. He thought her pupils were mildly dilated. Was it desire? He wanted to spit right alongside his disgusting prisoner.

"I outta know if he's a piece of shit. He's my cousin. And she's a lousy lay."

"Ah, nothing like a little inbreeding to make things interesting." McKee taunted. "Time to take a nap with the roaches." Intended to make Kendall understand the conditions in the holding cells. She wouldn't want anyone to lay her down on one of those filthy cots and then run a rough hand over her delicate, pink nipples.

McKee felt a tightening in his middle at the thought. Kendall made him crazy. He'd been tempted to go to her every night since they'd had sex. Instead, he'd taken cold showers and dreamed about being with her in the desert.

Frank let out a string of curses that should have made Kendall cringe. McKee looked over to see if she demonstrated any disgust. Didn't she get it, yet?

Frank would tear her up.

McKee desperately wanted to be the one to slide his fingers inside of her sweet flesh until she was wet. He wanted to pull her to the end of the cot and press his cock deep inside of her while she arched and cried out with pleasure.

Instead, she wanted Frank, the beast. McKee shook his head.

However, he couldn't stop the images uploading into his mind. He'd sit on the cot in the cell, as she knelt with his cock inside those moist, soft lips. Sucking.

Just then, Frank struggled impotently against the handcuffs. Distracted by his thoughts, hot and bothered, McKee looked over at Kendall's beautiful face. Unfortunately, she seemed to have the same avid interest, watching with fascination the leashed violence of the prisoner.

It made McKee angry enough to want to smash this prisoner into the wall. Instead he just pushed Frank forward, toward the cell.

"That's brutality." Frank declared.

"I'm surprised you know such a big word." Rider said, "I doubt you can spell it."

"My lawyer can sure as hell spell it."

McKee met Frank's small hard eyes. "I don't think a court appointed flunky will help you much."

McKee had already read Frank his Miranda, so he stood waiting, while Rider locked the man into the holding cell. Trying not to loose his focus on the task at hand. Trying not to allow images of Kendall--naked and begging--distract him from his obligations.

"Sleep tight." Rider said as he turned from the cell. "Sheriff's gonna be away for a long time."

Frank let out a string of cuss words.

McKee turned from the cell; at that moment Kendall locked gazes with him. There was heat there. Was it guilt he saw in her hazel eyes?

"You don't know what you're looking at." McKee tried to keep the disgust out of his voice so he wouldn't have to answer any questions from Rider, "It's pure poison, Kendall."

"I..."

McKee wanted to walk over and shake her. He wanted to smash Frank's face, or Rider's, for taking so fucking long on a routine task. "Hurry. Rider. You move like an old woman. Let's get the hell outta here."

"I'm going. What's your hurry?" Rider tucked some papers into the file. "I'll just get these back to Lacy...I mean the law enforcement office."

"Fine. Kendall, we're leaving now."

"Okay."

She sounded meek. He knew she was anything but meek.

McKee took an impatient breath, reminding himself that it didn't help to piss off the staff when he wanted something. Even if he couldn't take his eyes off this particular employee.

"You sure you want me to go?" She asked.

Wearily, he rubbed a hand over his face. "Yes." Rider had already gone out the door.

McKee turned away from her. He fully intended to walk away, as well. Go to the bar. Get drunk. Forget. Instead, he walked through the otherwise empty jail toward the other end.

Did part of his destiny include wanting a woman, who wanted a man like Frank? It made him wonder if the creator had a warped sense of humor. *At least I'm acknowledging the creator these days.*

He'd been angry for such a long time.

A noise near the front of the cellblock caught his attention. Kendall came walking toward him, with a decisive click of her work heels on the cement floor.

"You couldn't help but come to check out the prisoner. Maybe let him go down on you for a few thrills. Right in there in the cell." He taunted. "I knew it."

The clicking faltered then halted altogether. Her eyes were golden pools in her face, and though he couldn't interpret her expression, he imagined he knew what she wanted.

She shook her head dumbly.

"You're sick. It's no wonder. Damn counseling shit screwed you up, just like it messed up Anne."

"I did have a few holes in my education. Fortunately, I've learned a lot here in Last Chance."

"Now you should go home before there's any harm done." Was he warning her or himself?

Instead, she took a step forward, click. Then another. Click. Stalking her prey. Apparently, sick with wanting him. McKee knew how she felt. He grabbed the bars of the nearest cell until his hands went bloodless and white.

She moved in close enough that he could smell the essence of her with every ragged breath, mixed with prissy perfume, and lotion. Beneath the facade, he scented a real woman who was sexually aroused. She almost brought him to his knees.

Letting go of the bars, he thought to reach out towards her hair, but hesitated. His hand shook. But he had to know for sure. "Do you really want Frank, the inbreed pig, to touch you? Pull your hair down and tangle his hands in it? Or you just want him to take you quick and hard against the filthy wall of his cell?"

"A man like that won't be interested in making sure you're soaking wet with desire. He won't care if you're slick and hot for him. Or that you smell and taste like heaven." McKee knew he radiated anger and sexual urgency.

"I want all of that," she confessed.

"He won't satisfy you. He'll leave you wounded and broken." The way her confession made him feel.

"Please," she begged. Her eyes wide with honesty.

McKee turned away from her. "You're dangerous not only to yourself, but also to this law enforcement agency. You are going home. I'm going to do the paperwork tonight."

McKee watched as her lips moved but no sound came out.

He answered the question he imagined she must be asking. "I stayed to stop you. To keep you safe." *Kendall drew him so strongly. He wanted her more than his next breath.*

Did she shiver? Was it fear? Did she finally understand his desperation? He'd never taken a woman without consent, wouldn't start now, and he was afraid that if he put his hands on her, he would erupt. He turned away from her to face the stark ugliness of the urinal.

"McKee?" A whisper.

He stopped. Turned. He felt as if his deadened soul was there in his eyes, hard and cold as stone, and he hoped it would be enough to keep her from saying something to stir him up.

"I didn't come for Frank. I came for you. Only for you."

It took a second. The words didn't quite register in the hot turmoil of his mind. Suddenly, he strode toward her with such violent intensity; she instinctively stepped back into the entrance of the empty cellblock behind her.

McKee swept her off of her feet, carrying her unrelentingly to the furthest, most isolated cell where unceremoniously he dumped her on the cot. He stood over her breathing in long slow gasps. He tried to slow the molten heat running through his veins.

Still, a victory chant ran through his head; she'd come for him.

Kendall pulled herself to the top end of the cot on her elbows. When her head bumped hollowly against the wall, she looked up.

McKee gestured toward the crude graffiti of hugely exaggerated penises and vaginas looming above her head. "I told you this was no place for a lady like you. I tried to warn you."

She looked at McKee with a wicked gleam in her eye. "I think this is exactly where I want to be as long as I'm with you."

Looking anywhere, but into her eyes, McKee shook his head to clear it. "You can't want this. Not this disgusting time and place. Not a man with violence in his soul."

"You have just enough renegade inside of you to excite me like no other man. You're honorable to the core. You're the only one who can make me feel this way. I thought you were a fantasy, but you're real. No place is disgusting with you. You excite me like no man I've ever met." Teasingly, her fingers opened a button on her blouse.

"Play prisoner with me."

His eyes moved to cover every inch of the pale flesh as she bared it.

"I've got no promises. Nothing to offer a woman like you."

"I've got something for you. It's free. A gift."

She finished unbuttoning her blouse then slipped a bra strap off of her shoulder baring one breast. Her nipple was puckered. She gave it a little tug as he watched avidly, enthralled, desperately desiring to touch.

Dying to touch her.

"What are you waiting for, McKee?" She complained. "I'm your prisoner."

"Take down your hair," He commanded. Turning and then going to the door separating the cellblocks, slamming it shut with a decisive bang. He stood for a minute, catching his breath. Then, he took out the key, and placed it in the lock.

If Kendall had a fantasy, he would do his best to provide the proper stimulus. The hollow sound of the metal door reverberated through his core as he actually clicked the lock into place.

Who had the fantasy?

"Oh," she breathed. "Did you just lock the door?" He turned and nodded.

"I guess I'm your prisoner." Kendall pulled the simple clip from her hair.

Waving the key ring on his finger, he told her sheepishly, "It's not for real."

Hair spilled over her shoulders like a fur cloak except where her breasts peaked out. She looked more wonton than his most graphic fantasies. "It's amazing. You're feeding my fantasy. You are my fantasy. It's just you now."

He'd noticed she been wearing her hair looser and softer, lately. He loved the silken spill of her hair. Didn't she realize that in many ways he *was* her prisoner?

She touched her breasts.

His body temperature went from hot to boiling in that instant. The anticipation of sex here had somehow taken on incredible urgency. *I'm just playing along with her desires.* He told himself.

But he wondered. Had he ever thought of it himself? Had he dreamed of having a woman when he'd been locked in this cell or one like it? If the pressure in his groin was any indication, he'd definitely experienced this as a wet dream.

Kendall pushed the hair back off of her shoulders, "I feel so incredibly hot." She taunted him.

"You're too beautiful to be here." He murmured. "Too beautiful to be real." He pulled the tab on the zipper of his jeans to relieve some of the pressure. He wouldn't touch her unless she really wanted it.

"You are about to be fucked by this beautiful woman. Come here, you renegade."

"You look mouth-watering against the bars of the prison." She told him. "A dangerous man."

McKee raked his fingers through his disheveled hair. She thought he looked like an outlaw. He certainly felt like one. "I may never let you out."

"I'd be disappointed if you did."

"I can't believe how arousing it is to see you here on this cot." It sounded lame. But it was true.

"You're so aroused that you're sticking out of your jeans like a knife, a rather long knife. Have I told you how much it turns me on that you carry a knife."

He watched avidly as she pushed her slacks over her hips and thrust her fingers in the wet heat between her legs.

The jeans slid off of his hips in that instant. As it turned out, demanding women were even more appealing than ones who begged.

"Come here and use that weapon on me."

"I might have to search your body cavities for contraband." He pulled his shirt over his head baring his chest. "I'll have to push my fingers inside. I might even have to restrain you first."

"Cuffs?"

He nodded. "Anything you want."

"I had a fantasy in the cruiser. I imagined you hand-cuffing me to the grate, then pushing your cock inside of me, when I was totally open and vulnerable to your every urge. I lusted after your thrusting cock."

"Instead I got the fire ants. You should make it up to me." Impatiently, she pushed her slacks off of the cot and on to the floor. Then she let her legs fall open.

The sweet scent of her desire wafted over him and he couldn't resist stroking his fingers over the soft pelt between her legs.

She writhed as his fingers found a path between her thighs. "More," she demanded.

He stroked the swollen flesh.

"Come here and use that weapon on your prisoner." Kendall insisted.

His hands shook with an urgency he hadn't felt since his first time. "Let me touch you gently." He tried to calm them both. "Remember who we are." He resisted falling on her like old Frank would have.

"In this fantasy, I demand to be penis whipped, pounded, and otherwise used and abused by my lawman." Her eyes were wild and her body arched against his.

I'm as much your prisoner as you are mine. He pulled her roughly toward him-to the very end of the cot where she dangled, open and vulnerable. Then, he pushed her legs up, holding them, while exposing her sex.

His fingers moved gently as he cupped her. His thumb circled her clit. When she moaned, he pressed, sliding his thumb inside of her. Once, twice, and then again, until Kendall began to thrash and moan.

McKee had to lock his jaw to keep from going with her as he watched her bucking beneath him. He had barely touched her, before she'd climaxed lustily. She was so exotically sensual. He rolled her over so her legs were supported. Sitting down on the edge of the cot, he stroked her hair while her breathing calmed.

"Oh, Lord, McKee. I didn't mean to go off like that, oh. My." She looked sweetly disheveled as she raised herself up on one elbow.

He leaned down to nuzzle the tempting tip of her breast where it nestled, so pink and tender. It crested in his mouth. His fingers caressed the other nipple until it budded.

Slowly, he ran his fingers between those breasts, down to her slim waist and over her belly button. She parted her thighs again. Opening to him. His fingers circled where she obviously wanted him to be until she panted.

"McKee."

Now she was begging, and he found it just as seductive as when she'd been demanding.

Her canyon-colored hair tumbled around them. He felt desire overwhelming him, driving him like a sudden impeding thunderstorm. So he opened the condom he'd palmed from his pants pocket and opened it to roll over his straining penis.

Her hands got in the way, trying to touch. Tease.

Afraid that he might burst before he entered the sweet cave of her flesh, he brushed her hand away then rolled on the latex.

He raised himself up on the cot, hips in the cradle of her hips, inches from the moist invitation of her sex. His hands went to the hills of her breast. He tugged on her nipples until they rose.

Her breathing quickened.

Soft kitten meows came from her lips. Those hips gyrated toward him. There was a plea in every move she made.

He didn't say so, but he couldn't have resisted the temptation of her flesh even if his life depended on it. He abandoned the hills of her breasts, placing his hands on the curves of her ass, pulling her close, possessing her with just the tip of his engorged cock.

Encased in her moist heat. Then pulling back. Bereft, he left her.

Full to bursting when he was inside of her. Kendall curved pliantly against him. A perfect fit.

With explosive urgency, he sank all the way into the moist canyon of her flesh. He drew back, then with a powerful thrust, like a lightning strike, they were engulfed in an inferno.

McKee give all of himself with each incredible thrust until Kendall screamed his first name out loud, a look of wonder came on her beautiful face and then he willingly followed her into the void.

Chapter Twenty-Two

Kendall didn't know how long she drifted in limbo; McKee obviously knew how to sweep a woman away. His lovemaking was more elemental than she'd ever experienced. Wow, even the stain on the mattress just inches from her nose didn't really bother her in her present state of sated, female, unreserved, sexual release.

It was a good thing he didn't want anything from her-but sex, because she was inept at everything but sex when she was around him. They couldn't seem to communicate at all.

Which would bother her when she'd come down from her sexual haze. However, there seemed to be a flip side.

Apparently, she was amazing at sex.

Or more accurately, *they* were amazing at sex.

It felt weird that given all of his prejudices against her, she still wanted him enough to do anything he might ask of her, she'd move heaven and earth to do it. Call her crazy.

Or she could just admit she loved him.

She struggled to raise her head and shoulders where she was trapped beneath him.

"Should I apologize? Was I too rough?"

Kendall knew when his Texas drawl thickened he was feeling vulnerable. However, considering what she'd just admitted to herself, he knew nothing about vulnerability.

She's just admitted to herself that she loved this man! And it wasn't just because of the sexual explosion strong enough to rock her neurons. In fact, it had been his tenderness that had done her in. When he'd rescued her from the carnivorous ants, he'd become the hero of her heart.

"Kendall?"

Time to use her quick wits to keep him from identifying any goofy, gooey expression he might see on her face. "What would you be apologizing for? The great sex or for thinking I wanted him?" She pointed at the section of the jail where they'd stuffed Frank into a cage.

McKee grinned.

The most relaxed grin she'd ever seen on his face.

"You don't think he heard us?" She asked feigning anxiety.

"Sure, I had you screaming pretty loudly. He probably thought I was beating a prisoner."

She chucked. "It's probably a technique he uses for foreplay."

"I guess I'd better go and check on him." Gingerly, McKee moved off of her.

"Where could he possibly have gone?" She watched from the cot as McKee pulled his jeans up over his ass. *What a shame to block such a view. Of course he'd cause riots if he went around like that.*

He turned around while tucking his black shirt, a little wrinkled from it's evening on the floor. His brow furrowed. "You'd better get your clothes on."

"In case someone comes?"

"No, so I'm not tempted to commit the same crime a second time." His eyes were hot.

She stretched provocatively running her hands over her breasts. "What if I promise you won't get caught?"

"I'm already caught." He growled taking three long steps over to her and then kneeling to bury his face in the side of her neck. "You smell heavenly." He stroked her hair.

Every one of her nerve endings was firing. Kendall wrapped her arms around his neck. "Promise you won't ever post bail."

Then a phone ringing from the office shattered their mood. "The machine will get it. It's getting late."

"I'll go and make sure."

"Jake?"

With a jerk he turned to look back at her.

"Will you take a walk with me in the town square?"

His hesitance made her heart shudder. "Please? Just a few minutes of your time?"

McKee nodded abruptly and then reached through the door of the cell to turn the key.

A little shiver of appreciation shook Kendall; he'd actually played into her fantasy. Then he'd exceeded it by miles.

But he didn't look back as he left the cell and then walked down the isle.

Hoping he wouldn't change his mind, Kendall dressed quickly in her slacks and blouse. Wishing she'd worn something simpler to the office. Her hair she finger combed then gathered into a loose ponytail.

"Kendall?" His voice came from the front.

"I'm coming." She tried to modify her response. No sense in scaring him off prematurely. Otherwise it would be a long summer in Last Chance.

"Who was on the machine?" She asked as she came into the main intake area.

"They didn't leave a message." McKee unlocked the door. "Probably a wrong number."

She nodded as he opened the door and allowed her to walk through ahead of him. They headed down the sidewalk in the middle of town. A few people were out and about in the relative cool of the summer evening.

"It's always so quiet in this town. I can almost see the appeal." She teased.

"It's usually peaceful."

She looked up. "And that sky. Now I know what they mean when they say big sky. I've never seen so many stars."

A nod from her stoic companion had her wondering what he was thinking about.

"The air's so warm. But it's a dry heat." She tried to get him to smile. But he looked so serious she finally gave up and just enjoyed the short walk to the town square.

Some teenagers saw them and with long looks behind them the kids turned, and walked off the other way.

"Do you think they're afraid of the big bad lawman?" He looked down at her.

"Yeah. Why aren't you?"

"I am." She said it sincerely. Wondering how could she bear to let him go.

She sat down on top of a picnic table in the old-fashioned town square and proceeded to swing her legs like she had when she was a girl.

He sat down on the seat just below her.

The silence tempted her to spew her feelings. So she filled it up with the first thing which came to mind. "Do you know picnic tables make decent beds, except those long benches? No matter how you try to keep your arms up they flop down and go to sleep. It sucks."

"I guess you enjoyed camping as a kid."

Did he sound condescending? Probably. A Native American probably wouldn't think much of modern camping. "Not camping exactly."

"What?"

"Nothing. She rubbed the goose bumps on her arms. Why had she brought this up now?

"Tell me."

"You wouldn't believe me. You have all of these preconceived notions."

"What?"

"Prejudices. You're a prejudiced person."

"I don't hear that from many people." He sounded bemused.

She shrugged. "It's true. You think you understand me just because you think I'm a type."

"Okay, tell me something that would surprise me."

Searching his expression in the limited light from the streetlights, she thought he might be sincerely interested. "Occasionally, when I was growing up, I was homeless."

"We've all felt homeless from time to time."

He wasn't going to give her a casual brush off-but he still didn't get it. "I mean physically homeless."

"What about the farm in Virginia?"

"My aunt's house."

"Where was your mother?"

Kendall took a deep breath. "She couldn't hang on to money, a job, or even stay in one place. She had itchy feet. Couldn't concentrate. Even though she loved me, she couldn't really be a parent. She could be fun. And she was streetwise, not stupid. The best I can figure is some sort of adult form of ADD."

"That's why you don't like Maggie."

"Actually, she's kinda growing on me. Do you know she came by the office to thank me for coming out with you? We talked a little bit."

He grinned as if he approved. "So when I said, physician heal thyself.

You were actually trying to heal your mother."

"Something like that."

"You've had to try and reconcile two very different worlds. I know a little bit about that."

"Two worlds." she agreed. Thrilled he would confide even such a little thing.

They sat companionably for a few minutes. Then she lay down on the top of the table. "Come up here with me."

"Gotta keep it G-rated out here in public."

"Sure. I promise."

"You feel so warm."

"You too." He felt amazing and she was tempted to make it more than G-rated.

"Is that why you get into fights? Because you feel as if you're between worlds? Or is it just part of being a warrior." She knew she was attracted to him because of his warrior ways.

He reached over and tugged on her hair until the ponytail slid out and her hair tumbled down. He petted her hair, running his fingers gently through it.

"I've been fighting myself." Kendall offered. "I realize it now. I've been trying to stamp out any quality, which I feel comes from my mother. I guess I associated it with the grief I felt when they took me away. I wasn't going to get hurt again, so I've been playing it safe. And of course my aunt and uncle encouraged me to fit into their world."

"I've been fighting because I can't do anything else. I can't even dream. I feel impotent."

"About Anne." She hazarded a guess hoping it wouldn't immediately shut him down. "Since, I can personally vouch for your virility."

She felt good when his arm tightened around her.

But the conflict of his emotions shone in his eyes. His chiseled features had paled in the dim lights and a weight of sorrow seemed to drag down his lips, which had smiled so enduringly just minutes before.

"I've been thinking of going back to the land."

"As a lawman?"

"No."

"But you love this job." She protested. She couldn't imagine him giving up the badge he sported so proudly.

"It has to have meaning. Balance. Justice."

"You mean closure."

"I guess that's the fancy name for it."

"There's got to be another way."

"I heard from my uncle." McKee held up a strand of her hair. "He claimed *a woman of desire* will save the man in darkness. Then he sent another postcard claiming *a seeking woman* would save me. Prophetic dreams run in the Shaman's line but I don't think he knows what he's talking about."

"I wonder if he means...well it doesn't matter." Kendall stopped. While she'd tried to talk to the man at the campfire, he'd ignored her, or he couldn't communicate with her because she wasn't of the blood. Yet it seemed he was aware of her presence in McKee's life.

Does he mean I'll save McKee by finding the answer?

"A sunlit blonde will heal the wounds..."

Kendall ran her hand over her auburn hair. *So much for hoping the Shaman means I'll save McKee. Well I knew what I was getting into and not all visions are accurate. What am I thinking? Visions are accurate? I'm using logic and evidence. I'll show the Shaman.*

"I know you've been searching for Anne's killer." Kendall said. Hoping McKee would confide in her this time.

He pulled away from her, accidentally pulling on her hair and hurting her. She didn't tell him.

"I'm at the end of the trail. The only place to seek her is in the spirit world. Eventually. Right now I need to concentrate on the case at hand."

"Maybe I could help you." She said tentatively.

"You?"

She sucked in a breath for courage. "I'm great at research."

The smile he gave her was wane. "You have an orderly mind, and unexpected depths. Those obviously come from the varied experiences you survived with your mother. But you have no training, no experience with this stuff. There's nothing you can do."

"I'd like to try. Ask me. Ask me to try. How can it hurt?"

"Why?"

Because I love you and I want to save you. "Because then you can make up for your prejudice about me. You actually owe me."

He resumed patting her hair. "Kendall, you'll just be wasting your time."

She shrugged. "I've got a lot of time on my hands, and what else is there to do now in Last Chance, but take this one last chance? Think of it as fated."

"I've exhausted all of the leads. I've been through her personal journal. We've traced similar scenarios. The autopsy didn't give us any fibers or prints. It's like it was a bad spirit. There's just no evidence." He ran his hand through his midnight hair.

And the one thing you haven't said is that you feel like her death and the disappearances are connected. You won't say it because you have no evidence. Just a dream. Wouldn't you be shocked to know I'm having your dreams?

Kendall wondered if any two people could be so close and yet so far away as she and Jake McKee.

"Maybe the fresh eye of a trained researcher could see something you haven't seen. You were too close to her and she haunts you." *She loved you too and maybe together we can make it right for you again.*

He shrugged. "I guess it can't hurt."

Kendall made a sound of agreement. Would he relent? Could he stop fighting himself?

A long sigh escaped him. "Kendall, I guess I'd appreciate whatever help you could give me."

Her heart leapt. The warrior had become wise.

She leaned in close. "Why don't you come home with me tonight. We could take a hot bath and get the yucky jail smell off of us."

"You have all those candles."

"Yeah I do. And we can stay up as late as we want because tomorrow's Saturday."

And tomorrow will be soon enough to confess my cyber crimes and tell him about my theories.

Perhaps, in time there were other things she could teach him before she went back east. But she could never expect him to turn his back on his blood debts and give up his heritage.

I guess I'll be the one going home feeling empty and impotent because I'll never love another man the way I love this one.

Chapter Twenty-Three

After driving back from Melissa's memorial service at Texas Tech, Lacy decided to just go home. Shedding her dress, she slid into a pair of ratty shorts and a tank top to keep cool. With the air conditioner humming full force, she set an ice cold Dr Pepper on the coffee table, along with an inhaler. Slumping down into her favorite recliner, she grabbed up her controller, preparing to do some serious channel surfing on the TV.

It had been a grueling day. Everyone had been devastated by the loss of such a young life. Something dark drifted in the back of Lacy's mind. Going back to Tech had triggered something she didn't want to think about.

I'm probably just sad that I never finished my degree. Because of that professor.

She felt her breathing quicken.

I have to calm down because I'm going to have an attack.

The threat hovered in the background. She'd been hyper aware of the danger all day. Lacy knew stress could trigger an asthma attack. She wasn't an idiot. She'd come home, and she was basically just being a slob. But instead of feeling relaxed, she felt alone and just a little frightened.

Jumpy.

Surfing through the channels she quickly flipped past the programs about police, dramas, and violence. Looking for a nice romance. Something happy.

There would be no happy ending for Melissa.

Lacy couldn't seem to rid herself of a series of imagined, grisly, mental pictures of Melissa's remains. Pieced together from the subdued and minimal radio chatter she and Kendall had monitored. The mental scenes were like something from a forensics show. One part really bothered her; the evidence team had picked up Melissa's skull last, carefully scooping it up, gathering up her matted and dirty shreds of hair.

Melissa's hair had been beautiful in the pictures today. Bright, blonde hair, not unlike her own, something whispered inside her head, some clue Lacy sensed only she had access too. But it was like trying to remember a name you just couldn't grasp, lost in her head.

You could help if you weren't so weak. If you could breathe like a normal person.

Even the thought of not being able to breath sucked the air right out of her.

Lacy reached for her inhaler.

Each time she tried to remember, her heart rate quickened and her lungs seized up.

But it seemed so important. Something…

I hate this weakness. I hate having asthma. I remember how I volunteered at the clinic where they were experimenting with a treatment for asthma…

Her breath immediately seized up inside her lungs and she had to force out the breaths in a series of huh, huh, huhs.

Huh, huh, huh,

huh….huh…Finally she sucked in a partial breath. Okay. Better. Maybe.

Tentatively she sucked in another shallow breath. Trembling.

She could feel her face getting flushed and her hands were shaking. Even though she was used to her condition, there was an overwhelming sense of panic waiting to pounce when she felt her lungs beginning to tighten up on her.

Asthma was common in her family. A long time ago one of her cousins had died in her mother's arms on the way to Lubbock…

Her chest immediately tightened.

Usually she didn't let herself think about it but tonight death seemed so close…

She started wheezing.

GET A GRIP! She told herself. This is not helping. You know better than to freak yourself out.

Grabbing her rescue inhaler—she took a hit.

Wait a minute, one minute, two, until the meds kick in. You will not have to go in for Oxygen tonight. Or steroid shots.

Get yourself under control.

It worked. She got the wheezing under control with her inhaler and finally felt confident enough to go on to bed.

Before sliding between her orange and brown striped designer sheets she carefully placed her fully charged phone and her inhaler on the nightstand.

Just in case.

As she lay, comfy, propped up by pillows, she thought about her fiancé. She counted the weeks until his next leave. Planning the fun things they'd do together besides jump each other and have incredibly hot sex.

She had to force Rider's face out of her mind. She loved her fiancé, but Rider was handsome and close by-the hero type and she felt so vulnerable.

I'm good. I'm okay now.

But she took another look at her inhaler there on the nightstand in the glow of her nightlight, just one more reassuring look before she drifted off to sleep.

I can look at Rider as long as I don't touch. She smiled at the thought and drifted off to sleep.

#

Frantically, Lacy woke up from a disjointed dream. Wheezing.

She lunged for her inhaler and in her panic knocked the inhaler off of the nightstand onto the ground.

OH, NO!

Calm down. CALM DOWN!

The ground looked miles away and her inhaler had rolled a good distance. Lacy wasn't sure she could get up and get it just yet. Her chest was so tight. She lay back down, still, telling her muscles to relax.

But her lungs got tighter and tighter.

They're not really shrinking-you're just afraid.

She reached out for her phone and hit the text button. Her vision dimming from the lack of oxygen.

Rider's number was the last one on her list. She texted him, 9 1 1 and then the phone slipped from her trembling fingers. *No!*

Breathe.

Breathe.

Breathe.

Breathe.

She would not be dead. She would not be a corpse with her blonde hair untidy and covered with dirt. Instead she snapped her teeth together, sucking in air with a long hisss.

I'm getting air she told herself. I'm getting air. Her phone flickered where it lay on the ground.

He's got the message. He's texting back and he's coming. Breathe.

Breathe. Suck in air. Don't want to be dead like Melissa. Never. I'm getting married. Got the dress. Picture myself walking slowly down the aisle.

Breathe.

Unless Rider's out, or he's too far away.

Should have gotten that life alert my mother wanted me to have, even if it made me feel like an old lady...

Rasp

Rasp

Rasp

Each effort was more of an idea than a full breath, more of a huff, and a little hitch. Each effort brought a puff of oxygen in her lungs.

Gasp.

Gasp.

GASP!

Damn him! Where is he? I thought he'd save me!

I may die after all...I thought death seemed close tonight. Tell...I loved him.

The darkness claimed her.

Chapter Twenty-Four

A song played in her dream. A song about a bad boy being bad to the…Kendall opened her eyes to the sound of the ringer she'd set for McKee on her phone. She blinked eyes dried out by the heat and the air conditioning. Yawning, pushing her ponytail off of her face, nearly alert, she finally grabbed her phone off of the charger.

Yeah, she'd missed a call from McKee. A booty call? It's 2 A.M.

Okay, she was…maybe…pretty interested.

After the memorial ceremony at Tech, McKee'd been so distant. He didn't say much. He didn't offer to come back home with her after they got back to town. He'd made an excuse to take off.

She sighed. She still hadn't gotten a chance to tell him about her research. She was procrastinating. After they'd talked in the park, she'd enjoying having him in her bathtub and at her mercy. Not that he'd seemed to mind. But there was no way to tell how he'd react when he knew what she was up to so she hadn't confessed. She didn't want to risk the fragile bond they'd established.

I don't even know what I'm up to. I don't have any real connection between the missing girls except that they went to Tech, and most of them dropped out, cleaned out, and walked away. Or were carried away…yeah I'll just tell him those girls are out in the desert crying in my dreams. He'll probably take me seriously. But I'm not ready to take those dreams seriously…

She hit the re-dial button.

His phone rang and rang on the other end. "Come on McKee. Answer your stupid phone."

After what seemed like an eternity, he finally answered.

"McKee did you call me? It's 2 A.M." She knew she sounded surly. She was definitely going to make him grovel for the booty.

"What? Lacy's in the emergency clinic? Asthma?"

"No, you don't need to pick me up." She looked down at herself. Naked and tousled was fine if he'd only wanted sex.

Kendall pushed Precious aside as she climbed out of her bed. "No, I don't need you to pick me up. I can drive. Yes, I can get there on my own. I'm not a child."

"Yes." She softened her voice. "Yes, I'll be careful. I promise."

She grabbed the jeans she'd laid on top of the dresser to prevent scorpions from nesting inside.

Don't want to get a big surprise.

The cat lifted her head, blinking big golden eyes.

"You know Precious, it does things to my blood pressure when he asks me to be careful. You'd think he actually cares about me."

#

"What happened to Lacy?" Kendall blurted out as she hurried into the nearly empty clinic.

Rider just nodded at her.

Lacy tried to smile from a hospital bed, with an oxygen mask strapped on her face.

"What's wrong? What triggered it?" It had occurred to Kendall on the drive over that Lacy might have heard some news about the missing girls. After all, Lacy was plugged into the local network, related to everyone. They didn't really need the local newspaper around here because by the time the paper came out, the news inside the paper was as stale as day old bread. Lacy'd be one of the first to know if someone had found Carrie.

"She couldn't breathe. She was rasping and as pale as a corpse when I got to her house. The inhaler had fallen and even a couple of hits on the damn thing didn't seem to do much. Scared the hell out of me. So I called Imogene to come and evaluate her. I keep telling Lacy that we need to evacuate her to Lubbock to a real hospital, but Lacy's being stubborn."

Lacy put her thumb up.

"It'll be okay." Kendall said, though she wasn't sure. Lacy looked pretty fragile.

"I knew she had asthma. But, holy shit when did it get so bad?" He rubbed a hand over his face.

Apparently he'd been doing it repeatedly because his glossy black hair was mussed.

Kendall thought Rider looked almost frantic for Lacy. She wondered what might have been if Lacy weren't already engaged. How sad that these two hadn't taken a chance to be together. Lacy had once said that she and Rider came from two different worlds. They hadn't even tried to be together. It sounded awfully familiar.

"She pushes herself so hard." Kendall told Rider. "And the funeral wasn't easy."

Lacy shook her head emphatically. "Even if she won't admit it."

Kendall looked at Lacy, "Why do you keep going when you feel the warning symptoms?" Kendall knew the basics about asthma because counseling could actually alleviate some asthma symptoms, indicating asthma was affected by the emotional well being of the patient.

"I push myself...so that I can have...some normal." Lacy huffed and puffed her way through the sentence. "I don...t waaaaant to seeeem we...k."

"If you relax. Your breathing'll get better." Kendall told Lacy.

"Rider, the steroids are... kick...in." This time Lacy made it through an entire sentence. "You can go. I'm go---ing to be fine."

Rider shook his head.

"Why don't you get her a Dr Pepper? You know how much she likes them," Kendall suggested.

He looked suspiciously at Lacy.

Lacy nodded, wide eyed.

"Okay. I'll be right back."

When he'd gone, Kendall couldn't help but scold Lacy. "Why did you push yourself so hard? You scared him to death."

"I woke up...I...could...n't...b.b.bre . . the." Lacy said.

"You couldn't breath."

"I it...s...cold ...er."

Kendall had heard those words before. From a dead woman. But she wouldn't let Lacy die. No way.

She patted Lacy's shoulder. "You're going to be fine. You're okay."

It's because she's thinking of those girls. It's worrying her to death. I don't mean death, literally. People don't die from asthma. Not usually.

Imogene, the nurse, came into the room and looked at them. "You can't talk to her or she won't get enough oxygen. I don't want to have to call her mother."

Lacy shook her head empathically.

Kendall smiled. Lacy was in good hands. Imogene was her aunt once removed or something like that and Imogene wouldn't hesitate to call in the relatives if Lacy needed anything.

Kendall reached over and gave Lacy a hug. "You rest. I've got something I definitely need to finish."

Lacy looked confused, but kept the oxygen mask firmly in place, with her eyes fixed on the nurse instead of asking Kendall the question she obviously wanted to ask.

Kendall hurried to the stairs, neatly avoiding Rider. She needed to get to the law enforcement office to finish the task she'd begun. At this time of night there'd be no interferences or distractions. It was time to end this mystery. Somehow she had to make the critical connection.

There was one important thing she could do for Lacy, for all of them. She needed to find a killer.

Chapter Twenty-Five

The dinger on the door of the law enforcement office sounded. Kendall shifted her head to look at whoever was coming in, but carefully, slowly, as her neck was stiff from being in one position for too long.

Sheriff Foley strode into the office.

Kendall blinked. She'd been reading, looking for the common thread connecting the possible victims since she'd left Lacy in the clinic with Rider. Hoping Lacy would feel a lot less stressed if they had an answer, that she'd literally be able to breath easier.

"Good morning, Kendall." Foley looked fish-belly pale where his farmer's tan had once been. His blue eyes were a little sunken. But he was alive. And obviously kicking. Sheer temper sparked in those eyes.

He looked grim.

He knows I'm in his computer database.

Still, her lips cracked a smile, becase he was alive and well. "Sheriff Foley it's so good to see you out of the hospital. How do you feel? Where's Janice? Are you supposed to be back to work so soon?"

"Kendall, what are you doing here?" His question sounded like an accusation.

"Working?" She looked at the clock. It was almost noon. She'd been at it nearly ten hours.

I'm trying to find a serial killer. I'm trying to figure this out.

"Working on what?" He demanded as he came around to view the computer screen.

It was tempting not to hit a button that would have exited her from the site on screen, but she resisted.

I'm not a liar. And I've got a good reason for what I've done. McKee asked me to help. Even if we never nailed down exactly how I planned to help him…

"I have a good reason to be on this site," She babbled. "Please listen before you say anything."

"You're using police files? On top of everything else."

"Yes. I've been trying to solve the murders. I've found more missing girls fitting the profile. I've developed a hypothesis that the killer's on staff at the university, with access to their database. He makes it looks like the women drop out of the university. Then they disappear. If you'd just give me a few more hours on this website. I could find the common link between the victims. Besides, the fact that they were all blonde at the time of their disappearance."

"Kendall. You're fired."

"What!" She heard him but she didn't believe what she'd heard. "What did you say?"

"Kendall, pack up your stuff and go home."

"Why? I told you I found something…this guy…and what do you mean on top of everything else?"

"You're fired. Give me your key to this office right now; I want you out of town by nightfall. I know you don't have much to pack besides that damn prissy cat of yours."

Those words went through her like a shot. It felt like her stomach plunged to the floor.

People had said her mother wasn't good enough, so Kendall had always done the right thing. Worked like a dog to do so. No one had ever said she hadn't done a great job. Excelled even.

This time she'd done the right thing too.

Not the right thing for her job. No, according to the rules of her job, she'd knowingly overstepped and broken laws. But something had changed inside of her heart.

This time she'd done the right thing for the people involved, for McKee, Anne, Lacy, and those poor young women.

She knew she was on to something. She knew it.

She pushed a strand of hair off of her face, trying to find a way to talk to him.

"I just need a little time here."

"I said you're fired."

"Because I went on the police website? Really?"

"No, not the hacking."

"Hacking? I wasn't hacking." Although the thought of being bold enough to break the rules both thrilled and panicked her. "You call this hacking? I was merely looking for information to aid in an investigation."

"It doesn't matter. You're fired. Fired. Go home. It's for the best. I want you to leave town immediately. I want you as far away from Jake McKee as you can drive tonight."

She found herself wiping at tears she didn't even know she'd shed. "I can't be fired. I've almost solved it. I practically know who's killing the girls. No more girls have to die."

"Shut down that computer. Immediately."

Her face felt hot, and moist, and most of all she felt mortified. "What are you saying? I've worked hard for you-I filed and organized the entire office."

"You don't understand what you've gotten yourself into."

What was he talking about? "I can't have a black mark on my record. I've got a shot at an incredible career. I can't get fired from a law enforcement office in a town with no stoplights. It could ruin everything. You've got to give me another chance."

"No."

"But…"

"I'm trying to keep your life on track. Believe me. I'll give you a good reference. Nothing negative will go into your file. I admit it's partly my fault. I wasn't here to keep an eye on you."

You weren't here because you had a heart attack and I saved your life.

She felt a small sense of self-assurance at the reminder that ultimately she'd done something heroic in saving Foley. How could she make him understand that she was still trying to do something heroic?

"I was just doing a little research. You don't understand what's at stake here." She couldn't exactly tell him about the ghostly voices. Then he'd have good reason for shoving her out of the law enforcement door.

"I'm going to hold the other party responsible. I'm going to make sure his superiors understand that he's unfit for his position."

"Are you talking about McKee? He doesn't know I've hacked into your computer database. In fact his passwords must be in his native language because I haven't been able to crack them."

Foley put a hand up to rub the side of his pale face. "I'm not stupid. Don't make me say this. You know what you've done. And, I know what I have to do."

"What?"

"This is my jail. I take precautions."

"Sheriff, you should sit down. You're looking a little shaky."

"We have surveillance, and computer security alerts."

"You knew I'd logged into the police database?"

He looked down at his huge boots.

She jumped to her feet. "What aren't you telling me?"

He looked up, his pale face flooded with color. Even his sparse eyebrows looked pink.

Could he be embarrassed?

Kendall grabbed the edges of her desk. *What was wrong here?*

"I have cameras in the jail cells, Kendall. Do you know what a brief viewing of one of those video tapes showed me about what my staff was doing in my absence?"

Suddenly she felt her face flame. "Oh, my God. Did you watch the whole thing?" She'd never had a father but right now she felt as if her father had caught her having sex with her boyfriend, mortified beyond belief.

I guess I acted like a juvenile, so I deserve it. I knew my fantasies would eventually get me into trouble...

"I watched enough."

"I admit it was the wrong thing to do."

"You admit it was wrong? You're my employee. I trust you to make better decisions than to be with McKee. He's trouble."

"What's worse? That I was indiscrete, or that it was with McKee?"

"Indiscrete? His eyes bulged. "Indiscrete!?"

Remembering all the things they'd done inside the cell created a sinking sensation in her stomach. "Okay. I royally screwed up." Then she shook her head. "I didn't mean that..." *Literally.*

"Okay," she continued trying to regain her composure. "I deserve to be fired. But, don't go after McKee. I'm a consenting adult. In fact, I'm the one who initiated our relationship."

"Relationship!" He roared. "You can't have a relationship with him. He's on the edge of self-destruction, and he'll take you down with him. I'm not going to hold it against you if you promise to leave town. Now. You're a victim in this mess."

"I'll leave town. McKee doesn't want me anyway. Not really, but one bad decision doesn't mean I'm wrong about the serial killer. You have to listen to me."

"Is that what you call having sex in a cell? A bad decision?!"

"I couldn't help it."

"Obviously."

She cringed. "He didn't force me or anything."

"I saw that too."

"I well, I forced him. Really." Foley just looked at her.

"Yeah, I came here to, well…sleep with a criminal. It's been a…fetish of mine. I'm not a good person. I've got this issue. I only seem like a nice girl." The confession came out of her all in a rush. The truth. At least it had been the truth.

That truth had been so much easier. The real truth was much more complicated.

"It doesn't matter." Foley shook his head. "This time I'm going to force McKee to get the help he needs. He won't be able to wiggle out of his responsibility this time. I have him by the balls and on the record."

She stood up. "Don't do anything to Jake. Don't let anyone fire him or transfer him. Promise me and I'll grab my stuff and leave town. You can give me a good reference or you can ruin me. I don't care as long as you never tell anyone what you saw on that tape."

"Dr. Waite? You'd really sacrifice all your hard work on that worthless lawman? Graduate school? A job in a clinic like you told Janice? You'd rather give it all up than see me fire him? Believe me he'll be better off if he has to face his problems."

"I influenced him. I told you. I'm not who you think I am." *I'm not who I thought I was.*

"I checked out your references I know who you are."

"Why would you conduct such an extensive background check? For an administrative assistant?"

"This is my town, and I'm very careful who I bring into my town. Under the circumstances I've cause to be grateful to you."

He's trying to return the favor by getting me away from McKee.

She shook her head. "I've underestimated you. I apologize. Please, let me go. I don't want to take anyone down with me. Especially not Jake. He doesn't deserve any more pain in his life. He's already lost Anne. He's lost his gift. If he's crazy, it's because of the dreams. I know all about how dreams can affect a person."

"You know something about McKee?"

"Yes." She sank down on the edge of her desk. "Yes. I do."

Foley sighed. "I'll make sure he gets some help. A suspension. I'll make sure he's okay."

"It's not enough. He won't go for counseling. He'll self-destruct. Give him my case notes. Let McKee solve the case, himself. That'll heal him. Everything will be okay."

"Why are you trying to protect him? Why?"

"Because I made another really bad decision, Sheriff Foley."

"What? He looked worried.

She pushed her hair back. Fiddled with it.

"Kendall?"

"I...I...don't worry about it."

"Given the mess we're already in, I don't think I have a choice but to worry."

"It's not that kind of mistake."

"What is it?" He finally snapped.

She sighed. "I'm afraid I've gone and fallen in love with Jake McKee."

The painful look on Foley's face was reminiscent of how he looked during the heart attack.

She shook her head. "You don't have to tell me how hopeless it is."

"Kendall."

"If you'll trust me for five minutes more minutes, I'll shut down the computer and retrieve my things."

As she shut down the computer she thought she could hear the ghostly voice wailing in protest.

I'm sorry Anne. I'm so sorry.

Handing Foley the thick file of work she's so painstakingly gathered, and her key to the law enforcement office, she told him earnestly, "I knew this obsession would cost me everything."

Foley just looked at her. He obviously couldn't reassure her everything was going to be all right.

And Foley didn't know how far she was willing to go for the man she loved...all the way.

Chapter Twenty-Six

She *was* going home to pack as she'd promised. Eventually. Foley had taken almost everything.

He'd taken the paper trail of evidence. Given his promise in return. Jake would be okay.

Hopefully, Jake would take her research more seriously than Foley, who couldn't seem to focus on anything other than the indiscretion.

There was one thing she had to do before leaving town; she had to see Jake. When she arrived at the motel, his Harley was parked out in front of his motel room.

Kendall got out of her car and let herself inside McKee's room. She smiled at the irony, Foley wouldn't be happy that she still had a key, especially a key to McKee's motel room.

We'll I won't have it for much longer. There was a catch in Kendall's heart at the thought.

Especially, when she saw him, her outlaw, sprawled, in a deep sleep, in a skimpy pair of black briefs. She took a long moment to admire him.

Disheveled, rumpled, and mouth wateringly sexy. He obviously hadn't heard her come in the room over the rhythmic racket of the laboring air conditioning unit.

He's exhausted. I wonder which ghost kept him up all night. She wondered if he'd gotten into another bar fight. Not that she cared.

I just want to be with him this one last time.

Kendall slid onto bed behind Jake, wrapping her arms around his waist and plastering herself up against his body. How could she ever get enough of him? How could she say goodbye when she'd finally found him?

But it was the only way to save him--the literal man of her dreams. She held back the tears caught in her throat.

They only had these few hours, this last chance to say goodbye and make one more memory for her days alone.

Kendall planned to make it as x-rated as possible. Foley would be so mortified if he could see them now. If she had anything to do with it they were about to set this ugly, orange motel bedspread on fire.

She scooted close, nestling her groin-to those tight ass cheeks. Stoking the fire simmering inside of her. She gave into her every fantasy by sliding her hands under the waistband of Jake's briefs, where she discovered McKee was already fully erect. His cock felt wonderful in her hands as she explored his smooth, hot flesh. One hand grabbed his rod, and she slid her other hand down to stroke his rough balls.

He moaned low in his throat.

"I'm taking this guy into my custody."

"Okay." He muttered.

"Okay? Honey it's going to be way better than okay. I'm going to ride you until you beg for mercy."

In one fast move he grabbed her arm to flip her over and under him. "Darling, you were on top last time. It's my turn now."

He completely covered her body. Fitting himself against her, his cock nestling between her open legs, probing and hungry. She tried to press against him. Wanting him. She ached to have that part of him deep inside of her body.

"What's taking you so long? Why do I still have my clothes on?"

"I don't know. Why didn't you get rid of them before you climbed into bed?"

"Would you believe I was anxious to get into bed with you?"

"Too bad. I hope you're not attached to this prissy work shirt."

"Why?" *Not that I need it anymore.*

"Because." He grabbed the front of her white button down blouse and ripped it open.

She shrieked as the buttons popped onto her neck and bounced on the bedspread underneath her. "What are you doing? You lunatic?"

She wished there were a mirror on the ceiling because she imagined they looked incredibly sexy with her ripped shirt exposing her skimpy fuchsia bra-one she'd ordered after she'd met McKee.

If there were a mirror she could see what she could only feel, her breasts straining against her bra, begging to be touched.

And Jake's golden skin, covering her pale curves.

"I'm getting rid of these clothes." He reached over to the nightstand and grabbed something.

She stopped breathing when he pulled out his ceremonial knife. Her bad guy.

Was it any wonder she'd always imagined he was only a fantasy? What other man understood that a woman needed a man with the courage to be both raider and savior, rough and tender, and merciless enough to hold out for his partner's screaming sexual surrender?

Pulling Kendall's hair up over her head, while she winced, hoping he wouldn't cut any of it. Jake slit the tight hair band to allow her hair to spill all around the two of them.

She felt her scalp tingle with the relief afforded by loosing the pressure on her scalp.

"I love your hair. It's so beautiful. I love to see it rippling over your skin."

"I'm not complaining."

"Good. He lifted the centerpiece of her bra up off of her skin. Her breasts swelled above the top.

"I'm going to use this on you."

"Okay." She panted. He made her feel so hot. The knife was just another dangerous facet of her Indian outlaw. "Please." She added when he continued looking down at her flesh, seemingly in no hurry. "Hurry."

"You want me to free your beautiful breasts?"

"Yes. Do it already!"

"You're going to have to make a sacrifice." He teased.

"Yes!"

Speaking in a totally different tone, he said, "You're going to have trust me, totally, Kendall because if you move at all this knife's sharp enough to cut you to the heart.

How appropriate.

With a quick flick of the knife he cut the center of the bra and it snapped away, leaving her aching breasts uncovered and the bra in pieces.

Jake loomed over her, with intense and admiring interest, with the knife in hand, darkly dangerous; setting her senses aflame.

Kendall panted. "Touch me."

"I'm enjoying the view."

"Touch me." She pleaded.

He smiled as he flipped the knife around. Using the bone handle he rubbed the smooth material around and over her erect nipples.

"I only use this knife on my helpless prey."

"I'm your helpless prey." If he'd bothered to look into her eyes, he would have known she spoke the absolute truth.

He leaned forward and took one nipple into his mouth, nibbling, and then increasing the pressure until she cried out. "Please."

He lifted his head to look into her eyes. She sensed his desire, and something else, in his inscrutable expression…

"I'll kill you if you quit now," she warned him.

He leaned on his knees, with a little pressure on her thighs. "Now for the pants."

"I won't be needing them anymore." He didn't seem to hear her admission.

It didn't matter. Nothing mattered except for this moment, their final moment. Kendall could feel her heart pounding. Her blood rushing in places she desperately needed him to explore. She started panting, knowing what he could do to her--what he would do to her.

Kendall gasped as Jake pulled the pant material up, off of her skin. She sucked in a breath, not daring to move, but wanting to writhe and scream when he began cutting the khaki material along the zipper. Above her most intimate place.

If there were a mirror on the ceiling, she knew she would see herself laid open to him, all defenses peeled aside, and vulnerable all the way to the heart.

Then he put pressure on that heart of her, with the handle of the knife. She thrust against it crying out at the fierce, intense pleasure.

McKee rubbed the surface of the bone handle against her clit.

Back and forth. Back and forth. Oh. Oh.

But before she could come, he moved the handle of the bone knife away.

She looked up into his eyes. Those beautiful dark eyes were glazed with desire. She wasn't suffering alone.

"This knife thing is turning you on, too."

"I love the way you make yourself totally vulnerable to me. What other woman would let me use my knife on her besides my beautiful Kendall?"

"It makes me tremble."

"But for the wrong reason, my reckless darling."

"I trust you. I've dreamed about you all my life," she admitted. Wondering if he'd remember after she'd gone. Would he finally understand why she'd given herself to him on that very first night? She'd known him forever. She'd loved him always.

"And, I've dreamed about you." It sounded as if the admission were torn out of his soul. He set the knife aside.

She looked at him. Wondering. He didn't give her any more time to think as he slid over her body, to claim her in the most brazen fashion.

He positioned himself, sliding his fingers over her clit, filling her first with his clever fingers and then pushing her thong aside and claiming her with every inch of his thick, hard, penis.

As he pushed himself deep inside of her, she closed her eyes, and memorizing every sensation, scent, and sound of him. Knowing that after today all she'd have left were memories and her dreams.

And she'd be grateful for them.

Chapter Twenty-Seven

Inside Kendall's dream, they sat in front of the tribal fire. The shadowy figure, the Shaman squatted just beyond the edge of the eerie bluish light. And the familiar shade of Anne lay nearby.

"What are we doing here?" Kendall asked Jake. No one answered.

"I have to leave town. I promised Foley." No one answered.

"I did it for you." She told McKee.

"And I did it for her." Kendall turned to Anne who lay broken and silent.

"What the heck's going on? All this time you were talking to me. And I felt like I was going crazy. And now this dream's gonna be silent. Does it mean you're all disappointed in me? Like Foley? What am I supposed to do? He means business. I never failed before but this time I've failed spectacularly, stupendously, screwed everything up."

Kendall reached out her hand and somehow McKee's ceremonial knife was there in her palm. She grabbed a hunk of the hair lying on her shoulder and cut the strands short, near her shoulder. The voice of the wind was keening for her losses as it blew all around them.

Grieving.

"I don't know how to fix this." Kendall sawed at her hair. Watching as large strands were picked up by the breeze and sent floating over the dry terrain as an offering.

"My heart's broken" Kendall looked down to see the shredded shirt she wore had a bloody hole in it and the flesh underneath gaped with an old, devastating wound.

The last strands of her hair blew away from her in the wind. Some of it fell into the dirt, discolored and dirty.

She'd finally fit it all together, accepted all the pieces of herself. Her sensuality, the wild streak she'd gotten from her mother, and her ability to 'see' the dreamscape and accept that there was more to life than science, that there was spirit, soul, and most important of all, there was love.

Kendall knew she'd be sacrificing the most important part, the love, because she wasn't the one McKee needed.

There were no answers in the shrieking voice of the wind, only grieving for all the losses…

"I'm so sorry." Kendall's eyes were as dry as the desert and no tears would flow. She fell to her knees. When she looked down there was no flesh, just bleached bones and the sand blew through her leg bones. Her hands were skeletal where they clawed the dirt. Most of one foot was already buried.

One foot in the grave.

Her clothes were rotting. They'd fallen away. Dirt lay thick on her clothes and the hunks of her discarded hair.

And she knew she was destined to become a victim of the man she'd hoped to stop.

Now you're going to be one of us. Said a chorus of chanting voices. There was the sound of a shot.

Chapter Twenty-Eight

There was the sound of a shot.

A sharply rap on the door to the motel room.

Kendall opened her eyes to a false twilight preserved by the heavy motel drapes and realized it hadn't been a shot. It was someone pounding on the door.

"What?" She asked, still fuzzy from the terrifying dream.

McKee was getting something out of the top drawer of the nightstand. His gun.

"Shhhh." He told her as he got out of bed and stood over her. "Who's there?" She asked.

"How the hell do I know? I'm not expecting company. I was anticipating additional sex."

"Okay." Kendall whispered. Admiring his beautiful physique. She also wanted an encore. One that would last a lifetime.

Jake looked through the crack in the drapes. "Looks like Highway Patrol." He pulled a pair of briefs over his erection and then pulled on a black tee shirt.

Kendall got up on her elbows. "Great. Foley told me I could take an extra day to get ready because I didn't sleep last night. And he knows I had to go to the clinic to see if Lacy was okay. I didn't think he'd send anyone after me."

"What are you talking about?" McKee turned from the window.

"I…uh…I."

There was a more insistent knock on the door. "I'm coming." He said loudly, calmly.

"Kendall, get dressed. I don't want anyone to see you like this." He stood at the door informing whoever was at the door that he was a law enforcement officer and would be opening the door in a minute.

Kendall looked down at herself. This could be awkward. She was naked and tousled and looked just like she'd been having sex. Her hair clung to her moist body. The sheet was tangled and lying on the carpet. The bed-spread with its bright orange pattern must have slipped down at the end of the bed. The options for covering herself were certainly limited. Especially, when her clothing had been so expertly cut from her body.

She sat up, then slipped out of the bed, and then hurried into the bathroom. She shut the door behind her.

She heard McKee open the door to the motel room. She heard him talking to someone. It sounded ominous. She looked over at some clothing Jake had stacked on top of a metal shelf. She pulled on his tee shirt and it fell to mid thigh. Then she walked barefoot out of the bathroom. How much more did she have to loose?

A man in Highway Patrol uniform was talking to McKee. Another officer stood just outside the front door of their motel room. Would Sheriff Foley have them drag her outta town?

"Miss Waite. How long have you been here with McKee?"

"What?" Kendall tugged self-consciously on the tee shirt and her hair lying haphazardly on her shoulders.

"Simons, I told you she's only been here for a couple of hours." "McKee I don't want to have to take you in but according to James Arranger…"

"Take him where?" Kendall interrupted. "Where are you taking him?"

McKee just shook his head. "I'll come with you. I already said I would. Just leave her out of it."

"It looks pretty bad that you're still in bed at this time of day, where were you last night?"

"I was camping out in the desert."

"Right."

"He doesn't lie." Kendall moved closer to McKee. "There was a funeral yesterday. He helped exhume the body of the missing college girl." It sounded weak because there was so much more to it, things which were essentially unexplainable. Things she was just beginning to accept.

"McKee, You'll have to come with me. Answer a few questions."

She jumped in front of McKee throwing her arms wide open. "No, he's not going to jail!"

Jake put his hands on her shoulders. "Kendall, my little warrior, this isn't making it any easier. You have to cooperate. Go and get dressed."

"I don't want to cooperate. Not if it means loosing you." She reached out to put her arms around him.

He took both of her hands in his, "Everything will work out. Just let me go and talk to them. Please." He kissed one of her palms and then another. Then he pushed her hair back, smoothing it away from her face, and leaned forward to kiss her forehead. He murmured something low, possibly in his native language, something she didn't understand, but it still brought her to tears.

I'll never see him again. But she backed up and sat on the corner of the bed, on the slippery orange bedspread.

"I have to put on the cuffs." The officer sounded apologetic.

"No." Kendall said jumping back up off of the bed. "You can't put cuffs on him. He didn't do anything." She sucked in a frightened breath and let it out with a sob. "I did it."

Both men turned to look at her.

The officer asked her curiously, "Are you confessing to beating Bart Arranger to death?"

Kendall's legs felt wobbly and she grabbed onto the nightstand. "Arranger? No, what are you talking about. I didn't hurt Arranger."

"His body was discovered early this morning. He's dead and according to his brother, James Arranger, Jake McKee threatened Bart on more than one occasion and in front of witnesses."

Kendall turned to Jake. Then she looked at the officer. "Jake didn't do it. He'd never do it. He had the chance to hurt Bart Arranger just a few days ago and he didn't do it. I was there. I witnessed the whole thing."

"I'm sorry but I've got to take him in anyway."

McKee looked at her. "It's okay Kendall." He grabbed his jeans and slid into them. Then he took his wallet off of the bed table and slipped it into his jean pocket like he was just going down to the corner store for coffee.

Kendall sank back down on the bed, biting her lip to keep from embarrassing Jake, by bursting into tears, as the highway patrol office apologetically cuffed Jake McKee.

She shook her head. Nothing was okay. Nothing made sense. And she just stood there impotently as the officer walked Jake out the door, and then both officers escorted him to the squad car.

Kendall trailed behind, them out of hotel room, watching, bereft and alone on the prickly doormat.

All she could do was cooperate and she hated it.

It didn't make her feel any better that Jake turned to give her a crooked smile before his head was pushed down so he could duck into the back of the car.

Kendall, the queen of cooperation, had finally had enough…

She ran inside the room and picked up the phone and called Rider Blue Storm. The words tumbled out of her mouth as she tried to explain the situation coherently, though she found herself breaking down into tears even as she tried to be succinct.

"I want to come in and testify." She insisted, knowing she sounded hysterical and stupid.

"I'm already on my way. Were you with McKee last night? Because I remember we were both with Lacy."

"I…uh…"

"I thought not. And don't even think of perjuring yourself. It will only get you into more trouble."

"How can I possibly get into more trouble?" she wondered aloud. Grabbing a tissue off of the motel desk.

"What?"

"Nothing. Rider, Swear you'll get him out."

"I will. Just don't worry and don't forget to check on Lacy."

"I'll check on Lacy."

After all, *I have to tell her goodbye.*

I have to tell them all goodbye.

Her heart shattered and her breath caught. She sank down on the bed where she wrapped her arms about herself and rocked back and forth understanding exactly what Lacy must feel when she couldn't breathe.

I finally found him. And I've lost him.

Chapter Twenty-Nine

Kendall didn't know what to do next. She'd changed into a pair of shorts and a bra tank top she'd had in a bag in her trunk for working out.

She didn't want to go home. She didn't want to think; especially not about the fact that they'd just taken her boyfriend to jail.

Again.

Not that he deserved it this time.

Hysterical laughter threatened. Tears threatened.

The buzz of the phone interrupted her pity party. It was Lacy demanding in all caps for Kendall to call and tell her why Rider had rushed out of her house a few minutes before.

"I'm coming," Kendall texted back.

"Door's open," return text.

It took two minutes to get to Lacy's house and Kendall lectured herself the whole drive.

I will not say anything to upset her.

"Thanks for leaving the front door open for me." Kendall said as she closed the door behind her. Lacy's house was ranch style, with sand-colored tile, and two sliding glass doors in the living room that looked out over the back yard pool, on calm blue water.

"I didn't have…a choice. Rider's coming back…to …ah check on me." Lacy sat in her favorite recliner with a black suitcase containing the portable oxygen at her feet and the O2 mask in her lap.

If Kendall had needed anymore proof she couldn't confide in Lacy, it was sitting right there in Lacy's lap.

"Aren't you supposed to be resting?"

"Very funny. Where....'d Rider go?"

"Jake got that call too. He said it wasn't what Rider thought. Just routine," Kendall lied though her teeth.

Lacy looked like she didn't believe it. "It'sss okay?"

"Yes. Everything's fine." Kendall pushed at her hair, which was tied up so tight it was giving her a headache. *I have to trust Rider to get Jake outta this mess.*

She forced back tears.

"Are you okay?" Lacy asked. "Sit."

Kendall settled into a comfortable armchair. "I've just got some of that wonderful red grit in my eyes; since the wind's picking up. And it's been a long day."

"Because of me. You were at the clinic in...the middle . . of the night"

Kendall shook her head. "We should just relax."

"I don't think...I'm set...up to relax." Lacy said apologetically. Kendall smiled sadly. Her chest felt tight. Lacy's chest must feel that way too. They breathed in unison, in and out. It was kinda intimate and soothing, but then reality of what had happened would hit her again and Kendall kinda choked on her next breath.

"It's getting better." Lacy rubbed her chest. "I really hate it...you know. Once I thought...I was going to finally get rid of it but I couldn't stay in the...study group. That Kolter guy was too fricken' scary. "

"Study group?"

"Yeah, this profess . . or, named Kolter had an asthma study. . at Tech. It'sss been on my mind all day, and I dreamed about it every time I closed my eyes last night."

Colder? Like c-o-l-d-e-r?"

"No, K-o-l-t-e-r."

Oh my god. Kolter. *How many times did I demand that Anne tell me the name of the killer, and Anne said, Kolter? But I wasn't listening. I was too afraid to really hear what she was saying. I thought she meant colder, like the cold of the grave. Oh my god. We've got him.*

Kendall leaned forward, impatiently waiting for Lacy to explain.

"The professor had this theory...that asthma is a physical symptom of an emotional event. He used hypnosis...Regression to infancy..." A puff of air came out with the last word.

"Slow down," Kendall, insisted, even though she wanted to scream in frustration.

Kendall felt the little mental click, as the final connection slid into place, or was she simply grasping at anything that might keep her close to McKee?

"His theory was so strange. He claimed children developed asthma from emotional detach…" Lacy couldn't find the breath to finish the word so she tried again. "A cold, unloving mother." She gave a little gasping laugh.

"That's an outdated theory. No one believes that theory anymore."

Lacy nodded. "That wasn't the theory pre . . sent…ed by the uni… Tech. Of course they're research…ing the effects of stress on asthma."

"How did you learn about the cold mother theory?"

"It was sorta his pet thing. Under…neath."

Kendall struggled to stay calm, realizing that stressing an asthmatic wouldn't get her the answer she needed any faster. "What happened?"

"I don't have a cold mother, but I was des…perate. My good friend Katie wanted to try it…so we app…lied." She pushed the blonde hair back from her face where a sheen of sweat attested to her struggle to breath.

"Did you get accepted?" Kendall could hardly control her combined sense of dread, and exhalation, and guilt. Lacy should be breathing oxygen, not reliving a difficult memory even if it might bring absolution to every-thing and everyone here.

"Yes, we both did…The guy was gorgeous…Redford type, academic, genius and very compelling."

The stats ran through Kendall's mind. Thirty-something, well-edu-cated, white males with superior social skills made up ninety percent of serial killers. She thought about Anne's journal entries, "Did he hypnotize you?"

Lacy grinned, obviously on her way back to sassy. "Turns out I can't be hypnotized. My mind's too…cluttered."

Kendall grinned.

"I got sick of not being able to go under, so I pretended."

"Then what happened?"

"I saw him looking at Katie, like he hated her. Touching…her…breast. It was unreal. Terrifying. I knew I was probably over-reacting. But…I told her and we…never went back." Lacy's eyes were wide with remembered horror.

Kendall suspected Lacy would have said so much more if she had more air. "More breathing and less description please."

Lacy put the O2 mask on. She closed her eyes.

"Katie was a small, blonde girl." Kendall guessed out loud. "Exactly like the eight other victims."

Lacy's eyes popped open. "Two," she mouthed.

"No, at least eight young, petite, blonde women have gone missing from the university in the last fifteen years. Many of them formally withdrew from school, but they never made it home."

Lacy's eyes widened over the mask.

"I suspected it was a staff member with access to the university database."

"What about...the...dorm stuff?"

"Did this professor Kolter have student aids?"

Lacy nodded.

"If you're inside the student's head during hypnosis you might ask them about their roommate's plans for a holiday or sports absence. The aid wouldn't be noticed in the dorms. Pick girls with little social life. No boyfriend. I think it could be done."

"But it's just a working theory. We don't know if Kolter's still at the University."

Lacy took the mask off of her face. "I think that man's cap... able of any...thing. He's cert...if...iable. I've...dreamt of him in crazy night...mares I hardly remembered until this funeral...finally made me remember."

"I'm guessing this professor was popular with the students and staff. I'll bet he's incredibly charming too. Everyone liked him."

Lacy nodded emphatically.

Kendall sighed. "I'm not sure how he's making it look like those girls dropped out and went home. I just know they never made it home."

"Maybe he did something different every time. If he's good enough he might use hypnosis to suggest the student actually drop out and pack up their stuff before meeting him somewhere."

"Since he's handsome, maybe he has a sexual relationship with them and then pretends he wants to take them away somewhere they can be together." Kendall ran her hand through her hair and it started to slip out of the knot on top of her head.

Lacy shook her head. "Someone at Texas...Tech is really killing them?

So many?"

"Yes. I'm sure of it."

Lacy let out a long breath. "How did you figure out there are more missing girls?"

"I may not be a professional researcher, but I got a lot of experience in grad school. I also...ah...had a little help from the police database."

"That's what you've been working on s s so hard, these lassst weeks."

"I just wanted to help."

"So you found a trail of missing girls."

Kendall nodded. "I also researched serial killers. I believe this one is escalating his pattern. I think Anne confronted him. I think he had to get rid of her and it freaked him out. It triggered a change in his normal pattern, or, subconsciously, he wants to be stopped."

"They do that sort of thing?"

"Yes."

"Not this guy. He's arrogant. If the professor's your guy." She coughed, and then she took a sip of water. "He's a real egomaniac."

"Even the arrogant ones lose their edge. The real world seeps into his psyche. He may not have a conscience, but he lives in a world where it's normal to have a conscience. Neither Melissa nor Carrie dropped out. My guess is that on a subconscious level, he wants someone to stop him."

Lacy sat up straighter. "Then let's stop him."

"Okay." Kendall dug a notebook out of her purse.

"Why were you looking for missing blondes...sss in the first place?"

"Because of Anne's diary."

"You have Anne's diary?"

"McKee dropped it on his first day in the office, and I happened to pick it up." *Lacy doesn't need to know about the voice in my head. That would send her into a full-blown attack.*

"Right. But you didn't return...it."

"I read the dairy. It was disjointed. She talks about being afraid."

"How nosey of you and how frigh...ting for Anne."

"Yeah, she didn't like being afraid."

"If Anne had anything to do with Kolter then she was right...to be afraid."

"Anne started having flashbacks to the time when she'd been hypnotized at Texas Tech. It haunted her. She talks about 'the study' and not being able to breath but never came out and said it was because of asthma.

I thought Anne couldn't breath because she was frightened."

"Maybe she doesn't want to remember him by name. Maybe she feels safer if he was nameless. The guy I remember is one cracked dude. I don't even like remembering his cold hands on my skin."

"He touched you?"

"I might have been fricken' hypnotized, I though he touched me but how do I really know for s…sure?"

"Anne didn't feel sure of what happened in the sessions either. In fact I'm sure her journal started out as a dream journal. It just feels like she's documenting her irrational fears."

"That's why McKee didn't take anything she'd written serious…ly." Kendall smiled. It felt good to share it with someone who understood.

"And he'll think I'm irrational for taking Anne's journal seriously."

McKee wasn't going to believe any of this theory because there was still one very large stumbling block.

"We don't have any way to determine if asthma is the connection? Do we? Neither of us know if Anne had asthma."

"We can…find out." Lacy bounced out of her chair.

"Calm down or you'll have to put the oxygen mask back on.

"I'll call my aunt. She knows the family history of every person… in the coun…ty." Lacy trailed off into a coughing fit and it took twenty minutes of oxygen to get her calm enough to get her aunt on the phone. "That'ssss the pow…er of sma…ll town connect…ions."

Kendall thought she'd go crazy waiting for Lacy to get off of the phone with her aunt. It was slow going because Lacy had to stop and catch her breath after each sentence.

Impatiently, Kendall paced back and forth on a cowhide rug practically memorizing the pattern of reddish brown spots.

Finally, Lacy set down the phone. She'd gathered enough breath to report, "Anne had had mild asthma in childhood. She hadn't had symptoms in years but she told her mother that she'd worried about the childhood illness keeping her from being in law enforcement…she wanted to be an officer so badly and worried herself sick over everything…"

Kendall was shaking with excitement. "Lacy, you did it."

Lacy nodded thoughtfully. "She was afraid asthma would keep her from going into law enforcement; she wanted to make sure it was really gone so she took a chance on this program when she was at Texas Tech."

"She was like you, Lacy. She didn't want it to keep her down. But something about Kolter made her uneasy so she quit the study but she didn't forget. Not really."

"Until something in this investigation connected her to the memory again."

"I wonder if she remembered something from when she was under hypnosis. Something he said or did. Something damning."

"You knew her Lacy," Kendall leaned forward. "What would Anne do? How would she react? Would she just barge in and confront the man?

"You said it yourself, she was a trained investigator. She wouldn't just rush over there." But Lacy didn't sound convincing.

"A trained investigator with a crazy hypothesis and a memory she couldn't trust because of the hypnosis."

Lacy was nodding.

"And a gut full of the fear of failure." Kendall thought of her own motivations for coming to Texas. "You don't always react logically no matter how much training you have."

I know all about that.

"Sometimes feelings overwhelm your good sense. I think she went to talk to him. Convinced herself she was just confused by the experiences under hypnosis and he killed her for it."

"Why petite, blonde women?" Lacy mused with only a little wheezing.

"He's got a cover story, and a respected following, and plenty of financial support from some pretty prestigious intuitions but…Kendall shook her head.

"My guess is that underneath it all he's targeting his mother or a lover who rejected him, over and over again."

"Okay, we've got a theory and a possible motive but we don't have any proof." Lacy said. "We can't just barge in and question him." Her breath hitched a little at the end of her sentence.

"I'm a trained counselor. I might be able to get something out of him." Kendall got up from the chair and started pacing back and forth in Lacy's small living room.

"You're crazy. Anne was a professional and she got herself exe…cuted." Lacy started wheezing again.

"Anne was emotional about the situation. The residue of the hypnosis made her vulnerable."

Lacy shook her head. "I don't think she was as emotional as you're assuming. You can't think of doing…this…alone. We have to call Rider and McKee."

"Of course, I'm speaking in the abstract." Kendall said as she wound her hair back into a knot. "I wouldn't think of confronting a possible serial killer. I'm a secretary at a law enforcement office. Not a police woman."

Lacy's face got red and she started sputtering. "Pro...miss...me."

"I promise. And if you get anymore upset you're going to end up in the hospital."

"You can't do thisssss."

"I'm not doing anything. I swear. I'm going home and tomorrow when you feel okay, we'll look online. Find out if this Kolter guy's even still at Tech."

Lacy shook her head and concentrated on her breathing.

But her look was penetrating. As if she could see into Kendall's mind and heart. As if she could see that her friend was blatantly lying.

"I'm texting McKee, telling him to keep an eye on you tonight and tomorrow." She held the phone so Lacy could see her send the messge.

"Okay, text away." *His phone is in evidence by now, anyway.*

"You really will wait until we tell Rider and McKee?"

"Of course. Do you think I could find Kolter tonight even if I wanted too? He's not likely to be answering his office phone this late on a summer day—even if he teaches summer session. And what the hell would I say to him?"

"I don't know. I just feel so helpless. Useless."

"You've been incredible. You solved the case. I'll be here in the morning, around ten a.m. I think we should both sleep in. It's been a rough couple of days."

Lacy nodded, but her blue eyes were worried.

"Call me if you need anything?"

"I've got the O2. I'll be fine."

"Okay." Kendall stroked Lacy's golden hair. Knowing that whatever happened tomorrow, she'd never see Lacy again in Last Chance.

Chapter Thirty

Kendall drove through the desert, her little car buffeted by blowing red sand and an eerie hollow, pre-storm silence, which even Anne hadn't dared disturb.

Not that I need to hear her warnings or complaints to know this is crazy.

Even Precious failed to grumble aloud, though her glowing eyes glared accusingly at Kendall through the silver bars of the carrier sitting on the passenger seat.

Allowing the sand storm to take up all of her concentration was a simple matter. Both because Kendall had never seen a real sand storm before, and because she was afraid to dwell on the potentially deadly consequences of the meeting she'd arranged.

I should turn tail and drive back east without stopping.

Torn between terror and tenacity, she could feel the sweat sliding down from under her hair where it just touched the back of her neck.

Good thing I used deodorant.

And that sweet perfume.

Because a predator can smell fear.

Once she got to the edge of civilization, she made one important stop. Then she followed the GPS directions to the Texas Tech campus, finding her way quite easily because the streets were numbered and lettered in an orderly fashion.

I might actually have had a better chance of survival if I'd gotten lost.

Once Kendall hit the huge parking lot near Kolter's office, she picked up her cell phone and called Lacy.

"Hey girl how are you feeling?"

"Neglected I thought you'd…come by."

"Do you have the oxygen handy?"

"Uh oh, I have the feeling you're going to upset me."

"I didn't come by because I had to pack all of my stuff. Except the cat, she's in a carrier at the Holiday Inn, in a room registered in both our names. I sent you a text with the address and room number. If anything goes wrong will you take her? Please."

"You promisssssed!"

"I lied. I've spent my last night in Last Chance. I kinda overstayed my welcome. I got fired. McKee went to jail."

"What?"

"It's okay. McKee's out of jail."

"What? What are you talking about?"

"Just listen. Rider bailed Jake out sometime this morning I think. And I really want to talk to him but I haven't been answering his texts or calls. Because I can't tell him…anything. I've got it all worked out though. I've already failed at just about everything out here so I can't fail Anne, McKee, or the other girls. Not now."

"What…why?" Lacy was wheezing.

Kendall ignored her guilt at upsetting Lacy. Soon enough this would all be over. "I need you to call Rider, ASAP. Tell him to drive to Texas Tech and use the lights."

"I'm sending you a text message with the exact address where I'm scheduled to meet with Dr. Kolter. I'm going to record my conversation with Kolter on my phone, so the police will have the evidence they'll need to convict him."

"No way, don't, do thisssss. Please wait for them. What makesssss you think it'll turn out any…better than what happen . . ed to Anne?"

"Because I'm not doing it alone. I trust you. I trust Rider. I trust McKee to come riding to my rescue. I know I need my hero to come and save me. Anne felt she had to do it all alone. She had to prove something. I just want to make him talk to me before the good guys come and take him away. I have to do this."

"What if…they…don't get there in time…wait. . Kendall."

"Oh I know they'll come in time. I imagine McKee's already getting the message."

In more ways than one. He's probably already plugged back into the spirit world. I have to believe it. Otherwise there's no point.

"I won't keep your damn cat...I'm allergic. She'll starve...don't do thissss."

"You'll find her a good home."

"What if...Rider doesn't answer his phone?"

"He'll answer for you. You've got two great guys that care about you: your fiancé and Rider. Count yourself super lucky. On the other hand, McKee's gonna be so pissed he'll probably kill me, if Kolter doesn't."

"When did he go to jail? What did I missss?" Lacy hissed. "Oh my God. Kendall. Don't do thiss. Please! Just wait for the guys."

"No. I'm done waiting. I've got to end this now. I'm going to put all of my expensive training to the test and see if I can get Kolter to tell me something we can use against him. Don't worry. I love you, girl. And don't you dare stop making that jewelry!"

"Kendall..."

Kendall hung-up the phone.

She looked in the rearview mirror, hardly recognized the woman she'd become. She pushed a strand of hair off her face.

I can do this.

There was only silence from Anne.

I just hope the posse gets there in time.

Chapter Thirty-One

In the Psychology Department, Kendall walked past a long row of familiar looking college cubicles, while making her way toward the lair of a serial murderer.

It looked innocuous, just one of the larger offices, and a name printed precisely in the frosted window of the door, Dr. Thomas Kolter PhD.

She took a deep breath, gathered her courage, and knocked. She almost backed away as a large, intimidating figure approached from the other side of the glass ominously blocking out the light.

Dr. Kolter opened the door. "Hello. Kendall. It's so nice to have a visit from a fellow scholar."

He welcomed her with a high wattage smile that didn't dim the frost in his eyes as he gripped the edge of the door to his office.

Kendall pushed her hair over her ears, wondering why Dr. Kolter hadn't offered to shake hands. Then, it occurred to her that he'd probably used that hand to kill young girls.

She barely held back a shudder.

"Thank you, I've, um, been fortunate enough to be mentored by gifted men in the field."

"Yes. What an honor that you're working with Bill."

"Yes, if you'll let me know when you're going to be in Virginia next, I'll talk to him, I'm sure he'll want to meet you for dinner."

Once Kendall had verified Kolter was still at Tech. She'd spent the whole afternoon changing up her Face book, Twitter, and Instagram homepages to lure Kolter, even making up a research relationship with a colleague, Dr. William Fox, an influential man in their field whom he'd be desperate to meet.

Kendall had then changing her profile appearance, and made weak-minded comments so she'd sound exactly like one of Kolter's preferred targets.

She'd reached out to Kolter via Facebook, and he'd responded almost immediately.

It was actually terrifying how quickly it had all fallen into place. "From what I've read, you're the one doing cutting edge research, Sir."

Kolter stood there with his hand on the door as if he were blocking her entrance to his sanctum. "There are brilliant young minds in my program. I assure you that I'm simply a mentor—pointing my students in the right direction."

For a minute he looked almost haunted. Did he suspect something? Kendall tried to project a bad case of hero-worship and she gushed, "I've found your theories fascinating. Especially the study you did in 2007. After the Touchier results came out. You're sure to create the benchmark for treating traumatic asthma."

"Yes, well, I happen to believe all asthma is the result of emotional trauma." The professor preened as he finally stepped out of the way, allowing her into his office.

"What a beautiful office." She blurted out.

"Thank you. Dr. Waite. I'm afraid my interest in teaching in Texas doesn't include a cowboy motif."

"Yes, I've discovered Texas is another country." She forced a giggle. It sounded ridicules, but he immediately loosened up. Kendall's mother had always insisted that insecure men liked women to behave like little girls. It wasn't a brilliant idea considering what Dr. Kolter liked to do to little girls—even if her mother was freaking brilliant for suggesting it.

"It's not a civilized place." He sniffed.

She sat in a straight back chair made of blond oak with a blood-red leather cushion and there she blabbed on and on about all the sunburns, stings, and bites, she'd experienced first-hand while living in West Texas. She finished up with a complaint about the sand storm they were presently experiencing.

I hope this weather doesn't slow the guys down or the Texas weather will literally be the death of me.

Kolter's body language was sympathetic as he listened.

Of course, I'm telling the truth.

Now I just have to get him to tell me the truth.

"Miss Waite, would you like something to drink?" He offered cordially, when she'd finally run out of complaints.

Silently, Kendall debated the safety of drinking anything a serial killer might offer. "No, thank you, I just finished an iced tea in the car."

He grimaced. "Do you mind if I finish my hot tea?"

"Not at all."

She watched as he sipped his tea with a fussy precision. "Umm, that smells so good."

His smile was confident. "Yes. It's imported."

I'll bet. "So, I don't want to take up too much of your time. I wanted to shake your hand and tell you how much I admire your work. I intend to tell Dr. Fox all about you. Of course."

"Are you looking for field experience this semester?" He asked tightly. "I don't think I have any openings right this minute, but I could keep you in mind."

You should have at least two openings at this moment. "Thank you, I've got several interviews lined up. But I'm flattered you might consider me."

"I'm flattered you've taken the time to come." He sat back in his leather chair. "Do you have any questions?"

"Oh, I have a number of questions." She leaned forward as if excited by the idea of getting to ask him about his work. "I'm personally interested in your idea of origin." She tried to look embarrassed and vulnerable.

His muddy eyes widened, "My dear, do you suffer from asthma?"

She shook her head. "No, I grew out of my asthma in grade school." It would be difficult for him to check on the lie.

"Did something in the family dynamic change?"

Kendall was ready for this line of questioning. "My mother was able to stay home with us when my father got a really good job. I guess it made a big difference."

"Many things can make a difference."

"According to my research your approach's a little different."

"Yes. I use hypnosis to try and discover the root of psychological stress. Still, we have more questions than answers."

"Regression." Kendall fiddled with her purse strap. "It must leave your subjects feeling pretty vulnerable."

He sat back. "My successes speak for themselves."

"I've often thought a lack of maternal warmth inhibits many great accomplishments."

"An old theory." He looked honestly interested. "Why do you bring it up?"

"I thought we might have that in common, I've seen some of your early published work."

"I'm presently pursuing the effects of stress on asthma symptoms."

"Of course. But sometimes old theories have some truth in them."

"I no longer believe that theory's relevant."

"I suppose I'm being immature and unprofessional. In a way, I'm also trying to heal something in myself."

He leaned forward. "You are safe in this room. Tell me what you're feeling."

Safe?

Isn't that what those young women thought before you discarded their bodies in the desert?

Kendall rubbed her hand over her mother's good luck pendant, a gaudy piece of costume jewelry. She hoped Kolter would see the naked truth in her eyes as she confessed. "Here on the edge of becoming a professional. I've been worried about my buried neurosis.

"I feel I can confide in you. In fact, I suspect it's the real reason I've come to Texas, to ask for your professional guidance."

"What?" His eyes were intent. "How can I help heal you?"

In that instant, his attention dissolved her fears like a warm shower, rolling, tenderly over her. There was nothing in the world, but his undivided attention. He swallowed all of her concerns with their intimate connection.

His hand moved and a glint of light reflected off of his ring. Once. Twice, three times, Kendall watched the light as it swung back and forth and back and forth.

The truth poured out from her tattered heart. "I realized I'm in this field because of my mother. In so many ways I'm hoping to cure myself of her influences."

He nodded. His understanding lapped at her wounds, "I know how you feel."

Tears threatened. Only the light seemed to hold her interest. "How could you?" She whispered. "You don't doubt yourself."

His eyes were golden pools of understanding, golden like the light. She felt as if she were falling into them.

"Ah, but I do understand. Intimately. Kendall."

She sniffed. "You do?"

"Yes." His smile was so poignant. "My mother was frigid. She denied me the love that should have spilled freely from her along with her mother's milk. My research is successful because I understand pain and alienation."

Instinctively, Kendall clutched at her mother's necklace; the hard edge where it had been broken years ago, bit into her finger.

Get a grip. He's hypnotizing you. Anne's pragmatic voice sounded so real in her ear.

Shake it off. He'll kill you.

Kendall struggled to surface.

"I feel so woozy." She confessed.

"It's probably the afternoon sun. The Texas sun can be blinding. Let me close the blinds."

Don't be his mark, Anne's voice again. Or was it her mother's voice?

Kendall tried to keep her eyes open, but they only fluttered.

"Is that better?" He was moving around.

She kept seeing the flashing light. How?

"Relax, and look at the light, Kendall. It'll take you places you want to go. Back. Back to innocence."

McKee will go over the edge if you let this guy win again. Kendall pushed the sharp metal deeper into her finger.

"Kendall, where are you?" Kolter's voice flowed over her.

She hoped she looked relaxed, like she was just fiddling with the necklace. Then she let her hand slide bonelessly from her neck to her lap.

"I'm in an apartment. It's so cold. We've had the heat turned off." She'd been too stubborn to sleep in her mother's bed despite the promise of warmth because she'd been so angry…

"How old are you?" Dr. Kolter leaned forward talking to her in that sing-song tone.

Kendall didn't think she was still under the influence of hypnosis. She was just recounting an old memory. But if she were wrong she could end up dead…

She made her voice sound petulant. "I'm seven, and I'm mad because it's cold. I want to go to my Aunt's house for Christmas because they have nice presents!"

He didn't ask. He seemed caught up in his ability. "Of course, you want to go somewhere warm and safe. I'm going to take you there." He held up a golden pendant and started swinging it.

Kendall tried to look as if she were going under, while not actually going under.

"I think you're fighting me, Kendall. How can I cure you if you don't tell me about your pain?"

"I'll tell you." In fact she'd been exploring and exercising that pain for weeks now.

"We need to go further back."

Kendall relaxed against the back of the chair, let her head fall, made inarticulate noises. She'd seen it in many films. She hoped he'd be convinced.

I hope I'm not just dreaming that I'm resisting.

"Good. Good. You are most responsive." Dr. Kolter sat back in his own chair. "Now, when you awaken you'll have a sudden urgency to leave this university. Furthermore, it will make you uncomfortable to discuss this visit with anyone."

Fat chance.

"Kendall, I believe we've got a problem." Unwittingly, Kendall eyes popped open.

He snapped a handcuff on her right wrist.

She pulled at the restraint. Not relaxed. Not amused. "Let me go." She demanded. Trying to see where the cuff was anchored beneath the chair or the cushion.

Apparently he's got this down and you thought you could handle him.
OMG.
Don't panic.
I'm not panicking.

"Let me go." She sounded panicked.

"No, I don't think I'll be letting you go." This time when he spoke, his eyes looked different. Feral. Evil. The knowledge of the damned was in those eyes.

Kendall realized she was facing real evil. She thought she might be sick.

"Let's talk about this like true academic professionals," he suggested.

"It will be a pleasure to be honest with someone enrolled in such a prestigious program with mentors like yours."

Don't wig out. Just make sure he confesses while your phone's recording.

"That's high praise from someone like you. But what will I tell Dr. Fox?"

"I'll have to arrange a meeting through some other associate. I'm afraid you're going to be…missing."

"Is that what you want to tell me? That you've been killing the students who resemble your cold hearted mother?"

He jerked in his seat like she'd stabbed him. "Why would you assume such an absurd thing?"

"You tell me?" She shrugged, and the cold unrelenting metal of the cuff reminded her that she was taking chances with her very life.

"I release girls who are in terrible pain."

"Release? Is that what you call it?"

"Therapy." He rubbed his hands together.

She needed something solid for McKee. He'd never be whole unless he knew what had happened to Anne. "Why did you kill Anne? Why didn't you just cure her?"

His reaction was subtler but she saw the twitch in his cheek. "That name's familiar, but it's been such a long time, I'm not sure she was a student of mine. Really, Kendall you're being most melodramatic."

Kendall rattled the cuff. "Really?"

He grinned. A sweet, sexy grin apparently aimed at her heart or libido, but at this late date she was cured of wanting bad guys unless they had unruly black hair and…

"I won't confess. I haven't done anything wrong." He told her with oozing charm. "My little experiment has shocked you, and I'm sorry. Let me help you." His cool charm was more frightening than the cuffs.

"His little experiment is to handcuff me to the chair." Kendall said for the record. She could only pray her two favorite officers were doing one hundred fifty miles an hour down the empty Texas Highways riding to her rescue.

And that the sand storm hadn't intensified to the point where they couldn't see where they were going…only in Texas.

"Why did you kill Anne?" she prompted Kolter. Hoping her phone wouldn't end up buried in the desert with her body

Kolter ignored her.

"Did you slaughter your mother, and leave her out for the fire ants, too?" Kendall shuddered at the thought.

That shocked Kolter.

He turned to her with fury, putting his hands on her forearms where they rested on the leather padded, wooden arms of the chair. He squeezed, bearing down with all of his considerable weight. "You don't have any knowledge. You certainly don't have any proof. You're merely speculating about things which are not your business."

"How old were you? I'll bet you were young. So young the cops never even considered you a suspect-it would have seemed obscene. I think you've been killing for so many years, that it's become second nature. You're not human. You're a predator. You're not intelligent. You're an animal masquerading as a sentient being."

The pressure on her arms was agonizing. She rocked back and forth against the back of the chair, squirming to get away from the terrible pain.

"You'll shut your cunt face."

Kendall nodded. She wasn't proud of her lack of courage as tears and snot trickled down her face.

"You can't prove anything." He said quietly. "She couldn't prove anything. Stupid women, it's not enough that you withhold your love, but you come here to threaten me. Well, I can defend myself and I'll retaliate."

Part of Kendall's mind was icy clear. "How many times did you retaliate?"

"Many times." Kolter rocked back and forth a wild look in his eyes. "Wait, I don't know. I didn't kill them. They just died."

Each time he rocked backwards, the pressure on her arms eased, allowing Kendall to take a ragged breath.

She had no regrets.

She'd found love and reveled in it.

She'd discovered that the human spirit was infinite. And, even though she didn't want to leave this plane, she knew she wouldn't be completely gone.

She'd even gazed into the eyes of true evil and found she had no desire for an evil man.

There was only one more thing to do before this insane man killed her; save McKee.

"Anne. Why did you kill Anne?" she choked out. "She wasn't a threat?" It was part query. "You could have pacified her and sent her away."

"She accused me." He growled. "I didn't do it. I didn't. But they keep disappearing." He began beseeching. "I'm guilty? Am I guilty?"

"Anne triggered something. Something important. When she was hypnotized you sucked on her breasts. She wrote in her journal that it was just a bad, surreal dream. It wasn't a dream. She must have looked very like your mother."

"She was a whore!" He thundered. "Unworthy. She threatened all the important work I'd done."

He couldn't seem to separate Anne from his mother in his thoughts. A push. This was the area he needed a push. So Kendall could get a confession for McKee. "Perhaps your mother sensed you were an evil child. How could she love an animal coming from her womb?"

The humanity fled Kolter's face, the stark lines of the monster glaringly visible, "She created me." He shook Kendall so hard her neck felt like it would snap.

"She didn't want you."

"I killed her. But she keeps coming back."

He reached into his desk and took out a revolver. Kendall grabbed the arms of the chair with hands as stiff as boards. She felt her bladder weaken.

Okay, so she actually had regrets. Many regrets.

She also felt vindicated. This was probably the weapon he'd used on Anne and it could be traced.

I solved it for you McKee. You've got his confession on my phone and probably my body for evidence. If you can't close this case then I'm going to haunt you for sure.

But she wasn't dead yet. "You can't afford to kill me in your office."

Kolter put the gun down on his desk. "In fact I'm going to take you on a little tour of the rough side of this state."

Her heart whimpered. The thought of fire ants made her skin crawl.

Breathe. In and then out, like Lacy does. It's only an anxiety attack. Breathe while you still can.

"Then I'm going to introduce you to some of the local scavengers." He bent his head and routed around for something in his desk drawer. He came up with a prescription bottle. "First you're going to have some tea, after all. Then a little nap."

It figured, she thought hysterically. The Texas critters had been gunning for her since she arrived, and now she was going to be served up.

Just when she'd acclimated.

McKee, I really really need you to save me!

Anne can't you whisper in his ear? I know he was dreaming on our last night together. I think your reaching him. Help me!

At that moment, something behind her crashed, and then shattered in an eerie explosion and the air was suddenly full of what looked like diamond dust.

There was a heavy thunk.

Kendall found herself looking at a familiar bone-handled knife that had pierced the heart of Kolter's framed PhD, just inches from Kolter's head.

She wrenched her neck around and caught a glimpse of Rider with the butt end of a gun, which he'd obviously used to shatter the fancy window in the office door.

McKee threw open said door which banged against the wall with a sound like the shot they had not fired.

Kolter screamed, the thin scream of a wounded animal "How dare you? How dare you? I'm an educated man. I'm...

"You are under arrest. I'm officer Jake McKee, put your hands in the air." Jake's voice resonated through the office.

Kolter grabbed the gun off of his desk, shooting wildly.

Kendall closed her eyes, waiting for the explosion of pain. But it didn't come.

Neither of the men rushing into Kolter's office faltered or fell.

Then, they were on Kolter, restraining him. Kolter swore and struggled but was no match for her heroic lawman.

When Jake's eyes met hers, she let go of the horror. Fainting.

When she surfaced, the first thing Kendall noticed was that she was cradled in familiar arms, Jake's arms.

"Why did you take the chance? All we needed was the lead." He scolded.

She brushed the hair from off of her face. "I needed to prove myself. It turns out that I'm a hell of a therapist." She chuckled. "I might even do some profiling. Hell, the sky's the limit."

Uniformed policemen came in and then they escorted Dr. Kolter through the jumble of furniture. The man cursed and struggled while Rider held the man's shoulder in a tight grip. At the door, Rider turned to grin at them, a triumphant grin.

Jake watched impassively.

Kendall leveled herself by resting on one elbow, curling her legs under her. Her grin felt as big as Rider's, and equally cocky. "I got him. Jake! I got him! I got him!"

"Are you done impressing yourself, counselor?"

She leaned forward and kissed Jake on his firm, unsmiling lips, tasting the banked passion and the power of the man she loved. Then she leaned away from him. "Okay, so you made a grand entrance through the door, McKee." She laughed. "But you have to admit, I helped. And my cell phone was recording the entire confession."

"Yah, you got him." His mouth finally curved upwards. "We got him."

A beam of light from the window struck the hair spilling over her shoulders.

Jake lifted it to catch the light. "Damn shame. You cut your hair."

"Yeah but it was for a good cause."

He stroked the unfamiliar, sunlight color of her hair with one finger.

"Kolter fixated on blondes," Kendall explained apologetically. "That was part of the profile. I updated my Facebook page with my new look. He called back once he got the opportunity to see my picture. I also flattered him and lied my ass off, telling him I'd introduce him to the most prestigious professor in the field. Kolter wouldn't know I haven't even met Professor Fox, but his ego wouldn't allow him to resist the possibility."

She blinked several times. "These colored contacts feel a little weird, but when I looked in the mirror I felt Anne looking back at me. I felt like she approved, and that she was watching over me. I know she's in your spirit world after all." *And someday soon I'll tell you I've been hearing her in my dreams.*

McKee tightened his grip. "You could have been killed. You took an awful chance. Anne had everything to live for and he put her in the ground with a single bullet."

She could hardly breathe, but she didn't mind this time. It struck her that Jake was looking at her with more honest emotion than she'd ever seen him express before, and suddenly she felt like he'd kicked her in the guts.

"Is that why you're looking at me so tenderly? Because I look like Anne? Do you love her after all?"

His honest confusion was a beautiful sight. "You look like my beautiful Kendall. My beautiful, brave, Kendall who faced a demon from hell to solve a murder."

She snuggled against him. Almost content. Too bad she couldn't change her nationality as easily as her hair color. It would solve all of their problems. "I have to go home to Virginia. After I get this handcuff off of my hand. I mean."

"I don't think so."

"Foley fired me." She could feel herself blushing.

"You need a job. We'll find you a job. If you're willing to give up Virginia and move to Texas."

"Oh, my God. We solved the murder. We got the bad guy. What else do you want, Jake?"

"You."

"I thought you'd made a solemn vow to your Shaman?"

"His postcard said I should look for a woman of light." McKee held up a strand of the hair she'd cut, bleached, and colored up to catch the sunlight from the window.

"I thought it said, beware the woman of desire?"

"That's the problem with being cryptic. It can come back to haunt you."

Kendall wondered; what was he getting at? "You can't seriously think he'd fall for a change of hair color?"

"No. But Cody Bluestorm, our Shaman, knows that the gods act in mysterious ways."

"I don't understand," she complained.

"The old man knows how to ride the winds of fate, he won't be able to resist taking credit for a woman of light coming into my life, and helping me solve the mystery."

"He might accept me?" Her heart beat a little faster at the thought.

Jake looked smug. "Your gift of prophetic dreaming will certainly seal the deal. He won't be able to resist the idea of grandchildren who dream."

"How did you know I was dreaming?" She repeated dumbly.

"You talk in your sleep and that last night, you were obviously addressing Anne. I just got uh, taken away, before I got a chance to talk to you about it."

"Jake, I've been dreaming about you all of my life-I just didn't think you were real. But the dreams about Anne started that first night we were together and for a while, I thought I was exhibiting signs of mental illness. I'm still not sure about this mystical stuff. I'll need a resident expert to tell me what to expect."

He hugged her awkwardly around the cuff. "Damn things."

"The dreams or the cuffs?"

"Both. But Kendall, you can't fight your destiny. Believe me. I've tried."

"So, we were meant to be together?"

"It's been written in numerous postcards. Of course, I'd have run like hell if you'd been a blonde."

She laughed; she couldn't help it. "I'll change my hair color back. I promise. But, really, what about your uncle?"

"If he has any doubts, I'll just have to explain I can't live without you." He looked at her so lovingly it took her breath away. "You really are my light."

She cried happy tears. "How romantic."

"It's more like lightening…"

She laughed and cuddled and wanted him naked.

Judging by the sounds coming from the adjoining room, officers were ransacking the files. Kendall hoped they'd find everything they needed to keep Kolter in prison for a long time. After all, most serial killers kept trophies connected to their victims and…

Jake gave her a little shake. "Kendall, it's your turn to say something."

Did he look worried? Could he possibly believe she didn't love him with all of her heart? "I guess I could say that I came to Texas and caught myself a renegade." She teased, looking squarely at the bone-handled knife stuck in the middle of the diploma on the wall. "It's not much to brag about."

"You're perfect for me--the only possible man. And I've found out that I'm a bit of a renegade, myself." She rattled the cuff on the one hand, reached up one handed, to squeeze her mother's pendant, finally, accepting all the pieces of her heart.

Jake looked down beyond the necklace. Down into her blouse; his gaze settling on her cleavage.

He gave her a slow, sexy smile. "What do you say to using my uh, handcuffs, tonight when we're alone?"

"I'd love to, Jake. I wouldn't have it any other way." She laughed.

The End